CAVE OF SECRETS

LYNNE GOLODNER

SCOTIA ROAD BOOKS

Cave of Secrets by Lynne Golodner

First published in 2024 by Scotia Road Books (www.ScotiaRoadBooks.com)

Copyright © 2024 by Lynne Golodner

ISBN (paperback) 979-8-9876501-4-1

ISBN (epub) 979-8-9876501-3-4

Library of Congress Control Number: 2024905858

Interior by Scotia Road Books

Cover design by Susan Jones and Patrick McEntaggart

Printed in the United States of America.

In memory of my father, Norman Cohn.
I love you, Dad, and miss you every day.

BOOKS BY LYNNE GOLODNER

Fiction

I Love You, Charlie Tanner (2025 winner, PenCraft Fall Seasonal Book Award for women's fiction)

Cave of Secrets

Woman of Valor (2025 winner, American Fiction Awards for religious fiction; 2024 honorable mention, Eric Hoffer Award for spiritual fiction)

Nonfiction

Forest Walk on a Friday: Essays on love, home and finding my voice at midlife

The Flavors of Faith: Holy Breads

Stand Out from the Crowd: The Your People Guide to Beside-the-Box, Funky, From-the-Heart, DIY Marketing, PR & Social Media

Hide & Seek: Jewish Women and Hair Covering (Lynne Schreiber)

In the Shadow of the Tree: A Therapeutic Writing Guide for Children with Cancer (Lynne Schreiber)
Residential Architecture: Living Places (ghost-written for Dominick Tringali)
A Patient's Guide to Understanding Cutaneous Lymphoma

Poetry
Driving Off the Horizon (Lynne Cohn)
Living Inside: The Poetry of Prayer (Lynne Schreiber)

PRAISE FOR CAVE OF SECRETS

CAVE OF SECRETS is an award-winning novel! This title won a Bronze Medal in the 2025 IPPY AWARD for multicultural fiction, was a 2025 Finalist in the American Fiction Awards for Romance and General Fiction, was a 2024 Finalist in the Reader's Choice Book Awards for Romance and was a 2024 Finalist in the FOREWORD INDIES Award for Romance & LGBTQ+ Fiction.

CAVE OF SECRETS transports readers on a timeless journey to Scotland while weaving a captivating tale of love, identity, and legacy. Lynne Golodner highlights family history and expectations that eventually force her characters to make difficult choices. Sprinkled with secrets and a touch of magical realism, this novel is a must-read.

Merle R. Saferstein, author of *Living and Leaving My Legacy, Vols. l and ll*

A masterful blend of suspense, romance, and self-discovery, CAVE OF SECRETS is the tale of an intrepid young archivist's pursuit of history, unveiling a secret love affair and a powerful family's hidden Jewish roots. Golodner's gorgeous prose and skillful narration will bring you to the edge of your seat, yearning for the next revelation. A must-read for anyone craving a story that explores the layers of identity and the enduring power of love.

Lisa Williamson Rosenberg, author of *Embers on the Wind*

Tackling the topics of antisemitism and homophobia, Cave of Secrets, is an engaging, thought-provoking read, illustrating the power of courage to unveil past secrets, make tough choices, and live an authentic life against all odds. Golodner exquisitely crafts a layered story full of heart, wisdom, hard truths, and explores the journey of self-discovery and the deep need for human connection. A touching tale of love, loss, and the fortitude to pave a new path forward.

Annie Cathryn, multi-award winning author of *The Friendship Breakup*

What begins as a journey to unravel an historical romance reveals deep secrets that a family has tried to hide for decades.

CAVE OF SECRETS not only addresses forbidden love of the past but also brings to light the struggles of love and relationships today along with the search for acceptance by one's family and the outside world. Lynne Golodner's writing encompasses the feelings and emotions of each character in a way that allows readers to empathize with each of them.

Michelle Glogovac, award-winning author of *How To Get On Podcasts*

Chapter One

*E**ve, July 2014*

If Eve had known a storm was coming, she wouldn't have set out on a four-mile hike through the forests around Loch Lomond. But she was two miles in as a rush of cool air pimpled her arms. The first drops fell cold on her face, and she scanned beyond the trail for a place to shelter as a crack of thunder split the dark sky and fat raindrops drenched her hair.

Before the rain pelted down, Eve had sat on the nub of a hill and stared over the fault line that traced from the summit all the way down to the Loch and along three islands evenly spaced in the glassy water, the dividing line between the Highlands and the Lowlands. The line between the person she had been and the person she was about to become.

She had no time to pull out the gray rain jacket she'd bought before coming to Scotland because it promised to be easily packable and lightweight. It was balled up in her backpack, and as the skies opened up, she didn't want to stop to find it and risk drenching the notebook she took everywhere to jot down thoughts and questions for future research. Eve ran into a thicket of trees, ducking under the fragrant arms of an evergreen for cover. She was at the plateau in the climb, with a perfect view of the black water, which drank in the rain. The soil under her feet darkened as it turned gummy with mud. Deeper into the trees, Eve spotted an opening, and she went for it, darting beneath branches and over knotty roots until it came clearer into view.

The cave was wide and quiet and humid. Ducking inside, she sank to the ground to catch her breath, sliding off her pack and dropping it in the dirt as her eyes adjusted to the darkness. "Hello?" she called, her voice rippling back to her in echoes.

The cave calmed her and warmed her prickling flesh. Heat emanated from the slate walls. The ground was flat and moist, the silence soothing. After a few minutes, Eve walked deeper in. She shook the rain from her arms like a dog wringing out fur. The storm was unlikely to go long. She would wait until the rain slowed and the skies brightened, and then she'd tread carefully down the slick mountain paths.

A hundred yards into the belly of the cave and somehow, she could see better. Light was coming from somewhere inside, a cleft in the mountain that created a skylight. Still, she pulled a flashlight from her bag, glad she'd remembered to pack it. Spotlighting the space, she saw she wasn't the first person to seek shelter here. Burnt logs and broken twigs were scattered in an alcove where someone had lit a fire to keep warm. She grazed her fingers along a piece of wood—dry and brittle. The fire hadn't been recent. Farther still, flat boulders had served as a tabletop. Toffee and biscuit wrappers left by careless hikers littered the surface. Eve stuffed them in her pockets to dispose of later.

"Aieeee!" she called, just to hear the trill of her voice vibrate back to her and smiled as the high pitch bounced off the stone walls.

The dim light glinted off a flat surface where the rock wall met the sandy floor. Eve knelt closer, trying to see what had caught the light. A leather-bound satchel lay half-buried, half-revealed in the dirt. She poked into the soil, drawing open the earth. Palming the package, she slowly peeled it open to peer inside. The pages were smooth and not too soil-streaked, the letters faded but readable.

The first page read like a letter, though there was no date to identify when or by whom. Eve squinted in the low light to make out the words, which brushed across the page in elegant formal script. The author certainly had exquisite penmanship.

My darling Benjamin,

I have counted the days until you would return to my waiting arms, my insistent kisses. But now I know you never will. The telegram arrived to the Foundation offices in London, and a messenger ferried it to me here. News of your demise, your sinking at sea. Oh, my dear Benjamin, how will I continue without you? I write here in the privacy of my rooms, all the things I wish I could say aloud. I can tell no one that this baby I carry is yours. No one to wail to about the loss of my life's love. Hugh suspects, of course, for we have lived as sister and brother all these many years since I found you and released him to his secrets. But he will wear the face of father for this baby, who will never know his true lineage, never know his kind, patient, selfless father, whom I loved more than I have ever loved anyone. Now that you've gone to your eternal rest, I

will go about the business of raising my children, the last of whom will carry your gleaming smile, your tender eyes, your open heart, your giving soul. I will hold you in my heart always along with the memories of our enduring love. I pray that the brief time we had will be a beacon, brightening my days and softening my nights as I gaze at the round moon alone, without your tender touch, without a companion, without you, my darling. I remain forever yours.
    Shira

The paper was yellow with age but soft between the leather covers.

Eve scanned the cave's perimeter, looking for more, but found nothing. She laid the satchel on top of her pack and knelt where she had found it, clawing at the ground. Soft dirt coated her hands, sifted under her fingernails, and still she kept digging hoping to uncover companion pages. *There must be more,* she thought. A month into her fellowship at the National Archives of Scotland had taught her this much. When she'd gone three fingers deep into the ground and still come up with nothing, she sat back on her heels and swiped the sweat from her forehead. There would be more of a story to discover, but she wouldn't find anything else today.

Eve smeared her dirt-streaked hands along her jeans before unzipping her pack. Pulling her raincoat from the bag, she wrapped it around the journal for protection then slid it back in and zipped it closed. Then she hoisted it over her shoulders and headed to the mouth of the cave. Streams of rainwater spilled over the opening, runoff from higher elevations, not new rainfall. The storm was over. Where before there had been dark clouds, now pillows of lavender floated across the sky. Eve turned her face to the cleansing baptism of water draining over the cave as she headed out. On their hikes together in Ann Arbor, when she was younger, and on harder hikes during northern Michigan vacations, her father, Sam Waldman, always mentioned something about how nature does its thing without worry or want, and everything turns out as it should. He wished humans could mimic the ease and flow of nature — that he could. For years, she hadn't known what he'd meant but had sensed a sadness in her only parent, and as a little girl, Eve had reached for her father's hand and clasped her fingers around his for reassurance. They were each other's whole world, and she knew how hard it had been for him when she'd accepted the year-long fellowship in Scotland. But he hadn't asked her to stay in the States. He would never do that, clip his daughter's wings to absolve his own loneliness. And she loved him even more because of it.

She reached for her phone to tell him of the letter but had no signal this high up on the mountain, so she tucked it into her pocket and started the descent.

The wind was light now, breezy. On the trail, she fired off a text: *Daddy — You'll never guess what happened on my hike today. I found letters buried in the dirt. They look old, and the content that I read is intriguing. I'll call you soon and tell you all about it. Luv u*

The cave sat just below the tree line before the mountain rose like a naked shoulder of yellow-green. It was where the wind blew loud and harsh, even on a bright sunny day, across the open expanse of the meadow. While the day had lightened as the rain eased, the wind was still fierce at this elevation, drowning out the fervent cries of birds in the trees below.

By the time she reached her car, Eve's phone was buzzing. "Daddy?"

"Darling! Tell me about the buried treasure." She smiled at the comforting hum of his voice. Cobwebbed from the silence of hiking alone, she coughed her throat clear.

Buckling into her seat, Eve thrust the car into Drive, switching the phone to speaker over the console. "It's a satchel of smooth leather on the outside and oiled on the inside, which has protected the pages. Inside, I read only the first letter, but there are many. The script is beautiful and it's a love letter—an homage to a lost love. So beautiful, Daddy," she said. "Of course, David will be chuffed that I've handled it without gloves, but I didn't have any archival tools with me. How could I know I'd find something buried in the mountain?"

"Exciting." She could hear her father's smile in his voice. "Like you were meant to do this work, honey."

"The names are Jewish: Shira. Benjamin. In Scotland," she said. "Not a place known for its Jewish population."

"How interesting! You'll try to track them down, figure out who they were?"

She was nodding as she directed the car along the narrow road, under lush trees, hugged by stone walls. It had only taken a few days to adjust to driving on the right side of the car and left side of the road and now, Eve leaned into the turns as she whipped around the bends in country roads, no longer fearful of the narrow lanes.

"It sounds like they had quite a love," she said, her voice wistful. "We can talk more later, Daddy. I'm ducking into a pub for a bite and a dram."

"You already sound so Scottish," he laughed. "Cheerio!"

"That's English," she laughed. "And I'm not sure they actually say that. Talk to you later. I love you!"

Eve parked in the gravel outside Monteith House and grabbed her pack. The bottom of her pants legs were streaked with dried mud, her boots gray with it. Eve checked her reflection in the car window and pulled her chestnut-brown hair away from her face, twisting it into a low bun at the nape of her neck and securing it with a hair tie she'd kept around her wrist like a bracelet.

"Good enough," she muttered as she strode across the car park and into the open door.

Chapter Two

Mac, 2014

Mac threaded a dishrag through the belt loop of his jeans, gripped two plates and two empty glasses from the bar and dumped them in a rubber tray. Then he swiped the counter clean in preparation for the next guests.

The pub throbbed with people. Midafternoon on a summer Sunday in high tourist season, the pub on the lip of Loch Lomond was a natural stopping point for hikers along the West Highland Way. It had become a revolving door of hungry guests sweaty from difficult hill-walks and thirsty for cold local brews. Dark wood beams punctuated the low ceilings. Wooden tables filled the room, with another room for guests behind the reception area. In summer, tables were scattered outdoors too, in front of the establishment, and people clamored to sit under trees and along the sidewalk to soak in the meager rays of sun that broke through the daily rainclouds.

Monteith House, also an inn that offered twelve private rooms en suite, had been part of the Monteith holdings in the Lomond Valley for nearly three centuries.

It was unusual for a son of the fifth Earl of Monteith to man a pub, even a second son, who was not the natural heir. But it was what Mac had insisted on when he finished university, his football career a bust. His parents hadn't been pleased—neither by the career-ending injury nor his decision to adopt the life of a working man. Or rather, his mother wasn't pleased, and his father went along in support of his wife.

"It's unseemly," Margaret Monteith had insisted when Mac announced he'd work in one of the family's many real estate holdings—country estates, village pubs, storefronts on several High Streets and open land that reached high up into the mountains and across the Highlands. "The Monteiths have managed the working class for generations, not become part of it," she'd said, her nose wrinkling and her arms folded defensively across her chest.

Mac had resisted rolling his eyes or releasing an exasperated sigh. He would not engage his mother's snobbery. While his sisters were all too keen to engage in verbal warfare with their proud and proper mother, neither Mac nor his older brother Collin would tolerate it. His father, Alexander, the rightful Earl of Monteith and inheritor of the long-held family estate, whose chums called him "Alex the Great" with a gale of hearty laughter, had set his lips and nodded when Margaret went on a tear about position and propriety. But his eyes had gleamed with a more laid-back message. Mac's father had never cared for title or class, and it always perplexed Mac why his mother clung so fiercely to these haughty ways when her aristocratic-born husband cared so little for it. Although he'd never said it aloud, Mac sensed Alex was not only proud of his son's independent streak but admiring of his gumption to choose a different and unexpected path. He hoped one day he could broach a conversation with his father about his own desires and dreams, but he resisted the urge for fear of ridicule. Scots were more passionate than the English but shared the same insistence on propriety and appearance, and after decades of marriage, Mac's father had assumed aristocratic poise more than he ever had before meeting Margaret.

A chalkboard displayed a list of available local whiskies, beers and gins. The interior was darkened by plaid carpet and heavy wood tables buffeted by chairs with iron buckles and lattice backs. Deer heads on the wall and stuffed pheasants on shelves were from family hunts, some Mac or his brother or father had caught, killed and preserved. The Scottish ancestral motif was completed with pictures from those festive hunts and of family ancestors as far back as a hundred and fifty years, when the first photographs were being taken.

Clan artifacts—shields, swords and trophies from Highland Games—were displayed on the walls and in glass cases around the restaurant and lobby. Mac loved the intersection of Highlander glory and English aristocracy that was his family's history. He'd traced the conversion from fighting clansmen to proper loyal subjects of the King, uncertain how he felt standing on the English-sympathizing side of history. He was embarrassed that his ancestors had fought with the English at Culloden, defecting from the Highland clans who would be subdued and sent away after the Rising of 1746. Of course, doing so had ensured their wealth and landowning legacy, which had endured for centuries and from which he now benefited. But it had been a transactional move, rather than one steeped in meaning or belief, and that made him uncomfortable. Funny that now his life was all about transactions, but he saw it as offering people an experience that made them happy, so it was worthwhile work.

The host led a foursome through the restaurant to a table under the oak tree in front of the building. As they passed, he listened to their loud, American voices.

"My best friend swore this place was the best in the area," one woman insisted.

Mac smiled. He'd worked hard to achieve that designation, and he was grateful for the easy spending tourists brought to the region he called home. The summer rush kept Monteith House going year-round without need to advertise or promote in the off-season, though he did both to build allure and reputation. And the tourists didn't seem to mind the higher prices from May through October—they competed for a spot in the small inn and a reservation at the always-full restaurant.

He leaned against the bar and watched the animated faces and fast-moving mouths of his customers. His mother might not like that he worked for a living, but Mac was exhilarated by the pace and buzz of the place. It energized him to walk through the doors, nod and smile at the people he'd hand-picked for hire and nurtured through the training regimen on up the ladder to leadership. He was a good manager, teasing out his employees' talents and strengths and allowing them to shine, never threatened by an ambitious worker.

And he liked working. It was a privilege to not have to and one that had seized him with guilt during his teen years and early twenties. At 28, he'd made peace with the fact of things and come to love managing the inn, even if it wasn't a career he'd worked hard to build, rather than been given.

As he weaved between the tables, nodding and smiling at patrons munching and sipping, he tried to ignore the coquettish looks of women whose eyes followed his movements. He was used to it but never comfortable. While he could be as rowdy as his mates when they were bagging a Munro, clinking bottles of local brew around a campfire or racing kayaks on the loch with whoops and cries of competition, Mac grew quiet in a crowd of strangers. That drew women to him even more, which magnified his unease. It wasn't a tactic; he'd always been that way, even as a boy, in the shadow of his boisterous older brother, his voice shrinking as Collin's grew louder. What people never saw, until they knew him well, was the soft side, the tenderness, the concern for the smallest and frailest—find a baby bird injured on a trail and he'd stop to caress its soft, warm body and fashion a splint from whatever he could find in the woods. He particularly loved children and yearned for a family of his own, but that wasn't something he could openly admit in his crowd of uber-masculine friends. And if he said it to his mother, she'd badger him more than she already did. Margaret was relentless about the family legacy and the importance of guaranteeing a future for the Monteiths.

Mac had been in love only once, in his early twenties, with a bold lass named Sheena, and he'd thought finally, he'd found someone he could be himself with. Open, revealing, vulnerable—traits he'd never embraced with anyone other than his youngest sister, Emma, the only person he'd ever known who had not pushed him to offer more than was comfortable. But

Sheena had packed up and moved to Australia a year after they met, and she didn't ask him to go with her. That had been answer enough to his questions of where their relationship was headed. He missed her sometimes but never regretted staying in Scotland, where he belonged. If it had been real love, they'd be together.

So he dove into the demands of Monteith House, playing to the desires of tourists and hikers, creating a welcoming setting for visitors to fall in love with this gorgeous place and its storied culture. If he stopped long to consider it, he might admit he was lonely.

When she walked in, his breath caught in his throat. The din of noise faded and the motion of customers and servers froze. He watched her walk toward him, her brown eyes on fire, her warm brown hair in a loose bun that accentuated her long cheek bones and athletic body. She was beautiful, but he was struck more by the confidence of her gait and the fact that she was all alone in the pub. The place attracted solo hikers, sure, but usually they were men who looked like they didn't want to be bothered with human company. In the six years that he'd run the pub, he'd never met a woman who had soloed the West Highland Way. They always came in packs.

Which didn't stop Mac from having plenty of one-night stands. As the owner of the most popular pub on the shores of Loch Lomond, he was a character in their story of a dream vacation in the wild north. Hikers passing through and tourists who came to Scotland were spurred by the promise of romance and intrigue from countless romantic and historical novels and

TV shows, and many were all too eager to bed him and then continue on their way with a story tucked into their pack.

"Mac-o!" a deep voice called from across the room. Collin, waving a scrap of family plaid above his head. Restaurant patrons paused mid-bite and turned to stare at his beefy older brother, whose amber hair blazed. Mac pressed his lips together and heaved a hard sigh. He swung his hands, palm-up, in a question.

Collin skipped across the room to where he stood behind the bar, as the guests resumed their table conversations and cutlery clinked against plates. "Pour me a dram of your finest," his brother bellowed.

"I live to serve," Mac murmured, grabbing the nearest bottle of cheap whiskey. He didn't want to waste the good stuff on his brother. Collin's green eyes sparkled.

"Don't give me that swill!" He pushed the bottle away and gestured to the twelve-year Tomatin single malt. "That's what I want, brother. And since it's a family holding, be generous with the pour."

"What have you done now?" Mac asked as he searched the room for the woman.

Collin drained the pour instantly and stamped the glass on the counter to signal his desire for another.

"This is a paying pub, you know," Mac hissed.

"What do you care?" Collin spat. "It's not like this comes out of your pocket, ever. Pour me another, man."

Mac filled the glass with a finger's length of whiskey. "It's broad daylight," he chided. "You don't need to be the family drunk. There are many other roles you could fill."

Collin inhaled the liquid and swiped a hand across his lips.

Mac scanned the room. Where had she gone?

"I bear a message from our mother," Collin said, affecting the stiff demeanor of a formal messenger. "She requests your presence at Sunday breakfast." He winked. "A request that is really a demand, my liege."

"Cut it out, you fool." Mac swatted at his brother. "Why couldn't she text me?"

"That's not how Mum operates, and you know it." Collin batted his eyes at Mac and tapped his glass for another dram. Mac laughed. His brother was a goof who avoided work, but he wasn't a bad guy. Just lazy and spoiled. Which annoyed Mac, but he couldn't fault Collin for it.

"Third, and you're cut off," Mac said, tipping the bottle to pour. "Now go away. And tell Mother I might come, but I can't promise."

"It's your funeral," his brother said and drained the glass before pushing off from the bar. "*Au revoir, mon amour*," he said as he leaned over the bar and planted a loud kiss on his brother's cheek.

Mac winced as he swiped Collin's glass from the bar and deposited it in the dirty dish bin. He tucked the dishrag beneath the counter and stepped around to search for the woman who'd caught his eye. Just then, she emerged from the lobby restroom, swiping her hands along her pants. She was electric with energy. He smoothed his dark curls and licked his lips. She was coming right for him.

But then, she walked past, not seeing him, not stopping to say hello. *Silly man. She doesn't know you.* Mac scurried back to the bar and set himself behind it in an authoritative pose just as the woman slid onto a stool.

"What can I get you?" he said.

Chapter Three

*E**ve, 2014*

Eve scanned the drinks menu on a tall chalkboard behind the bar. "I'll have a Windswept Wolf," she said.

"Good choice," the bartender said, popping the top off the bottle and setting it on the bar. "Mug?" Eve shook her head and sipped from the bottle. "Nice," he said.

"Hmmm?" She wrinkled her eyebrows as she tilted her head back to swallow.

"I don't bother with a glass, either," he said in a deep and soothing voice, the sound she thought the beer would make if it could talk.

She nodded, smiling. She'd always preferred drinking straight from the bottle.

"Mac," he said, reaching a hand toward her. Eve clasped it, warmed by his firm grip, and shook.

"Eve."

"You look done in," he said.

"Hmm?"

"Tired. Ragged. Worn."

"Ah, yes. I was hiking, and the storm…" She laughed. Her hair was no longer dripping down her neck, though she hadn't minded the coolness of its trickle after the long hike. "Or hill walking, as you might say. Though it was more than a hill, more of a climb than I had expected."

In the hearth, a fire blazed. A busser fed new logs in to keep the heat going. Servers cleared empty bottles as they brought full ones sweating with condensation to the guests. Greasy fries and sandwiches and stews arrived to tables. Night was coming on slowly, and the few windows in the place revealed a lavender sky mellowing behind the trees.

After another sip of the dark beer, which tasted like nectar from the gods after the hard hike and soaking downpour, Eve pulled a notebook from her purse and set it on the bar. She peeled back the cover and started to write, lost in thought. He was watching her, quirking an eyebrow but saying nothing.

"I found a letter in a cave."

"Up on Conic Hill? A cave?"

She nodded, staring at his blue eyes, which seemed to shimmer.

"I've walked that hill a hundred times and never found a cave," he said.

Eve shrugged, sipped her beer. "Maybe it took new eyes."

How many times had she walked the same Ann Arbor trails, not really seeing them? And now, here she was in a foreign place, discovering its secrets because her eyes were open to the possibility. It was arrogant to think that just because you'd always known a place, you could ever really know it. She thought of the brittle paper of the first letter, wanting to retrieve it from the car, but she didn't want to risk damaging it with the oils from her fingers, or worse, a spill in the pub.

"Don't quite know what it is, but I'll find out." She looked up. Mac was staring at her but not in a jarring way. Eve smiled, and he returned the soft look. "I work in an archive—the National Archives of Scotland, actually," she said. "Learning to become an archivist, to track down history and preserve it."

"I don't know that I've ever heard of that career," he said.

"Most people haven't," she snorted. "But it's quite important. I mean, think about how we even know about earlier generations and societies—all the documents and photographs and portraits and historical items of value and import. Cultural details. Historical relevance. The events of history. Someone has to decide what to keep and what to forget."

"And you are one of those people," he finished.

"Well, not yet, but someday," she said.

She went to sip from her beer but found it empty. Mac must have noticed, too, because he nodded at it. "Another?"

Eve nodded. "Thanks. And some food? I'm starving."

He handed her a menu and cracked off the top of another bottle, swiping the empty one into a crate of recyclables behind the bar.

"Fish and chips or Scotch pie?" Eve handed the menu back to Mac. He was quite good-looking, his dark curls gleaming black in the shadows of the firelight. And strong. The sinews of his arms were taut ropes as he lifted and cleaned.

"Scotch pie with mustard," Mac said. "The crust is made here every day by a wonderful woman I've known all my life. You'll love it."

"Great, then let's have it."

Mac called the order through to the kitchen then turned back to Eve.

"Don't you have more important things to do than talk to one American customer?"

Mac shrugged. "People are happy. Content. They have food and drink and they're warm. Plus, I'm not the only one here to tend to their needs." He swept an arm across the pub. The tables brimmed with happy, chatty people, leaning in close and relaxing into the hard chairs. The fire roared. Outside, a line of eager patrons waited for tables to open up.

Eve heaved a sigh to release the stress from the storm that had settled into her bones.

Mac nodded at the notebook on the bar top. "Are you writing about the letter? How does one go about finding clues to history?"

Eve shrugged. "I'm still learning."

A bell dinged, and Mac squeezed his hands dry on the towel hanging from his belt loop, then strode to the kitchen window and palmed the plate of Eve's food. He carried it to the counter and slid it onto the hardwood.

"Careful, it's hot," he said.

True to his promise, the crust was crispy and golden, steam rising above it. Eve cut into it, and a thicker column of steam puffed out from the pastry. She looked at Mac, waiting for the food to cool enough to take a bite.

"It's a bit like doing a puzzle, I suppose," she said. "Take the pieces I know and connect them and then work toward the outer edges, where there is little or no information."

Mac was nodding and smiling. "And the journal?"

She shook her head, as she stared off beyond him at nothing in particular. "I've always journaled," she said, not looking at him as she spoke. "I guess it's how I make sense of the world around me. How I figure out what I think, how I feel."

She cut a wedge of pie and forked it into her mouth, chewing slowly. "Damn, that's good." She smiled, gulping a sip of beer. "And still hot." She waved a hand over the plate and chuckled.

"Okay, so what *do* you know?" Mac leaned his elbows on the bar and leaned toward her.

Eve took another bite before answering. "Well, it's a letter and quite old. I have no idea how old, at least a century, maybe longer. Though I have nothing to base that on. I'm really just guessing." She laughed. "I know the first name of the writer and the person she was writing to. Someone died at sea, a lost love. And something about a fatherless baby whose true lineage no one would know."

"All that from a single letter?"

She nodded, closed the notebook and sipped her beer. Her fingers were wet from the sweating bottle. "Exciting, isn't it?"

A small smile played on his lips as Mac nodded.

Lone hikers ambled in and settled at the bar. Mac took orders, delivered drinks, then circled back to Eve, who swept the flaky pastry and meaty chunks through the spicy mustard. She sipped from yet another beer. From the speakers came the sound of traditional pipes and the low, slow whistle of flutes. There were favorites like Dougie MacLean's "Caledonia" but also snippets of contemporary acts like Young Fathers, Paolo Nutini, Nina Nesbitt. She was beginning to recognize songs that she'd never heard across the Atlantic— "Pauper's Dough" by King Creosote was melancholy but beautiful, and she loved the beat of "Two Travel" by Beerjacket.

When she finished eating, she laid her fork and knife together along the plate and pushed it away. An empty bottle stood beside the empty plate. "Maybe a tea now?"

Mac nodded and pulled a mug from a cupboard. "I'll start the kettle," he said. He slid a glass of water toward her. "To hold you over until it's warm." She sipped at the water and pulled out her notebook again.

She scrawled across the pages, stopping every so often to think. He peered at her writing—neat, even script across small pages.

"I'm writing notes about the cave and questions to ask my boss."

"Should you have kept the letter? Perhaps it wasn't meant to be discovered?"

"Well, it's been there for ages, and only now it came loose. If I didn't take it, someone else would, and perhaps destroy it or not recognize its significance. And it's a clue to local history," she said. "I mean, someone cared enough to write it but then buried it so it wouldn't be found. Why not destroy it? Burn it in a hearth fire? Tear it to pieces and throw it away? Someone wanted it to be found someday."

"And now it has," he said.

"And now it has," she agreed.

Eve's cheeks burned. Her whole body buzzed with passion for the words on the page before her.

"But local history," he said. "Pardon me, isn't that outside your domain? I mean, you are an American, not a Scot. My family has lived on this land for generations. We have more right to its forgotten stories than you do, don't we?"

She cocked her head, her eyebrows scrunching, her eyes serious. Was he threatening her? Challenging? But he had a point. Who laid claim to history? Who had the final say over its dissemination? Was she a dreaded interloper, interested in a romantic image of Scotland after centuries of invasion, incursion and foreign control? She stared at the strange man across from her, wondering if she had made a mistake by talking about the letter at all.

"History should actually be handled by impartial people who don't have a stake in it," she offered, feigning confidence.

She chattered on about proper handling of historical documents, clucking her tongue at the lack of protective gloves at her disposal on the hike. "I didn't expect to find anything, so why would I bring archeological tools? I hope the way I've treated it doesn't harm the life of the letter," she said.

The life of the letter. She believed history to be alive, pulsing. Eve's cheeks were warm from the meal and the beer and the heat of the room. Mac's hand hovered above hers as she told him about the research and the temperature-controlled stacks of material in boxes and crates and folders kept in the Edinburgh headquarters of the National Archives where she worked.

"You're here for a hike but live in Edinburgh?"

She shook her head. "I live here."

"And work in Edinburgh? Are you mad?"

She smirked. "My colleagues think so. It's a long commute. I take the train from Stirling."

"Every day? But it's at least a half-hour drive to the train, and then what, an hour in? Barring stops and blockages and cancellations. That's a very American thing to do. Scots don't commute for work."

"Not the first time I've heard that," she said, draining the water glass.

The kettle whistled. Mac flipped the switch off and poured the steaming liquid into a ceramic tea pot, which he set beside the mug on the counter. He pulled a tiny pitcher of cold milk from a refrigerator below and slid a sugar bowl toward Eve.

"I lived in Edinburgh for the first month that I was here, but I'm not a city girl," she said. "I prefer country air and a slower pace, so it's worth the commute. I spend the time thinking or reading, and when I arrive at work, I am already mired in my projects. Plus, my boss is very generous—he lets me work at home Mondays and Fridays, so it's only three days a week."

Her hair was coming loose from the bun, fuzzy tendrils framing her face. She brushed the fine, soft hairs away from her eyes.

"Have dinner with me tomorrow," he said.

Eve pressed a napkin to her lips then laid it on the bar counter. She studied his face, the long lines of his neck, the shadow of stubble along the slope of his cheeks, the inky-dark waves of his hair.

"Sure," she said, scribbling her phone number on a corner of paper torn from the journal.

"Tomorrow, then," he said. "I'll come for you at six."

He slid a scrap of paper under her plate, which Eve assumed was the bill, and walked away. She watched him go, watched his body move, his back so strong and assuring. He disappeared around a corner and down a hallway until she could no longer see him. She turned the paper over, reaching for her wallet, but saw only a heart with two dots for eyes and a sliver of a smile, quick swipes of pen, another surprise on a very interesting day.

Chapter Four

S am, 1983

Memories of his early years aware that he was a gay man flashed back to Sam. As an eleven-year-old in yeshiva, not wanting to roughhouse with the other boys, disgusted by their lewd comments about girls. And years later, at nineteen, when his new wife, Shaindie, learned of his true inclinations, the searing burn of her disgust and threats. "You *ever* tell a soul about this, and I will leave you and take your child with me and tell the whole community, and no one—no one!— will allow you to see her. You're a poor excuse for a man."

His wife had ranted about how he'd been less than honest with her, with the *shadchan*, the matchmaker who recommended them to each other's parents, and the rabbi who had vouched for him. She stomped around the tidy apartment, threatening that she could leave him and the community would support her. It would be as if their marriage had never happened, and he'd be *persona non grata* in any Orthodox community, but she wouldn't do it, not then, because she was expecting and she'd keep his secret, if he played the part of the doting husband. So he promised that he would because everything she said was right. His family would reject him. His community, too. He'd be alone, with nowhere to go and no one to show him the way, so he soothed her rage and hid his urges.

Sam was the eldest son in a family of five siblings in Oak Park, Michigan, part of an Orthodox Jewish family and a world he never fit into. He went to school, followed the religious rules as his father taught him, and when he started noticing other boys in ways that made him feel ashamed—admiring the curve of a shoulder or the angle of a nose, such sights stirring a tingling in his stomach and a flutter in his groin—he kept these feelings to himself. With no training or education whatsoever into human sexuality, he didn't know how to make sense of them. Did other boys think like this? Feel this way toward their friends? And why didn't he see what the other boys saw when they looked at girls?

One night, when he dreamt of another boy naked and woke up drenched in sweat and other stickiness that he couldn't name, he was terrified that something was wrong with him. Still, he said nothing, afraid of his father's belt and penetrating gaze. He distracted himself with books from the public library, his only refuge.

Walking distance from his family's ranch-style home and also his school, the library was Sam's only exposure to the outside world. There, he saw people of all walks of life—different skin tones and modes of dress, men interacting with women, young people flirting, touching, unburdened and free. He became close with a kind librarian in A-line skirts and blouses with Peter Pan collars who saw his loneliness and helped him find answers to his questions. She ordered books for him from other branches, taught him about the broader region around his small enclave, including an open-minded town called Ann Arbor, forty-five minutes away and home to the prestigious University of Michigan, where she had studied. There, she said, people were "liberal as hell and accepting of everything," smiling and adding that it was "a damn shame more places couldn't be like that."

He spent hours after school lost in fanciful stories, immersed in nonfiction books deep in the stacks. He learned how babies were made, which horrified him, the thought of his body and a girl's interconnected so intimately. He sought out books about his fantasies and learned that there was a word for a man who desired other men—and when he looked deeper into it, he connected the term homosexual with the Hebrew from Leviticus, *to'eva,* the worst kind of "abomination." He'd read the text in school, felt the fiery reactions of the rabbis as they told the boys that a man laying with another man as he would with a woman was grounds for expulsion from the community and the deepest depravation. Sam cowered on the carpet beside the metal shelves of old books and wept.

For high school, his parents sent him away to a yeshiva in Skokie, Illinois, where he was called "a pansy" and bullied by the other boys for being too quiet. He learned to avert his gaze when other boys changed in the locker room or joked in the dormitory's communal showers. And as other boys talked about girls and the rabbis pushed marriage and the holy mandate to produce big families to replace all the Jewish souls lost in the Holocaust, he wondered how he would ever be able to be alone with a girl, let alone do what was necessary to create a family. Once, home on a break, he tried to ask his mother, but she turned red and looked away, saying it was a question better posed to his father. But he could no more imagine laying with a naked woman than he could imagine speaking about it to his father, so Sam left the subject alone until he turned eighteen and his parents started talking to him about a match.

And thus, his attraction to men remained a secret.

At first, Shaindie seemed like the path of least resistance. He had to marry, didn't he? It was what young Orthodox Jews did. The purpose of the community, the way to build a brighter, stronger Jewish people. She was a pretty girl, with chestnut hair, a shy smile and blazing almond-shaped eyes that glowed golden when she felt strongly about something. She wasn't short like his sister and mother, though shorter than Sam, who at five feet, ten inches, was the tallest person in his family.

On their first date, they sipped water from clear glasses at her kitchen table as their parents made small talk in the living room. The hum of their voices lulled Sam into feeling safe with this young woman and with the idea of moving forward with his duty, if not his desire.

"How many children do you want?" she asked.

His face warmed with embarrassment, even though he knew this was a typical first-date question in his quiet community.

"I don't know," he stammered. "I haven't really thought about it."

"I have," she said, her voice definite and firm. "Six, at least. And I can't also be the only income-earner. It's just too much. I've seen my mother do it, and I don't want to be tired and worn by the time I'm thirty."

He peered at her blazing eyes, saw the gold flecks glimmer like a late-day sun. Where did she find such strength? How did her parents allow it? Though his brother Moshe had a similar defiant streak which their father tried to beat into submission, the rest of the Waldman family was meek and obedient. Shaindie was a breath of fresh air.

"That makes sense," Sam said calmly, quietly. "I'm training as a bookkeeper, and I learn half-days in the *kollel*. Soon, I'll have a steady income. People always need help with their accounting."

She nodded as she considered the information. Was he attractive to her? Was he attractive at all? Sam had never evaluated himself in such terms. His dark, thick hair and dark eyes were standard issue for the community. His body had long, lean lines, and his hands were strong. What did she see when she looked at him?

Shaindie leaned in. "This could work," she said, searching his face, not for agreement, but almost as if she were inspecting him for flaws or secrets. He coughed, lifting a fisted hand to his mouth and looking over her head at the clean kitchen behind her. The house was small, like his childhood home, but it wasn't quite as worn, despite it being fuller with activity with nine children and a variety of nieces and nephews who lived within a three-block radius. How did religious women manage such demanding home lives? Sam wondered.

They were too nervous on their wedding night to do anything intimate, another secret to add to the pile Sam kept in his emotional filing cabinet. His rabbi and his father had insisted that for a marriage to be official, it required the public ceremony under the chuppah amid an audience of witnesses, and the consummation act afterwards, which used to happen in a quiet room right after the ceremony but in modern times was trusted to the young couple alone on their first wedded night. They had danced on separate sides of the ballroom of the Hilton, as required by religious custom. Alone among the men, Sam felt more at home than he had in the presence of his bride. His peers, even the ones who had relentlessly teased him, danced to entertain the groom as was the custom, donning bright-ly-colored hats with chiming bells, squatting for the Kazatsky dance, grabbing his hands and pulling him into a fast-moving circle of sweating, laughing, heaving men, and hoisting him on a chair high above the celebrants, with chants of "Oy! Oy!" to the pumping beat of the hard-playing band on a raised platform decorated in tulle and flowers to match the chuppah.

He didn't even peer into the women's side of the dance floor, as most grooms did. As most *men* did, poking their heads between openings in the dark curtain between the two sides, watching the women's bodies move, their glorious, unbridled laughter lighting their faces and their bosoms bouncing as they spun faster, faster. He had no interest nor curiosity, and gazing onto the fair skin of his wife would no more send tingles along his limbs than would her naked body on their hotel bed later that night. Sam pushed such thoughts from his mind and closed his eyes to the revelry, letting the men's laughter seep into his skin, feeling for the touch of their warm hands as they danced in circles and lifted him up.

"We have to do it," she said early the next morning.

Sam was flat on his back on the most comfortable mattress he'd ever slept on. It was his first time in a hotel because his family only stayed with friends or community members when they traveled for a wedding or bar mitzvah, and they rarely took vacations. It was the way of the Orthodox to keep costs low and stay in walking distance of their brethren and a synagogue.

He opened his eyes and turned his head on the pillow to look at his bride.

"You know we must," she said.

He nodded.

"Don't you want to?"

He couldn't say no. This woman was his wife. He'd spend his life with her, and it couldn't begin on a foundation of lies. And he didn't want to hurt her feelings. It wasn't her fault that he wasn't attracted to the female body. He turned on his side and leaned on his elbow. He was wearing the striped pajamas his mother always bought for him and his brothers, long sleeves, buttons down the front and long pants to just above his ankles. She was in white satin with thin straps, the pale skin of her shoulders and the swell of her breasts in plain sight. He'd never seen a naked woman before, except for illustrations in library books. The satin shimmered under the early light coming in from the window, the gown snowy white all the way down past Shaindie's knees. The fabric didn't mask the dark triangle below her stomach, and he swallowed, unable to dislodge the clog in his throat.

"Sure," he croaked, reaching a hand to her arm, trailing two fingers along the bone of her wrist. She closed her eyes, leaned back against the pillow.

And then, an image of his study partner flashed into his mind, his focused gaze on the shared page between them, the long lines of his pale fingers following the delicate Hebrew script as he read aloud. Sam's heartbeat quickened as he pictured his friend's pale skin and golden hair, and his body started to harden. He moved closer to his wife, remembered how the rabbi had instructed him to be gentle, to go easy, that the first time was often painful for a woman and to say nice things to make her feel at ease.

"You are a beautiful woman," he said.

Her legs went wider, and he slid a hand down the length of the satin—it was so soft, so delicate!—and under the lacy hem to the warm inside of her legs. Her breath came in quick rasps as he traced his fingers higher, the images in his mind making him throb. She was wet between her legs, which surprised him, though he didn't know why, and he pulled off his pajama bottoms and nestled between her open legs and thrust inside as he imagined what his study partner would look like unclothed. In an instant, hot liquid shot out of him and into her, and he grunted, his heartbeat pulsing in his temples.

His face flushed with heat.

"I'm sorry," he said, scurrying back to his pillow and shimmying his pajama pants up to his waist. "It was fast, I know."

She licked her lips and looked at him. "That's okay," she said. "It was just the first time."

"Were you okay?"

She nodded.

He chewed on a fingernail, then thought of his father's bitten cuticles, the inflamed skin around his nailbeds perpetually infected, and he pulled his finger from his mouth and wiped the saliva on his pant leg. He would never be like his father.

This could work, he thought. He would perform his duty, spurred by images that actually aroused him, and she'd never have to know. He could live with secrets...couldn't he?

CHAPTER FIVE

*M*argaret, *2014*

There were times when Margaret wandered in the hills behind her home that she marveled at how the slate undergirding of these mountains had built the tenement estates in Glasgow where she had grown up as little Mags Allan. What a journey! And one that she banished to the far recesses of memory, never sharing with the women in her aristocratic circles the true origins of her life.

Was it fear of judgment? Concern that she'd be cast out from the inner circle, recognized as one who would never truly belong to, nor deserve, the posh upper classes? Or was it an unnamed fear that she might never fit in anywhere?

It wasn't that she lied to her friends. It was what she chose not to share, the tiny details of her childhood, which, frankly, were no longer relevant this far into her life with Alex as the mother of a whole new generation of Monteiths. Without her, the family legacy would not continue, she convinced herself, never considering that if Alex hadn't fallen for her within days of meeting at university, he might have found some other girl who was eager to partner with the sweet, puppy-like man who became her husband.

Sometimes she felt like the Great Pretender. Borrowing from old Scottish lore and the nickname for the rightful king, the Bonnie Prince, and invoking the rebellious zeal of the Jacobite cause of the 18th century, she was the furthest thing from a rebel—unless one counted leaving a plain and disappointing childhood of poverty and loneliness as rebellion. Margaret only wanted her rightful place at the top of society, unable to be ousted. She believed she deserved a life of wealth and ease, which is why she'd started going by her formal given name of Margaret the minute she stepped foot into the university. She'd earned it, after scraping her nails against the stones to get by, working her little bum off at university to build a better life. She rarely admitted to herself that she should properly thank her generous and doting husband for lifting her out of the gray and ordinary lanes of her early life. She hadn't earned anything. She'd been lucky, come to wealth and ease and sprawling land and a hefty real estate portfolio in the Scottish Highlands because Alex fell in love with her and he happened to be an earl. He would have called her Mags if she'd let him, but even she knew that no upper-crust peers would take her seriously if she kept the dogged nickname of her youth.

Sometimes she wondered why, exactly, he'd fallen for her. At uni, Margaret had been studious and quiet, preferring not to talk lest her classmates make fun of her obvious accent or mistake her for the cleaning lady. She'd worked so hard to escape the Glasgow estates. She'd earned her place at university, dammit! She never wanted to go back. The echoing halls and stone foundations of this old, revered place were a better fit for Margaret's quick mind and serious posture. She was finally where she deserved to be and she didn't want to lose it.

Which was why she never considered love as a worthwhile prize. She kept her head down and her eyes forward-facing, acing exams and paying close attention in lecture hall to win the respect of her professors and peers. Alex admired her grades, yes, and her dedication to academics. He'd said so on their first date, a walk through the university parks with a coffee after in a little café off the High Street. It was Margaret's first date ever, a detail she never shared with Alex, for fear of showing her embarrassing innocence. He might have mistaken her shyness for humility, and she was a beauty back then—still was, by all accounts. She let him speak more than she did, and she listened intently, curious about his upbringing and then in love with the magic of it, as if this man had stepped from a fairy tale book right into her life. She paid close attention and got the sense that few people hung on Alex's every word, which she was happy to do as he regaled her with tales of a childhood in the verdant Highland hills and the buffoonery of his school years, tucked away at Radley College in the Oxfordshire countryside. She loved the long sinews of his arms from years of rowing and the sweetness in his eyes. Most of all, though, she loved the attention Alex lavished on her.

As a young girl, alone after school, Margaret waited for her mother in the public library, lost in books until the shadows of evening darkened the windows and her mother arrived to take her home. A kind grandmotherly librarian led the young lass to books of fantasy and fairy tale, and Margaret dreamt of being a princess. As she grew older, she read about the different classes of British society, yearning to rise from the tenements to a single-family home in the countryside. She read about royals and, as a teen, began working in a local market to be able to bring home thrifted garments to "dress up" from her station.

"Such a clever lass," the librarian said on more than one occasion. "You have a mind for education. That's the way out from here."

She'd wink at Margaret and share brochures from top universities in the United Kingdom and leave the hungry girl to pore over the words, building a belief that she, too, could land a seat in the hallowed halls. "That's where you start a new story, dear," the librarian said.

And so she studied vigilantly, dragging heavy books on weekends to the library tables and, to soothe her racing mind, flipping through the pages of magazines about aristocrats, politicians and members of the royal family to learn how to speak like them, stand like them, dress like them.

It wasn't hard to ace her A-levels—Margaret was a smart girl—and land a spot at Oxford. It was an unusual place for a poor kid from Glasgow estates, and her peers often reminded her that their origins, their place in the world, would never be the same. But once there, Margaret was determined to transform. She never looked back, rarely went home on school breaks. She read her mother's letters but never wrote back, erasing her background and ignoring her roots as she adopted a completely new persona, with the hope that one day, others would see her as deserving of all she had earned.

It helped that Margaret met Alexander Monteith in her first days at uni, drawn to his easygoing nature and ready smile. She loved his undivided focus, loved the way he listened to her talk about her classes and her hopes for the future. He loved her zealous focus on studies and her intense intelligence. She never lied about her background, but she also didn't offer too many details, only answering the questions posed to her and insisting she came from "humble roots." When he wondered why she stayed in the dorms over the holidays, she brushed it off as a need to work to maintain her tuition payments, and he didn't press further. Before long, when they became an item, she followed him home on breaks and poured all of her energy into fitting into the Monteith clan as if she belonged there.

Margaret always knew it could all disappear in a second if she wasn't careful. If she didn't hold on tight. Marrying into ancestry didn't make it yours. Her children inherited history; she had adopted it. And though adoptive parents insisted they loved their nonbiological child equally as much as one who continued their bloodline, Margaret didn't quite believe them. It was what was said, not felt. The entitlement that ran through the blood of the true inheritors was not something that came naturally to those who married in. Margaret believed it took a generation before the dust of the interloper settled, two until the memory of difference was forgotten. She might not live to see the fruits of her efforts. And so she pretended like she belonged. Played the part she had studied so carefully all those years ago, continued to read about the upper crust and the royal family and mimic their posture and tone, hoping one day she would believe it was true.

It was easy now with social media. She didn't have to let anyone know what she was researching. She'd been an early adopter of the latest technology only because it gave her a front seat to the class she aspired to, hearing voices in the videos and watching the carriage of the real princes and princesses as they sauntered, heads high, on their mission.

Margaret Monteith was tall and swan-like, with dark glossy hair and bright-blue eyes. She lived a lonely childhood in a Glasgow estate, gray and scattered with glass shards and rubbish. Her mother worked hard as a lady's maid for a posh family, and her father came on Sundays to take her for fish and chips and a smoke by the quay. She had no siblings, and though her mother was kind, she was quiet, bringing home hand-me-downs from the family she worked for. It wasn't quite pity that she carried in those paper bags full of used clothing. It was more the shame of it that shrouded Margaret in despair, anxious that someone at her school might question where her clothes came from, how such a poor girl could afford such fine threads. For all the years that she could remember, Margaret went to school in someone else's clothes. By her teens, she knew the only way to a better life was to excel in her studies and earn a place at one of the best universities. She aced her GCSEs and A-levels and landed at Oxford, where she was to study math and become an economist or an accountant. A practical career that would always be well-paying, where she could always find work, where she could sustain an easy life and afford everything she could imagine wanting.

She met Alexander Monteith on the second day at university. He was following in the footsteps of his ancestors, who were highly educated leaders in Parliament and industry. The degree didn't really matter to him—it was duty that demanded it, and he'd return home as an Oxford man to preside over the family estate.

She liked his smile but refused to let a man distract her from her studies. He was like a puppy, hovering, hoping for scraps of attention, and in time she learned not only that he would not threaten her mission, but their union could actually hasten it. And she liked him. He was easy to be with, a warm presence. She felt safe with him and seen. He was kind and caring and attentive to her desires, and she felt herself soften in his embrace, breathe easy at his side.

The first time Margaret visited Loch Lomond with Alex to meet his parents, she was struck silent by the beauty of the loping hills. Rounded slopes furred with trees and bluebells and intense shrubs that could not only withstand the harsh winds, but bend to their will and not be cowed. Like those shrubs thriving in the harsh winds and devastating cold of a Highland winter, Margaret would prevail.

Alex didn't mind where she came from, and he didn't judge her for it, but she was embarrassed nonetheless, afraid that if too many people knew, they'd reject her, and he'd cave to the communal consensus that she just wasn't enough. She lived in constant fear that Alex would abandon her for a more appropriate girl whose single strand of pearls hung consistently along the neckline of her pale-pink cashmere crewneck.

It was a late night, strolling through campus, when she admitted that she was not an ideal match for an aristocrat.

"Margaret..." He caressed her hand with his soft, pale fingers. Ran those fingers along the long lines of her bones, the smooth ovals of her nails, painted the pink of ballet slippers in slow, even swipes. He stroked her fingers as he gazed on what she considered her too-thin lips, into her gray-blue eyes, which she considered steely but he said were electric. "Nothing will stop me from loving you."

Her heart thumped. How could he promise enduring love? Too many people said things they didn't mean. Too many people left. Like the father she'd never really known.

"How can you be sure?" she whispered, not daring to look into his glinting green eyes.

"I just know." He was smiling, and his whole face matched the pink of her nails. His red hair in droopy curls made Alex look playful, boyish. It was something she liked about him—envied even. The man was as he appeared. No secrets, no hiding, no façade. "You'll have to trust me, Margaret."

"I grew up poor, Alex." Her voice was steel, flat. She didn't want to tempt emotion to join her, to dangle the promise of acceptance in front of her then reel it away. "Dirt poor. I wore used clothing from the families my mother worked for. I was a bastard child. My parents never married. I come from shame, out of wedlock, from the tenements of Glasgow. If your mother knew, she'd shun me immediately." It took such careful concentration to downplay her accent and sound refined. She was tired from all the effort.

In the silence of night, the click of a fellow student's shoes on the stone walkways echoed against the thick walls of the quad. Streetlamps shone pools of light along the lawn. The campus was quiet until it wasn't. A foursome of drunk young men tripped and laughed, and Margaret turned her face away so they couldn't see the tears pooling in her downturned eyes. So Alex couldn't see her vulnerability. She blinked them away, held her breath to pen in the emotion that threatened to run free.

He moved closer, hooked two fingers under her chin and lifted her face to his gaze. "Poor Margaret," he said quietly. "Believing you aren't worthy of love because of your station? Wherever did you get that notion?"

She choked back tears, didn't trust herself to speak. Could he be this kind? Was this real? And would his parents echo his sentiment or send her on her way as soon as they learned of her dark and dirty origins? She still didn't turn when people called her Margaret, though she was trying to respond to the more formal, proper name—the name she'd told them was hers. She still felt like Mags, as if she were playing the part of the upper-crust co-ed. In the United Kingdom, station was a badge one wore or a torn sash one hid in the back of the darkest drawer. Class and money and generational legacy were everything. They were written along the walls of the clubs you belonged to or were sprayed like graffiti on banners outside the clubs to which you might never gain admittance.

"When I say I love you, please believe me," Alex said, his voice stronger now. Louder. His deep baritone echoed against the stone walls of the very old and storied buildings. He backed her up against one of them and leaned close, the warmth of his body buzzing against her thin frame. His fingers were still under her chin, and she continued to look up at him, exhausted from all the pretending. She sagged against the stone wall and let

Alex cover her like a weighted blanket. He nipped at her earlobe, dotted her neck with little kisses. She closed her eyes, and the tears finally let loose, spilling silently from her eyes and streaking her cheeks. Her nose ran, and he continued to kiss her, to warm her, to make her feel less alone.

And that's why she married him. Hoping their love was real and true and could last, that she could have a better life and find happiness with this man, without it all being a rude, bad dream.

So why, thirty-some years later, did she feel hesitant still, reluctant to believe that she was once and for all a Monteith in every sense of the word?

Chapter Six

Mac, 2014

By eleven, most of the crowd had dispersed, and Mac was left to lock up. He waved to the last two as they pushed through the door and into the cold night.

That girl. He snickered as he pushed chairs against tables and straightened benches. The fire was down to coals, which he doused with a bit of water and listened to the hiss. Most people came to the pub because it was their local, the closest to their home, and they wanted a comforting meal, a cold ale and familiar faces, or they came as a stop on a whirlwind tour of Scotland, checking off all the important places. Rarely did a beautiful woman lope in on her own, plant herself at the bar and look for conversation.

She was beautiful in a different way than the lasses Mac had known. Chestnut wavy hair down past her shoulders and warm brown eyes with hints of gold making them shimmer. She wasn't too tall, nor too short, just the right height to tuck beneath his chin—Mac was a solid six feet standing—and she was athletic, with solid calves, strong shoulders and proud posture. She was something to look at, and no one had piqued his interest in quite a while. Not since Sheena, really, and it had been six years since she left for Australia. Dinner with Eve couldn't come soon enough. He wanted to know more, dig deeper, let her talk and talk while he listened and watched.

He wouldn't tell her too much about his family's wealth. Not yet. He wanted to see if the chemistry between them was real before she knew too much about the prestige behind his family name. He'd had too many close calls with women who liked him more the minute they knew about the family holdings—even after they realized it would all one day go to Collin, not him. He'd only just met her. But she was American...did they care about these things the way too many British girls did?

Mac shut the lights and locked the back door, running a hand over surfaces to make sure he'd swiped away all the stickiness. It had been a good night for the pub, plentiful receipts and good craic. Much of the usual crowd with a steady stream of visitors to round it out. They'd cleared out of fish and chips; he'd increase the order with the fishmonger tomorrow. It wasn't easy running a pub, but he loved it, much to his family's dismay. His brother thought he was crazy to work when he didn't have to. Mac didn't need this job; he wanted it because it made him more normal, more like the average Scot living a decent life. More down to earth.

When everything was shuttered and secured, Mac stepped outside and locked the last door behind him, shoving the key into his pocket and whistling as he walked into the night. It was calm and cool, with few rustlings among the trees. Only the sound of his feet scattering gravel as he walked home.

Although he'd grown up deep in the countryside on a sprawling estate that sat atop rolling hills and acres upon acres of family lands, he had moved to a small cottage half a mile from the pub soon after leaving uni. He loved living alone and being part of a small community of good people. In summer, he enjoyed the walk. But truthfully, even in winter he chose to walk home unless the snow was blowing or the night chill too deep in his bones. The walk offered time to clear his head and review the day. In high summer, this far north, it was only beginning to darken, stars winking in the night sky. The darkness wouldn't linger, either—daylight blinked its feathery eyes near around three in the morning. He cherished the long hours of light because he knew the short days of winter would come soon enough and last for far too long.

Before he reached the cottage, Mac thought about his last long hill-walk with some mates from uni, the year prior. They trooped along the ninety-six miles from Milngavie to Fort William every other summer, taking near on two weeks to complete the stretch, though they could go faster if they wanted to. They camped on the windy shoulders of mountains and took their time climbing to the summits, lingering in the occasional bothy to sing sea shanties and old Gaelic favorites, drink and tell stories. It wasn't about the hikes so much as it was reconnecting with friends who had splintered off into adult life with little time for laughs and lagers most of the year. This being an off year, Mac missed the camaraderie of his chums and wondered whether they were staring at the same night sky wherever they were planted these days, missing their shared journey, too.

Soon enough, he reached the house, which was cast in shadow. He'd forgotten to leave on an exterior light. Mac pushed through the door, which he always left unlocked, stepped out of his boots, and turned the knob lock behind him. He kept the lights off, finding his way in by memory, peeling off his shirt, releasing his belt buckle, unbuttoning his jeans, and dropping each piece of clothing as he went. He had left windows cracked in all the rooms, and the place was cool, moist air tickling his skin. How long had it been since a woman had visited? He couldn't remember. Maybe it was time to invite someone in.

CHAPTER SEVEN

*E*ve, 2014

Eve's house sat back from the road in a little village with a narrow gravel path winding from the A811. It was shaded by birch and ash trees and sat atop a carpet of damp, dark soil. Eve dropped her purse on a chair and pulled out the leather satchel of letters. Who was Shira? Benjamin? Hugh? When had the letter been written? And could there be more buried in the cave or somewhere nearby?

There were seven in the slim satchel. The leather was honey-hued and soft, the inside carefully oiled to protect the papers. Whoever had packaged this up wanted the letters to be readable in time. It was as if the writer had wanted to hide them, but not forever. She wanted them found eventually.

But why?

The first detailed the writer's heartbreak. The second, third and fourth letters were older, written from Benjamin to Shira, but the dates had been smudged beyond readability. One detailed a visit to the holy city of Jerusalem, another to villages in Poland and the third letter was full of disbelief about the differences between Jewish communities in America—in the cities, many lived in squalor but in smaller towns they thrived quietly, protective among the Gentiles.

The final three letters were again from Shira. One seemed to be written to herself, questioning her choices—why she had married for position rather than love, wishing she could turn back time to share her Jewish observance with her children and several sentences hinted at secrets that needed to remain hidden or everything would fall apart. What the secrets were, Eve had absolutely no idea.

She fingered the crisp paper, glanced over the script. It had been a lovely hike and now she was glad for the interruption of the thunderstorm. She'd go back and look again, scour the cave with a flashlight and a shovel, poke around to see if she could find anything else. And maybe, if it was a beautiful, clear day, she could complete the hike, reach the summit, gain a full view of her new home.

Or she could wait to return to work on Monday, show the letters to David, her boss, and ask him how to proceed. Maybe he'd even offer supplies, tools and time to return to the site and complete the work. Yes, that would be the wiser move—turn to the expert, let him lead her in the proper next steps.

Eve had rented the small house an hour north of Edinburgh and just a half hour from Loch Lomond a month after she arrived for her fellowship in June. She'd wanted to get the lay of the land before choosing where to live, and though she knew it was far from the city center, she hadn't wanted to reside in the bustle of Scotland's biggest city, even if she had to work there five days a week. She'd never lived amid mountains and deep lakes before, and if she were going to give a year to a place, she wanted to know it intimately and well. Plus, she loved the quiet of the countryside.

Eve had lived in cities, big and small, all her life. Ann Arbor, of course, the bustling college town an hour from Detroit, where her father still lived in the cozy bungalow he'd bought when she was eleven. And then New York City, thanks to a scholarship to Columbia University, where she studied journalism and history. After graduation in 2006, she landed a job as a reporter at the *Detroit Free Press*, an honor for a straight-out-of-college aspiring journalist who had, to be fair, stacked up several impressive internships during college that led to the plum post-college placement. Interning at the *Chicago Tribune, Midwest Living* and the *LA Times* had paved the way to pretty much any journalism job, and after spending summers in big American cities, she wanted the pace of a metropolitan daily to feed her enthusiasm, but in a smaller city. Detroit was perfect and not far from home.

Still, she didn't live there. She moved home to Ann Arbor and made the long commute by car each day, which was why a commute from a country cottage to Edinburgh didn't daunt her. She wanted fresh air on her face and the sounds of birds outside her open windows even if only in the early morning and late night. She wanted to wake up to the scent of pine and birch and see stars light up a darkening sky.

Eve was surprised by how little she'd enjoyed the newspaper job. After seven years, moving up from cub reporter to beat reporter to city desk editor, she'd wanted work she could love more than chasing stories. And she'd always been fascinated by history. Hers, in particular.

Eve could still remember the empty look on her father's face when she asked why she didn't have grandparents like her friends did, why they had no family visiting on holidays, no gifts shipped from far away by people who loved her. It was fourth grade when Eve first asked her father about why she didn't have grandparents like the other kids. He looked sad, and she felt bad for asking, but she really wanted to know.

"You do have grandparents, honey, but they aren't very nice people, so we don't see them," he said.

She wanted to know more, but the pain in his eyes stopped her from probing further. So she asked for a diary with a key and a lock for her next birthday and when she received it, she started writing her questions on its lined pages, hoping to one day find answers. At night, she fell asleep with images in her mind of fleshy grandmothers hugging her close to their warm bodies, wishing she had at least one relative who could read her stories, bake brownies for her, pull her onto a waiting lap.

By middle school, her friends became her family—friends like Kate, Melissa and Molly, other kids from the liberal hippie synagogue they went to on some Saturdays and most holidays and her father's work colleagues. But she wished for someone to claim her whose blood ran under the thin veil of her skin. She was alone in the world except for her father, who loved her nearly enough to make up for all the people she didn't have in her life. Almost enough.

And so, when she discovered the archives at the Walter Reuther Library on Wayne State University's campus as a place to research some of the stories she was reporting, Eve wanted to know more about the place and all the history it held. Other people's deep and detailed history. If she couldn't have her own, she'd immerse herself in the meticulously saved details of other families. Peruse the photographs and the letters and the protected documents detailing lives worth remembering. The unassuming building on Cass Avenue and the quiet librarians in the reading room who helped her locate a photograph or a letter or a document attesting to an important moment in history. The saved things proving the existence of meaningful moments. Moments that were historical pivots changing the way we thought and acted and moved forward in time.

Where were such moments, such historical research, to prove her own origins? A telling photograph, an intriguing letter, a document of historical importance that proved something beyond what she knew today? As a preteen, she'd turned her father's house upside down one careful, secret search after another during her teenage years, always when her dad was at work. Rooting through drawers, combing through closets. Carefully digging beneath her father's socks and folded shirts to see if he'd hidden anything that might be a clue to her history. But there was nothing. No remnant of his past or hint at her own. And after, she felt shame and guilt clutch at her throat. How could she betray her loving, doting father who worked quietly all day and pulled her close every night? Still, if she could learn to become someone who collected history and protected it, perhaps she could find out more about her own familial past. There had to be something to discover. No one emerged from total darkness.

Her friends and colleagues were surprised when she quit her plum newspaper job to move abroad. *Why?,* they asked. *Why flee across the sea for a year in a foreign land? What was there that wasn't here?* In their eyes, Eve had everything—an upward trajectory in an enviable career, a cadre of good friends and a revolving door of love interests. But what one could see from the outside never reflected the way it felt on the inside.

Chapter Eight

am, 2014

The house was lonely. It echoed in the night, and while Sam had never longed for a different life, never dared to imagine a partner in the home that was all his, under the immense old oak whose shade made air conditioning nearly unnecessary in the summer, he didn't always revel in the aloneness. Even when gay marriage became legal in Massachusetts and started its slow progression across the country, Sam couldn't imagine a wedding ceremony with him at the altar and another man gazing at him under the chuppah.

Unless it were Simon.

"Going for drinks?" a co-worker called to Sam as he clicked off his desk lamp and pushed in his chair. The reporters had all left, and while Sam had long ago shifted from the business side of the newspaper to the newsroom, he was usually the last to leave at the end of the day.

Sam looked up at the young man. Trevor, he thought his name was. He'd only just started a few months earlier, first as an intern and then, after graduation, as a new hire cub reporter. He smiled at Trevor's eager eyes and jaunty messenger bag slung cross-body. His dark blue jeans pressed stiff and rolled at the ankles, boat shoes and a pastel plaid button down tucked in at the waist, where a brass-buckled leather belt pulled tight. He was a good-looking kid, Sam thought, blushing with shame and attraction. *He could be your son,* he reprimanded himself.

"I don't know. Maybe I'll get there when I finish," Sam called, turning his gaze back to the computer screen and the glare of the white page half-filled with words.

Trevor waved as he headed for the exit. "See you there!"

Sam nodded and tried to return focus to the article he was writing. A detailed report of the latest city council meeting, including referendums about cannabis retail licensing, further urban development in an already crowded downtown, and a call to protect natural lands along the Huron River. It wasn't due for two days, but Sam liked to finish his stories early so he'd have plenty of time to reread and edit.

But he didn't need quite this much time. He could work on it the next morning and join his colleagues for a drink and some conversation. When had he last done so?

He saved the draft and powered down the computer. He tucked his notes into a neat pile and took his coffee mug to the communal kitchen, where he scrubbed the dark gritty grounds out of the bottom, rinsed it clean and dried it with a paper towel. Leaving the clean mug on his desk for the next morning's first cup, Sam pushed in his chair, stuffed two books by local authors that he planned to read and review into his backpack, and scanned the newsroom.

Summer light backlit the wide second-floor windows. The sky was a mix of late-day yellow and sunset orange. As he switched off the fluorescent lights, the waning summer day bathed the space in warm light, casting kaleidoscopes onto the old carpet.

He took the stairs to the ground level and pushed out into the warm, thick evening. Only seven o'clock—they might still be at the bar. He walked long strides to Conor O'Neills on Main Street, a long-and-true Ann Arbor favorite, especially among the journalist set. No college students would go there, and the dark wood and loud music were a perfect backdrop to loosen the stress of the day in a mug of ale.

When he pushed open the door, Sam was happy to see five of his colleagues around a sticky table in a far corner littered with empty beer mugs as they held the next round in hand. He dropped his bag on an empty chair near Calvin, the only co-worker he felt close to, who also happened to be closest in age to Sam.

"You made it, man." Calvin thudded his hand against Sam's shoulder. "You never come out with us! Glad to see you."

Sam's face went warm. "Why not? There's plenty of time to meet my deadline," he muttered, trying to smile and down-play his embarrassment. Sam had never liked being the center of attention, and Calvin's warm welcome turned the gaze of his co-workers in his direction. "I'll grab a beer," he said as he ducked away toward the bar, breathing in shallow breaths to steady his racing heart.

It had always been like this: embarrassment at being singled out, noticed, the source of other people's attention. He hadn't liked it as a boy when his father bore down on him for not knowing enough Torah, not saying a blessing fast enough, not being man enough like his brothers. While they wrestled on the living room carpet and came home with torn pants and muddy shoes, Sam kept quiet in a corner with a book or a notepad.

Sam fled to Ann Arbor in July of 1984 after the sudden and unexpected death of his wife, with a mewling newborn in his arms and no knowledge of what to do with her. It wasn't a well-thought-out or researched decision. Driven by the dream of that mythical place his favorite librarian had told him about, he left in the dark of night, convinced that the progressive college town would allow him to live freely. He could figure out what it meant to be a gay man in the 1980s, away from the judgment and pressure of the Jewish community. Shaindie was gone; she was no longer a threat to reveal his true identity, and no one else knew.

He left a note for his mother, saying goodbye, telling her he loved her, and promising to be in touch—though he doubted he would be, or if so, it would be years into the future, when he could stomach the explanation she would expect. By leaving, he was damning his daughter to a lifetime of anonymity but as he closed the door behind him and ran a hand over the gray brick of his childhood home to imprint its memory into his skin, he promised his baby girl that he'd more than make up for what she would miss. He'd be everything to her.

And while just saying the word *gay* aloud scared him, especially with news of the AIDS epidemic claiming newspaper headlines, he needed to come to terms with who he was. He couldn't make the mistake of committing to another girl. He never again wanted to touch a female body in that way or hurt a trusting, innocent young woman.

He'd been right about Ann Arbor being an easier place to live, but the adjustment had been hard. Not just because he was gay and didn't know how to live freely according to his instincts. Mostly because he didn't know the place and because he'd grown up in an insular world that paid little attention to academic learning, career training or social skills. His community had focused only on indoctrinating young minds to follow the rules of the Torah and the words of their parents.

Every day he thanked that librarian for showing him that there was another way to live! It hadn't been an option in his community. Whenever someone knew of a person who went *off the derech*, off the path of belief and Orthodox observance, it was whispered with head shaking, lowered eyelids and looks of feigned horror. God forbid it should happen in one's own family! Such a dereliction would scar a family for generations and make it impossible for their offspring to find good mates. A wrong move by one family member marred an entire family for generations.

Whatever befell his family they deserved. If they knew, they'd turn him away, slam the door in his face, utter nasty words whenever his name came up. His mother and sister would cry or shrink under his father's glare. It tore at his heart to think of his family hating him, being disgusted by his urges, pretending he didn't even exist.

Sam had to learn how to be a father and how to function in a fast-moving place where he needed a job for which he had neither education nor training. He needed to pay rent and buy food and find a place for Eve while he worked, and after all those needs were satisfied, he needed friends to escape the loneliness.

He snipped off his sidelocks, tossed the black yarmulke he'd worn morning, noon and night all his life into the trash along with the black pants and white button-downs that had been his uniform. He let his hair grow long. From thrift stores, he bought blue jeans and polo shirts and soft fuzzy sweaters in a variety of colors—reveling in the joy of being able to wear bright red or pastel pink without the inevitable teasing and condemnation of his brethren. Surely his childhood friends would sneer if they could see him in his new colorful life! But he didn't care. He was glad to leave them and his unpleasant past behind, pretend all the taunting of his yeshiva years had never happened.

He knew education was a key that opened many doors. And so while he found a small apartment on the Ann Arbor-Ypsilanti border in a less-than-pleasant neighborhood but with an eye toward moving to a better street in the heart of the college town when he could afford to do so, he also picked up a catalog for the community college. He found a job doing bookkeeping work from home for a small accountancy firm and studied to add skills to his resume of abilities. He was hungry for connection free of judgment or scorn. Everyone needed friends, a community; the only way he knew to find one was to enroll in school. And the only school he was qualified for was the community college, which was, thankfully, low-cost and where the professors allowed him to bring a baby seat with his cooing daughter as long as he kept her quiet while class was in session. At least he could save money by avoiding day care for a while.

He listened keenly to the conversations of his classmates because he needed to learn how to understand the popular culture references people uttered.

But he was lonely. Despite the relief of escaping the fear and loneliness of his childhood, he missed his mother and the familiar routine of the home where he'd grown up. He missed the steaming, aromatic Sabbath meals, the comforting homemade food on weeknights when he'd rush in from yeshiva and sit at the table, grunting through meals with his father and brothers and his dainty sister, who helped their mother in the kitchen, learning to build a home of her own. He missed the greetings on the street as he walked to synagogue on Saturday and the camaraderie of the men, their voices a rhythmic cadence filling the cavernous space, their hands beating on the podium and the backs of chairs and each other's shoulders as they chanted and prayed. He missed being part of something, counting for something. He missed the connection of a shared purpose, a communal focus. He missed the way his body knew what to do, on autopilot as he had shifted through the phases of his expected life.

In this new place, and this new version of himself, he had no route to follow, no familiar path. His life was full of choices, something he had never known as a religious youth. He could do anything, be anyone, live as he wanted, and it was so freeing, it was almost overwhelming.

And he wanted love. Tender love. Passionate love. A love that accepted and welcomed. A love that brought companionship and friendship.

After a year of classes, he landed a job as a bookkeeper in the accounting department of the *Ann Arbor News*, on the merit of his strong mathematical skills and good grades. There, he made friends and felt useful. Sometimes, they invited him for drinks after work, and he went, eyeing his watch for six o'clock, which was the latest he could pick up Eve from daycare. He joined a weekend playgroup at the community center, taking his daughter to be around other toddlers, talking with the other parents—mostly mothers—and fostering one or two friendships. He didn't know how to answer when the young moms asked where Eve's mother was, so he simply smiled and gazed at his daughter. He didn't want pity and he didn't want amorous advances, and so he just focused on his little girl and the joy she brought him. He worked hard and was rewarded with raises and promotions but mostly, Sam reveled in the idea that he was accepted at face value. No one asked if he kept kosher or observed the Sabbath or looked questioningly at his clothing. They saw only a man, and a kind one at that, and they smiled when they saw him, which set him at ease for the first time in his young life.

At first, Sam avoided the Jewish community, not wanting to address the confusing question of how or whether to observe at all. Jewish observance had scarred him—or rather, the rigidity of the way his family had observed. But every so often, he'd drive past a synagogue and wonder what the community was like, wonder if stepping inside might make him feel less lonely, be a compass to guide him in this new life. But he didn't want word getting back to his parents of where he was or how he was living. He assumed all Jews knew each other as they had in his home community, and he couldn't take the risk of cluing them in to his, and his daughter's, whereabouts. He was afraid they'd come after him, wrench his daughter from his grasp.

He was also afraid to step over the threshold of what he'd been taught were inauthentic Jewish communities. The people might be Jewish by birth, but the ways they observed were not legitimate in the eyes of the people who'd raised him. Could he be Jewish in another way? Any denomination outside of Orthodoxy was considered a *shanda*, a scandal, not legitimate. But as time passed, he reasoned that since he was one of the heathens now—a gay man *and* a single father—eating *treif*, enjoying the glorious flavors of non-kosher food, breaking every rule he'd been raised to keep, then he might finally fit into one of these odd but hopefully welcoming derivations of Judaism.

His daughter was thriving. He was surviving—even saving a little money. He felt safe, comfortable for the first time in his own skin. And the strange outside world welcomed him in without question.

Two years into his new life, his trauma softened with time, Sam sought out the most liberal synagogue in Ann Arbor, which was more of a hippie collective than a bona fide shul. He toted his toddler daughter into the lay-led service on a Saturday morning and sat in the back row. He'd brought books and soft toys and set Eve on the floor to play while he scoped out the scene. He didn't plan to stay long or speak to anyone. He just wanted to see what it was like, if he could find a community where he might belong, where he might raise his daughter with a sense of heritage and tradition. He wanted to see if he could be Jewish and gay and happy, all at once.

Turns out he could. And the loneliness started to dissipate.

When Eve was four and the father-daughter duo were entrenched in a flowing and full life, Sam thought it might be safe to reach out to his parents. He didn't imagine that they'd welcome him home with open arms, and he didn't want that—he'd never go back!—but he thought they might want to know their granddaughter. The synagogue community had become an ad hoc family, but he missed the deep connection of blood. Four years had passed. Surely that was long enough to forgive and forget and build a tentative peace.

His mother took his call but hid in a closet to talk to him, whispering so his father wouldn't hear. "You can't be in touch, Shmueli," she said, invoking his Hebrew name. "Your father won't allow it. He says you're an abomination."

Sam's stomach clenched, and all the air went out of him. "Mommy, you can't honestly think that of me," he muttered.

"Well, the Torah forbids a man to lay with another man," she said. "How could you do that? It's...disgusting...not normal."

How did they know? He hadn't had a relationship since he moved to Ann Arbor, didn't dare to bring a man home, in front of his daughter. And besides, he didn't even know how to begin meeting men in a romantic way. The closest he'd come was his friendship with Simon Tangers, a classmate from the college who'd also fled a religious family, albeit a Christian one, to live freely as a gay man. But Simon wasn't obligated to a child, so he felt freer than Sam. They were friends, even as the chemistry between them was palpable. Sam set boundaries, and Simon shared stories of his dates and hook-ups.

"Mommy, who told you?" His voice shook as he whispered the words, afraid to speak them aloud.

Her breathing was heavy on the line. It took a minute, maybe longer, before she dared to speak.

"Shaindie left a letter for her sister," she said. "She found it after the death, after you left in the shame of night. When she was packing up Shaindie's belongings."

Sam froze, his heart pounding in his chest. So they all knew. Had known for years.

What had Shaindie planned? To out him and have him banished? Or use it as leverage throughout their marriage?

He slumped, suddenly dizzy and nauseated.

"Bayla!" His father's thunderous voice bellowed in the background of the call.

"Shmueli, I've got to go," his mother whispered. "Please don't call again." And the line went dead.

Sam had been attracted to men, but never acted on it. He wanted to one day, when he could find a place for Eve and not risk word getting back to his family. But it wasn't safe yet.

Still, how could such natural, instinctive feelings be wrong? When a man and a woman felt such attraction, it was okay. This was the way God had made him—only, the liturgy in his world of origin taught that it was the worst perversion of human existence. The irony was that before he'd left his community of origin, he'd never been with anyone other than his wife.

A month later, a letter arrived from a Detroit law firm over-populated with Orthodox attorneys. His parents wanted custody of Eve, and they were joined by Shaindie's parents in the lawsuit. They cited his homosexual nature as grounds for taking his daughter from him, insisting that a father who defied "normal" could not possibly raise a child, let alone a girl child, in a healthy, nurturing and loving home. The words "depraved," "sick" and "dangerous" danced around the document. Sam was gutted and had never felt more alone. *Serves me right for even trying,* he thought.

It took the better part of a year and all his savings to fight them, but Sam prevailed. The Ann Arbor judge who heard the suit was liberal-minded, and Sam's new Jewish community testified about his character and his parenting in court, insistent that they'd never seen a more doting and attentive father whose personal life did not interfere with his parenting. In fact, these good people, who were good friends, had never even seen him have a personal life beyond his daughter. His father's outburst in the courtroom probably helped the judge rule in his favor. When the judge asked Rabbi Waldman why he believed his son wouldn't be a fit parent, the man railed against the misguided ways of the non-religious, which included the judge, who was a secular Jewish man dedicated to his ancestral faith and a regular member of a liberal synagogue.

Sam emerged vindicated as an exemplary human, though the emotional wounds were raw from a fierce rejection by his family. He would never again make the mistake of trying to rebuild their relationship. They were dead to him, as he'd been dead to them for years already. He would not give anyone a reason to consider him deviant from reasonable human behavior and would leave his horrid, hate-filled family in the dead-and-gone past.

"Killian's, in a bottle," he said to the bartender. The beefy blond man nodded and pulled one from the cooler beneath the counter, popping the cap off and handing the beer to Sam. "$3.75," he coughed. Sam reached into his pocket and pulled out a five-dollar bill. The bartender quirked his eyebrows, asking if he wanted change, and Sam shrank into himself, wanting to nod but afraid to appear cheap, so he shook his head, swiped the bottle off the bar and walked back to his friends.

What was I thinking, tipping that much, he thought. This many years later, he still felt awkward in a bar and second-guessed himself when trying to go with the flow. Buy a beer, leave a tip, not more than twenty percent, which would have been seventy-five cents, and look cool about it as you do. But he didn't want to haggle over fifty cents, and he no longer had to count his quarters to make ends meet. He had enough. More than enough.

"You're a man of habit," Calvin chided. "Always a Killian's! You like it that much?"

Sam shrugged, not wanting to admit that he didn't know enough about beer to make another choice on the spur of the moment.

"What are you working on?"

"They have me on the minority issues beat, and I can't decide if that's a compliment or a subtly racist insult," Calvin said. As the senior African-American reporter (with only one other in the newsroom, a young woman who'd been there two years and was vocal about wanting to move on and up to a larger newspaper in a more diverse metropolitan locale), he had become the authoritative voice on allyship, race relations, diversity and inclusion for the *Ann Arbor News*. "I'm researching home and property values in the whitest neighborhoods and comparing them to the communities closer to Ypsi. I think I know what I'll find, but I'm doing the research anyway. Not sure this is a story—it's an old story, if anything—but Mitch wants me to keep my finger on the pulse of fairness in this liberal town to see if we're making any progress."

Mitch was the long-held, much-loved editor-in-chief who had given Sam his first job in the business office and mentored him along toward a shift to editorial. He would always be grateful to Mitch for giving him a chance when he likely didn't deserve one. Also Jewish and highly distrustful of the Orthodox, Mitch had been sympathetic to Sam's situation. He even testified on his behalf during the court case to keep custody of Eve. He would retire at the end of this year; a three-decade reign at a newspaper was legendary, and he'd achieved some acclaim in the world of local journalism. Sam felt indebted to him to the point of always giving the benefit of the doubt, even though he sensed truth in what his friend was saying.

"Have you ever had a conversation with Mitch about it?"

Calvin drained the last foamy dregs of his beer and clunked the mug down on the tabletop.

"Ah, man, why bother? It's not like the guy is ever going to get it," he said. "He's so white, I sometimes can't see him in the sunlight."

Sam chuckled, then gulped from his bottle, the cool-sweet liquid coasting down his throat.

"I'm as white as they come, you know," he said. "And I get it."

"That's because you've been riding in my side car the better part of the last decade," Calvin said, patting Sam's arm. "We got each other's backs. And you're too Jewish to be white." He laughed. "Isn't it about time you stop looking shocked at what I say?"

Sam shook his head. "I'm always playing catch-up, you know."

"Yeah, I know." Calvin patted him again. "I know you, dude. You got to remember that. I know you deep. We're like brothers."

Sam smiled as a wave of calm washed over him. It was true. Calvin was an island in the rocky seas of being an outsider, and Sam was grateful for his loyal friendship. And for his patience in teaching Sam so much of what he never knew, but needed, to get along in a world that sometimes still felt foreign.

As the clock ticked toward eight, the group started to break up. Sam said his goodbyes and walked out with the others, who scattered like raindrops in different directions along the downtown. Sam headed for his car in the newspaper parking lot and drove the short distance to Burns Park, to his quiet home under the old oak. He took his time locking the car and swinging his bag over a shoulder, strolling the few steps up the walkway to the wide porch with its still and silent wooden swing. He lifted the lid of the mailbox beside the front door and found a postcard from Eve, three utility bills right on time, and a handwritten letter with the familiar scrawl that he loved so much.

Simon.

He fingered the paper, turned the envelope over in his hands, lifted it to his nose to see if it carried a lingering scent of the man from far away, the one who never left his heart, whose voice tickled at his ear. Only a faint whiff of musk, nothing strong enough to be identifiably Simon. He unlocked the door and stepped inside. The night would be better now, he thought, as he pulled a half-eaten casserole from the refrigerator and turned the dial to warm the oven. He laid the letter on the table, poured a glass of dark-red wine, kicked off his shoes and waited for the moment when the last dying embers of summer sun sank from view and the fireflies flicked on. The moment when he could tear open the envelope and take in the words destined from one heart to another, the words that he'd read over and over again until he knew them by heart.

Chapter Nine

M^*ac, 2014*

"I like this place," Eve said, scanning the low-lit room of the Clachan Inn.

"It's one of the oldest pubs in the area," Mac said, sipping from a tall glass of golden ale. It was early and the place was full. Soon, the sound levels would rise along with the temperature, as people leaned closer, laughed louder and sat longer over drinks. Some summer nights, people dallied outside the stucco front, waiting an hour or longer for a table, which was unheard of in rural Scottish towns during the rest of the year.

"What will you have?" A weathered blond woman of middle age stood over their table, half smiling, half challenging.

"I'll have the chicken liver pâté to start and then a burger, medium rare," Eve said.

"Cook does the burgers full-on, not pink and bloody," the waitress said. "Still want it?"

Eve nodded, handing over her menu.

"And you, dear?" The woman grinned at Mac. "What brings you to the competition, lad?"

"Ach, Miri, you know we're all in this together."

The woman grinned and clicked her tongue against her teeth. "We been here longer," she said.

"Well, I won't argue with ya, or you'll send me under the table with your facts and numbers, so I'll just ask for a half roast chicken on a plate tonight," he said, winking as he handed over his menu.

"That's more like it," she said, winking back as she walked away, menus tucked under her arm.

Mac turned to Eve. "Liver?"

Eve shrugged. "Reminds me of home."

"Your parents cooked liver a lot?" Mac leaned back. The hum of nearby conversations and low tinny music forced her to lean closer to hear him.

"My father is a wonderful cook," Eve said, sipping dark wine from a goblet. "He made chopped liver for holidays. One of my favorite dishes."

Mac watched her as she spoke, following the rise and fall of her lips as the words tumbled from her mouth. He heard them but didn't listen close, mesmerized by the light in her eyes and the soft lines of her face.

He sipped again from his ale, which was half-gone. "I'm going to need another." He tipped his glass. "How's your wine?"

"Nice. Soothing." Her cheeks flushed pink as she swallowed another sip.

"I can't remember my father ever cooking," Mac said. "But then, my mother's not much of a cook either. You mentioned your father. Where was your mother?"

Eve's eyes clouded, and her smile dimmed. "I never knew her," she said. "She died when I was born. I don't even have a photograph, just stories from my father. And only a few of those. When she was pregnant with me, her blood pressure rose dangerously high, and the intensity of the birth caused her heart to seize. They had to cut me out of her. She was gone before I took my first breath. It's a miracle that I'm here."

Mac nodded, his breath shallow. "Yes," he said.

The waitress returned to their table and lifted Mac's glass. "Another?" He nodded, and she cocked her head toward Eve, whose glass was still a third full of dark wine.

"Bring me another, and I'll finish this one," Eve said.

"So when exactly did you eat liver? Like, a normal school night supper?" he asked.

"Boy, you're relentless," she said, her face flushing again. She sat straighter in her chair. "Rosh Hashanah, Passover, Jewish holidays."

"I don't know that I've ever met a Jewish person," he said.

"There are Jews in Scotland, you know."

"I suppose," he said. "Not many. You'd think I might have met someone along the way, especially at uni, but I can't recall anyone in particular."

The buzz of the restaurant deepened. The heat of the room jumped a few degrees higher. The waitress slid a plate of pâté, oatcakes and cut cold vegetables onto the table. She set a full glass of ale in front of Mac and whisked away his empty one, deposited a new glass of wine in front of Eve.

"Tell me about Manchester," Eve said as she swiped pâté onto an oatcake. She sank her teeth in and closed her eyes.

"Good?" he asked, smearing a cake for himself. He took a bite and inhaled the smooth smokiness of the liver.

Eve nodded and took another bite. He loved the way she looked so satisfied. Is this how she would look in his bed? Mac thrilled at the thought, electric with wanting.

"I played football at Manchester," he said. "Crushed my knee in second year, so I hobbled through my studies to get a degree. It was devastating."

"I can imagine," Eve said, taking another bite. He liked how passionately she ate, without regard for him, without pacing herself, without the tepid hesitation of most women he'd dated. She was so free, so unabashed.

"What did you study? Or did you know you wanted to work in a pub?"

Mac took a bite before answering. He didn't want to admit to owning the pub as part of the family holdings, but he didn't want to lie either. Too many women had feigned deeper interest the moment they'd learned he was the son of an earl. But she was unlike any woman he'd known. Maybe it was time to take a chance.

"Well, I own the pub," he said, watching her face. "It's part of my family's estate."

She patted her mouth with a napkin and took a sip of wine. "Really?" She spread pâté on yet another oatcake as she spoke.

Her face didn't change. She seemed more interested in the food than in his admission. A thrill of relief coursed through Mac's body.

He held out a hand and said in a stiff voice, "Alistair Graeme Monteith—nice to meet you."

She looked up, confusion ridging her face. "What?"

He laughed. "That's my proper name. I started calling myself 'Mac' when I was wee and learned that our ancestral name was Macalaster. It just stuck. Means 'son' in Gaelic."

"Oh!" she softened with a laugh. "Well, okay then. Nice to meet you Alistair."

"No really, call me Mac. Only Mac," he said. "I hate formality, and honestly, I'm not a fan of my given name. Too proper."

He swiped a carrot through the last dregs of the liver. "We finished this fast," he said, swiping a napkin over his lips. "I love how you eat."

"What do you mean?" She snickered. "I was hungry, and it was good."

"I've never met a woman like you," he said.

"Because of how I eat?"

He shrugged and laughed. "Maybe. I don't know. I've just never met anyone like you."

"I'm one of a kind," she said with a smirk.

A line had formed outside the restaurant as eager diners waited for tables. Their main courses arrived, and the pub filled with laughter and loud voices. The manager propped open the doors to bring in the night air. Eve told Mac about Ann Arbor, leaving her newspaper job to work at the archives, her father, how little she knew about her family. He shared as little as he could about his family, highlighting only his sisters and changing the subject when she asked about his parents. He didn't want to introduce family drama too soon, and he'd already admitted to their wealth and position—though he wondered if she even noticed or got what a big deal that was in the UK.

They were so riveted in conversation that they almost didn't notice the server hovering over the table. She took their dessert order, then hurried off. They continued talking, learning about each other, until the dessert plates were in front of them.

"Most men think I'm too much," Eve said, swiping a finger through the trail of chocolate on the dessert plate, a thick wedge of chocolate cake drizzled in ganache and topped with a cloud of rich, fresh cream.

"Have you ever dated a Scot? We like our women strong. You won't be too much for me."

Eve nodded, growing serious. "We'll see," she said.

"Yes." He reached for her chocolate-covered finger and brought it to his lips. It was early and he was taking a risk, but all he could think about was how she'd respond if he pulled her finger into his mouth, how her skin would taste under his tongue.

Chapter Ten

*M*argaret, 2014

"Why can't I get your brother to come for breakfast?"

Margaret stroked her eldest son's red curls back from his forehead, palming his round face.

"Why would I know?" Collin shook her away and lifted the glass dome off the pedestal display of chocolate and butter biscuits, tossing one in his mouth whole. She swatted his hand but smiled. *Cheeky child*, she thought. And not a child—the man was thirty-two and no closer to marrying than any of her grown children, much to Margaret's dismay.

The grandfather clock in the front hall droned ten slow bells to announce the morning hour, and almost as if summoned, her daughters strode into the high-ceilinged dining room, air-kissing her smooth cheek and helping themselves to plates from the buffet where the staff had arranged scones, biscuits, poached eggs, bangers and hash, juice and tea. She wanted to reach for Shona's soft red curls, so like her father and eldest brother, but held back, knowing her headstrong daughter would not allow a moment of tenderness. Her face bore blazing green-gold eyes, a patchwork of freckles and a look that Margaret had never been able to read. It did not get easier with time. Somehow, Margaret had lost her way around her children. She felt awkward calling them up or starting conversations, probing for details into their lives. Served her right, after years of holding back, keeping boundaries between parent and child. Sensing her discomfort when the first baby came along, Alex had offered the assistance of nannies when they were young, and she fell into the routine of other people doing all the work of child-rearing. It had been a relief, she thought. But when had she missed the window of becoming close to her children?

Utensils clinked against China as three of her four offspring heaped their plates with homecooked food. Alex was already at the head of the table, his plate full, his coffee half-drunk, a maid fluttering around him with a hot carafe ready to refill when he smiled her way. He was always smiling. Which was why Margaret felt she had to be the stern one, play the role of overseer. She resented him for it. Nobody wanted to be the ballbuster, and yet she had to because no one else would.

"Emma, can't you find a pair of jeans that aren't ripped to shreds?"

Her youngest daughter glared. "This is the style, Mum." Emma. Dear Emma. Her thick, dark hair was cropped in a blunt shag, and her blue eyes held the sky in their shimmering depths. She wore a faded Culture Club T-shirt and jeans shredded at the knees over heavy black Doc Martens boots. Margaret had lost count of how many piercings dotted her ears. Although Emma had the most respectable employment of her four children—a financial counselor at a national bank—she was the one Margaret understood the least.

When the last of the family were seated and Margaret could hear no new footsteps coming from the entryway, she strode to the buffet and lifted a plate for herself. Mac wouldn't be joining them, then. Another Sunday family breakfast minus the rebellious son.

"Mum, are you joining us?" Collin called from the table, his fork scraping across a nearly empty plate.

"Coming, darling," she cooed, carrying a half-filled plate of scone and sausages in one hand and a mug of tea in the other.

"When is your next art showing, Shona?" Alex gummed a bite of scone while he spoke.

Margaret snorted in disgust. *Bloody man*, she thought. *Talking with his mouth full of food.*

"Mum, you look like a bull ready to charge," Emma snorted. "Chill."

Margaret pressed her lips together.

"I have an exhibit opening on the eleventh," Shona said to her father. Looking up and down the length of the table, she added, "I'm hoping you all will come."

"And Mac, too," Margaret chimed.

"Of course," Shona said. "Nothing without Mac." She rolled her eyes.

"When will you give up hoping for an appearance from the prodigal son?" Emma challenged. "He never comes on Sundays. Accept it."

Such rage, Margaret thought. Her youngest child, a roiling ball of emotion. Where did it come from? What did she have to be angry about? Any of them, for that matter. These were privileged children who'd never known a day's hardship! They had their futures laid out for them, financially secure with lots of choice. Everything taken care of. If anyone had something to be angry about, it was Margaret, for the way they didn't seem to appreciate all they'd been given, and she'd been trying to let her own anger go for decades now.

The anger perplexed Margaret because since marrying Alex, she didn't have anything to complain about. So why this festering anger that had grown in recent years to be more of a tidal wave engulfing her? In the lonely moments late at night when she couldn't sleep, she admitted that the anger was really a mask to hide her sadness at being so alone. Of course, she had only herself to blame for withdrawing from her husband years ago and holding her children at arm's length. At this point, she felt stuck. There was no way to turn back time, to rewrite history, and it felt like there'd been so many deep rifts between the people who were supposed to be closest to her that she had no idea where to begin to repair them.

She was trying—trying!—to let it all go, but the memories flooded her late at night when Alex slept soundly and she was alone in this big and lonely house. She'd traded one kind of loneliness for another. She knew Alex wanted to be an attentive and loving husband. He doted on her and wanted her voraciously whenever she'd let him get close. Which she rarely did these days. She knew it might benefit her to break down the barrier she'd built, but she feared what waited on the other side. Margaret hated vulnerability in anyone, least of all herself. It reminded her too much of her mother taking charity from those high-minded families she'd cleaned for. Margaret couldn't let emotion crack her armor if she wanted to keep everything she'd gained.

The conversation chittered on around her, but she barely heard the words. Something about a hiking trip with mates to Switzerland. (Collin) Something about a colleague at the bank. (Emma) Something about a painting in process and children in art class at the community center. (Shona) The ruffle of news-paper broadsheets being separated and smoothed over. (Alex) The scuffle of steps and the replenishing of platters and plates, the glug-glug-glug of the teapot being refilled and the coffee being poured. (All the various help in this massive echoing mansion.)

Margaret watched it all from the head of the table. The lonely seat at the end of a long, fine, shellacked walnut table carved and shaped by artisan hands and transported across many miles to fill this cavernous room with the hope that the people she loved would laugh around its smooth edges, clinking glasses, pressing napkins along their relaxed laps and lingering long into the night to make it feel more like a family home.

Chapter Eleven

*E*ve, *2014*

Eve tilted her head back, closed her eyes to the night and listened to the wind in the trees flutter their angelic whispers as his hands traced her body. When they pulled apart, she was dizzy with wanting.

"Something to look forward to," he whispered as he stepped back from her door and headed for his car. "Tuesday?" he called into the dark.

"Yes," she answered back, hiding her smile in the shadows of the cottage.

Although she wanted him to come inside when he dropped her off, Eve said goodbye to Mac at her door and watched him walk off into the night. She didn't ask him in, even after he spent fifteen minutes with his hands in her hair and his mouth on hers, the salty-sweet of his tongue dancing onto hers, exploring the cavern of her warm, wet mouth.

Eve knew he was holding back important details, but she was so entranced by his bright eyes and strong arms and deep voice and warm laugh that she didn't mind. It was only a first date after all. In time, he'd reveal more or he wouldn't, and this might determine whether she kept on with him or drifted away. In time, she'd understand why he took it slow. She studied the man across the hard wood table, in the flickering light of a fire on this cooling July evening in the mountains of Scotland. *Maybe it's too good to be true,* she thought. *Maybe when he sees how strong and assertive I am, he'll run like all the other guys.*

Though she was allowed to work from home on Mondays and Fridays, Eve rose early and headed into Edinburgh to share the letter with her boss, David MacLaren, a round, middle-aged man with dark-brown wisps of thinning hair sprinkled with the occasional gray. He had a friendly smile and a comfortable gait. Eve had liked him from the moment they met, on her second day in Scotland.

Two months in, they'd developed a flow. The fellowship was intended to train future archivists in the practice of research, document and photograph evaluation and writing. She'd learn every part of the archival process, shadow various professionals in the headquarters and some satellite offices as well. By the end of the year-long program, she'd be halfway to a certification in archival studies. And if she liked it enough, she'd continue on to a master's degree in library science with a specialty in archives and then look for a job managing a specific collection.

At the *Free Press,* Eve had done her share of deep-diving into backstory. And when she'd meander into the local archives for some deep, deep background context on an important story, she gained new respect for the people whose job it was to decide what was worth keeping and what to let go.

By the time David arrived to work, Eve had been at her desk for two hours.

"Hiya!" David called as he dropped his bag at the foot of his chair and swiped a mug from the desk. "Let me get my tea, and we'll have a chat."

Eve palmed her mug, watching swirls of steam snake up from the dark, hot liquid. She'd made the pot extra-strong, needing a jolt of caffeine. She smiled in David's direction. He hummed as he strode toward the kitchen at the back of their floor.

Ten minutes later, he was installed with his own steaming mug in a swivel chair across from Eve. She smiled good morning and sipped from her mug, which was finally cooling.

"You'll never guess what I found on a hike up Conic Hill this weekend," Eve spilled.

David cocked his head. "Tell me!"

She set her cup on the desktop, pulled on a soft pair of white gloves and bent over her bag to pull out the satchel. Placing it level on the desk, she opened the cover and gently pulled the letter from the middle pages and handed it to David.

"This."

He held the edges of the papers against his open palms, making them seem to hover above his desktop. He bent to read close.

"An exquisite find!" he muttered, peering at the words on the pages. "The paper is of an age that seems about mid-19th century?" It was more of a question than a statement. "Have you run these names through the database yet?"

Eve nodded. "Why do you think I've been here for two hours already?" She chuckled. "I couldn't sleep last night, with the anticipation of digging into the research. I've been dying to know who Shira and Benjamin and Hugh are and what the letters are telling us."

"And?" He sat up and stared at Eve, his eyes bright.

"I found a Shira and Hugh Macalaster—Shira Levenson Macalaster. Big history, David. She was the wealthiest woman in Britain before she married a Scottish lord. And Jewish. She came into her fortune young, after the death of her father. And while her family funded the royal court for decades, she was barred from the court when a wave of antisemitism swept through the country. Marrying Hugh Macalaster, the Earl of Monteith, gave Shira entrée back into the court's favor."

David opened a desk drawer and pulled out a pair of nitrile gloves. He slid his hands into them and smoothed over the paper sprawled on his desk.

"So who is Benjamin?"

"I have no idea."

"Couldn't find anyone in connection with their names?"

Eve shook her head. "Not yet. I can keep looking. But there's more, David."

He looked up. "Hugh was a Prime Minister of Britain after Shira's death. And"—her voice hushed to a whisper—"he was rumored to be gay. Carried on with his affairs in secret. The first gay Prime Minister at a time when homosexuality was illegal. And married to a Jew."

David returned his attention to the letter. "What are those squiggles in the far corner?"

Eve peered over his shoulder at the top of the page. "Looks like Hebrew," she said. "I don't know what it says, though. My Sunday school years ended with my bat mitzvah, so it's been a minute since I last studied the mother tongue."

"I didn't know you were Jewish," David exclaimed. "My best friend in uni was. He and his missus always invite us over for the Passover meal. All those cups of wine! Remarkable similarities to the Christian faith, you know."

Eve sniggered. "Well, we come from the same root."

"Okay take me through how you found this." David rolled his chair away from his desk and over to Eve's. "Every detail."

She described the hike and the thunderstorm and the cave. She told him about pawing through the soil and finding nothing else but wanting to return to dig deeper, look farther into the belly of the cave. She paused in her retelling and looked at him with wide eyes, almost pleading for permission to drop the other projects of her fellowship and focus solely on this one.

"Well, of course you must go back," he said with a smile. "Not solely because I can see how desperately you want to. This is actually an important document, and there are likely to be others. But you cannot work on this alone, mostly because you are a fellow and not a full employee. Liability and protocol and all that. I'll have to guide the dig because I am the licensed archivist in this division. I'll be happy to accompany you. And by the way, this eagerness to delve into history and dig for more evidence is proof that you are meant for an archival career."

"Fair enough," she said. "When do we go?"

David drummed his fingers on the desktop as he thought. "We'll need to learn all we can about Shira and Hugh first. That should be a day's worth of research, maybe two. Meanwhile, I'll gather the tools we'll need for the dig—a metal box for additional finds, trowels, duster brushes. I wonder if this is a historical site? Do I need to get the national historic register involved?"

He shook his head as Eve watched him debate with himself the merits of involving too many governmental agencies too soon.

"No, we'll search first, apologize later if we must," he decided. "We'll head to the cave by Thursday. I'll need to stay somewhere nearby. I can't be driving back and forth endlessly. I know you do it, but it's not for me to commute."

"Maybe the Monteith House has a room?"

"Did you say Monteith House?"

Eve startled. Her breath suspended in her chest, her heart beating rapidly. How had she not put the two together? Mac's family estate, the inn and pub that he owned, and the Macalasters—the Earl of Monteith.

"What?"

The color had drained from Eve's face. Had Mac known when she'd shown him the letter? And if he had, why hadn't he said so?

"I went on a date with a man who owns Monteith House," she said. "Do you think?"

David didn't seem as shocked by the connection. "Possibly. But the local lands are often named after long-ago landowners. Don't be too quick to accuse. He may not know anything or even be connected."

She nodded and let the breath back into her chest. But what if there was a connection?

Chapter Twelve

*E**ve, 2014*

By Thursday, Eve was eager to head back to the trailhead. She'd been up late, texting with Mac. Their Tuesday date had been as magical as the first, though she hadn't wanted to discuss the letter. She was enjoying the attraction too much to consider that his lineage might prevent them from moving forward. What if he found out she was digging into his family's sordid past and ghosted her?

Eve set the kettle on and dropped a PG teabag—one of the most popular brands of black tea in the UK—into a mug. Breakfast would be a fresh scone from the village bakery with strawberry jam and cream. She put two apples, a wedge of cheddar and two more scones in her backpack. David would bring the archival tools and she had a shovel in the car. She filled two bottles from the faucet. Outside, the day was lightening.

David met her at the trailhead. "My wife thanked me for leaving her alone for two days," he laughed as they set out. "We are rarely apart overnight, and I must admit, the room felt empty without her."

What must that be like, Eve wondered, *to be so close to another person that you miss them on a single night alone?*

"At Monteith House?"

David nodded. "And I met your man. Fine lad."

"You didn't say anything?"

"Course not! Do you take me for a fool?"

She sighed audibly.

"But it's not for you, dear, that I didn't say a word," David cautioned. "We don't know what we're dealing with yet, with these letters. If this is his family and we alert them too soon, we could face obstacles or legal fights before we know anything of significance. I've had wealthy families fight for control of a collection before, and I do not want to repeat it if I can help it."

Eve chewed on her lip as she nodded. Why had she only thought of the effect it might have on her burgeoning relationship? Selfish! How little she knew about this new field she was venturing into. She was grateful for a mentor who would guide her to avoid serious mistakes.

Eve tucked her phone into a pocket and hoisted the pack over her shoulders so she could carry the shovel more easily. She locked the car—one of only three at the trailhead car park this early—and set off, David behind her, leaning on hiking poles as the grade of the path increased. The route quickly looked familiar, and soon they arrived at the mouth of the cave.

In the light, it wasn't scary. Calm, rather, and inviting. Tree branches and overgrown shrubs shrouded the opening and hid it from view. The vegetation also shielded them from wind, which whispered today, compared to the screams of her last visit. No wonder the letter had remained hidden for so long!

All the greenery hid the cave from the path. David lifted some branches and Eve ducked under, switching on a flashlight as he followed her in.

She'd brought an electric lantern and plenty of batteries to flush the interior with light. Eve gasped in delight. Craggy walls of sedimentary rock were artistic in striations running horizontal along the perimeter. She ran a hand along the smooth, cool rock, walking deeper in. At first, the cave was cool and damp. But farther in, it warmed and became a palpable kind of quiet.

"Work to do!" Her voice echoed back to her. She found the spot where she'd pulled the letter from the soil. "This is where I found it."

David scuttled over to look.

"You already dug around here?"

She nodded.

"How deep did you go?"

"Two hands?"

He was nodding. "It's unlikely that Shira would have gone deeper—she'd be alone, with more primitive tools. She wouldn't have been used to working with her hands. Let's go wider."

He traced a path with the toe of his shoe. "I say we follow a trail from the first find backwards along the wall, deeper into the cave. We can dig along this vein."

It was well into the afternoon before they found another package of letters wrapped in oiled leather. Buried deeper in the earth, the second batch were fully caked in dark soil that had seeped inside at the corners, smearing the letters, which were less readable than the first batch. David carried the letters to a flat rock at the back of the cave and smoothed it, wiping away dirt with a brush. They could make out a few words, written in a different hand from the first. David held a magnifier over the top page.

Dear Shira,

I have arrived in New York Harbor and am grateful to the Foundation for the funds to make this journey. If you could see these stricken streets! Children, gaunt and gray, their eyes hollow, their hands pawing for scraps from rubbish bins. I had thought America was a place of great wealth and good fortune for those Jews who made it across the Atlantic. To be sure, there are Jewish families of means here, living the highest of comforts like the most fortunate Gentiles, but the depths of poverty are equally as extreme. Could this be what capitalism has wrought? Extremes of opportunity and despair, twin souls inhabiting the same streets?

Thanks be to the Levenson Foundation for outfitting our operation with enough medicines to minister to the sick and downtrodden of our brethren. Whole families live in single-room squalor, five and six abed, sleeping erect, never able to fully recline or repose, their faces stained red from wind and work. There is only so much we can do. Calling squalor home, in broken tenements, in buildings the city has forgotten, with dim light and fetid air, only perpetuates ill health. I can administer to the current symptoms, but I cannot change conditions. If only I could lift up the perpetual poor into a sunnier locale, into a structure that protects from damp and disease, from residing amongst vermin and all they transmit to the frail humans beside them.

When I return, I'd like to publish a paper proving the connection between living conditions and state of health. Might the Foundation find means of support for such an endeavor? With great gratitude and acknowledgement, of course.

For a moment, I turn from the work that calls me to the heart that beats within me. Which calls to you from across the roiling seas. My darling Shira, in the quiet moments between sleep and work, the few that I can grasp, I think of you fondly. I am indebted to you not only for the generosity and vision you share for this ever-important work, but also for the gift of your heart.

Until I can once again hold you in my grasp, I remain forever yours.

Benjamin.

"The date is smudged, and there're the same squiggles in the top corner."

"A doctor?" Eve said. "Administering to the poor. In my research, I found many grants from Shira's family foundation to such work around the globe. From the London archive that holds the Levenson Foundation collection, I've requested lists of doctors who received grants."

"Where are the family archives?"

"London," Eve said. "And Frankfurt. I have yet to reach out to them."

David brushed dirt from the letter and secured it in the metal box he'd brought to keep it dry and airless. He peeled off his gloves then gulped from a water bottle before saying, "What are you waiting for?"

"I guess to see if I can find the answers from London first?"

"Archival research takes time," David said. "Better to cast your line in multiple directions and see what you catch."

They broke for a late lunch. Eve bit into an apple, wandering toward the cave entrance to gaze at the hilly landscape. Wind cooled the sweat from her face. David approached quietly behind her, chewing on a curry chicken sandwich he'd brought from the market.

"We've done enough for today," he said. "We'll leave the equipment in a corner of the cave, but I'll take the metal box with me. We can start again at dawn."

She tucked the apple core into a side pocket of her pack. David covered the spot where they were digging with a tarp.

Chapter Thirteen

*S*am, 2014

"Why won't you come to New York?"

Simon's voice over the long-distance call was firm and probing. He'd been asking this same question in letters and during their long phone conversations since Eve announced she was going to Scotland. Sam didn't have a ready answer. Except to say that she'd be coming back or he liked his job or he owned a house, dammit, and why give up everything he'd worked so hard for just to move to a city he didn't know for a man he hadn't seen or touched in years?

Simon had had his share of hookups in New York, but never a love as profound and connected as he'd had with Sam in the years after the custody lawsuit. Shaken but finally secure in his solo parenthood, Sam had finally acted on his instincts one night when Simon was over for dinner and moved their friendship into the realm of romance. Eve was five years old and already asleep in her bed, and Sam could remember that first kiss as if it had just happened. They were already in love, though they hadn't admitted it to one another over the course of their friendship. They'd met in one of Sam's first classes at the community college and became fast friends because of their shared awkwardness and fundamentalist religious backgrounds. But Sam made it clear that all he could offer was friendship.

In New York, Simon could have finally put Sam into the distant recesses of memory and set out on the path of finding a viable love that could inhabit his days and brighten his nights. He tried. But as they wrote letters across the miles, he found no one enticed him in quite the way Sam did. When Eve graduated from college, he urged Sam to move to New York, to give them a chance, but Sam had lived too long alone that he was afraid to make a big change. So they reverted to letter-writing, and Simon prowled for love in the Big Apple. He came close a few times, but never fell hard and just when he came close, a letter would arrive from Sam, and he'd finger the paper and trace the lilt of his handwriting and sigh with frustration. He could have as much sex as he wanted, but the love of his life was a stubborn man in Michigan.

Now, though, he sensed a shift in Sam. Eve was overseas. They were so much older. Finally, they could be together. The excuses were dust-dry and old. Sam agreed to sell his house, to move to New York before the year ended. He'd written in several letters how eager he was to make up for lost time. Simon urged Sam to move faster, to get the house listed, to come look for places they'd live together, a home they could buy. Simon's career in theater design was thriving, and he assured Sam that he could find any number of journalism jobs in New York. Sam wanted this—he wanted Simon more than anything—but he was paralyzed by fear.

"I'm an old man, Si," he said. "Change isn't easy. I have roots here. It feels too hard to pack everything up alone. And besides, what if Eve wants to come home again?"

"I tell you what: let's take a trip. To Scotland. We can see Eve, and I can dig into my family's roots," Simon said. His voice was soothing, low, with a slight rumble that sent tingles through Sam's limbs and ignited a fire in his groin. "Just a trip. A week or two. Get to know each other again, in person."

The silence on the line was electric, pulsing. What harm could a trip do? Plenty! They could find there was no longer an attraction between them, which Sam had a hard time imagining. They could fight and get in each other's way, learn that they couldn't share space, and then the dream would die.

Or it could go better than he hoped.

"I'm running out of reasons to say no," Sam laughed.

"Then stop saying it."

Sam pressed the phone to his shoulder by tilting his head as he slid open the kitchen sliding glass door and stepped out onto the patio. The summer night was ablaze with the clicking of insects in the grasses and the swaying of leaves in the high branches of the old oak. It was a humid night, and the sun was long in setting. Sam sat in an Adirondack chair whose red paint had faded from exposure to sun and whose wood had softened from the elements. He'd bought the pair of chairs when Eve graduated college eight years earlier and left them outside in all seasons.

"Why didn't you fall in love with someone else long ago?"

Simon snorted. "Believe me, I could have."

Sam went cold. A chipmunk darted across the yard. A hawk winged overhead.

"Relax," Simon chuckled. "I tried. A few times. But what we had all those years ago—I've never find anything close. There's been plenty of sex, believe me, but I want more than that now. I want you."

Sam didn't know whether to laugh or cry. All of what he'd said was true, and yet he sat in a quiet night in the humid yard of a house he'd purchased nearly twenty years earlier, content but alone.

"You're the only man I've ever really loved, Sam."

The words were slow, quiet, the low rumble of Simon's voice reassuring over the miles. Sam released the breath he hadn't realized he was holding.

"Me too." His words were a whisper, as the phone shook in his hand. "I've been alone for longer than I was ever with anyone, you know. There'll be a learning curve."

"Fine. We'll deal with it. It's time," Simon said.

The loneliness was an ache that lived beneath his rib cage, perpetually. Despite the friends and co-workers and frequent heartfelt letters from Simon. Despite his doting daughter and their constant conversations.

"Let's go to Scotland," Sam said. "See what it's like to be together. A first step toward a future together."

The sky had darkened to a deep purple, and bats were circling low in the sky. The crickets were in full voice, throbbing.

He could almost hear Simon's smile over the line, could almost feel his hand sear heat into his skin. He was taking the leap—and he wouldn't fall flat on his face.

After, when the door was locked and the lights turned off, Sam lay on the bed, the covers folded back in the warm night. The air conditioning was on, but he'd left a window open to hear the night, and the air hung soft in his bedroom. In the dark, images of Simon's sandy hair and green eyes, the long lean lines of his body, his pink skin made Sam grow hard and warm. His body throbbed with wanting. He closed his eyes and imagined the man beside him, his skin tingling as it came into contact with Simon's body, his tender touch growing insistent, and he arched into the dark, cried out as if in anguish as his desire moistened the sheets and spread across his belly. He'd been alone long enough. If his desire could carry him this intensely when he was by himself, what might it be like with Simon beside him?

Chapter Fourteen

*M*ac, 2014

"You have to tell them," Mac said.

Emma slumped over the bar. "Mum won't take it well," she said.

"Does she take anything well?" He poured hot tea into his sister's mug, and she tipped the tiny pitcher on the counter, adding a swirl of cream. "Why now, anyway? To deflect attention from your notable absence? To distract from your new love interest?"

Mac pursed his lips and sighed. He ran a hand through his curls, tugging free an occasional knot. "It's only been a week and a couple of dates," he said. "It's nothing until it's something."

"It's something," Emma said, sipping from the steaming mug. "You can't stop thinking about her."

"Yeah, and why is that?" he laughed. "I'm all tied up in knots of wanting, waiting for a sign that she wants me as much as I want her."

Emma shook her head. "There is something lovely about having my partner all to myself, with no one even aware that she's part of my life," she said. "The minute Mum knows I have a girlfriend—and not some aristocratic, well-bred boyfriend—the magic turns to dust. The family becomes a nuisance. I don't want the questions, the disapproving head shakes, the whispers and the glares. No matter who I date, she'll never be welcome in the Monteith clan if Mighty Margaret has anything to say about it."

Mac laid a hand over his sister's on the bar. "Just show her your tattoo, and the girlfriend situation will seem like no big deal," he said.

Emma rippled with laughter. "Right. A daughter of Margaret Monteith with the Saltire emblazoned on her left bicep, a blue-and-white testament to my free-Scotland stance? She'd die of embarrassment on the spot!"

It was early on a Saturday, and the guests of the inn were breakfasting in the far room at the back of the building. Mac and Emma had the bar to themselves, with plates of sausages, toast and fried eggs. The tables in this part of the pub were empty, the chairs standing sentry, the surfaces still clean from the night before. Soon, the lunch crowd would begin to arrive, and then the place would hum with traffic all the rest of the day and into the night. Now was the time when Mac could think.

He swiped a corner of toast through a golden, liquidy yolk and crunched into it. Emma sipped tea and sliced a chunk of sausage.

He didn't get to see his sisters much. One, because he almost never went to Sunday breakfast, and two because Emma and Shona shared a flat in Glasgow and rarely made it home on a weekend. Emma had been dating Finlay for half a year now and was, in her own words, salty in love and restless at the possibility of their parents finding out and causing trouble. Mac didn't know how their mother would respond to having a lesbian in the family, but his gut told him it couldn't go well. Scotland was many things, including a champion of freedom fighters and rebels, but like the rest of the United Kingdom, it had been painfully slow in extending equal rights to LGBTQ citizens and even slower to build true acceptance after the laws changed, especially in smaller towns among the Highlands and Islands.

"Will I at least get to meet her before the rest of the clan?" Mac cleared away Emma's empty mug and came around the bar to hug his sister. Her eyes were blue as the sky, and when she wasn't working as a financial counselor at one of Glasgow's main banks, Emma favored old jeans and T-shirts emblazoned with the names of classic rock bands. Today, she wore a Rolling Stones T-shirt, the big red tongue dotted with tiny rhinestones.

"I'll show you mine if you show me yours," Emma winked at him, leaning against his shoulder as his arm came protectively around her.

"It's too soon for you to meet Eve," he said, stroking her soft hair.

She met his eyes and held them. "Let's say, if you're still dating her in a month, we do a double date in Glasgow?"

"You've got a deal, sis," he said, squeezing her shoulder and planting a kiss on the top of her head.

He would only work a half day, despite the inevitable crowd of a summer Saturday. His manager was capable of carrying on without him, a reassurance Mac appreciated that let him anticipate the evening ahead with Eve. He wanted to get her alone, finally, and move beyond the careful conversations that happen over a low-lit table in a crowded restaurant.

They'd been texting all week, plus two long, lingering late-night calls, her voice like the cool and soothing tumble of a waterfall. He would cook dinner at her cottage, thick steaks bought from the farmer up the A811 from Balmaha, with a sauté of fresh carrots, fennel and beetroot, and blasted potatoes, cooked to crispy and soft in the oven with heaps of butter. He'd make her a good Scottish dinner, light candles, play soft music, set the stage for a truly romantic evening.

But it was hours until then, and the day was gray, overcast, and a little blowy. She'd told him that it didn't feel like summer, then described July in Ann Arbor as sticky and hot, white-bright with very long days.

"Surely the days are lighter longer here in the north," he'd countered. And indeed they were. He wondered what she was doing while he was at the pub, getting in the way of the people who worked for him. The restaurant manager kept sending him wary glances, and finally Mac took the hint and waved off, leaving for good to get ready for his date.

The gravel kicked up as Mac's Land Rover turned in toward Eve's cottage. Mac shut the motor, grabbed two bags of groceries from the back seat and walked to the door. She opened the door and stepped into a spotlight of late-day sun. Mac's breath caught in his chest. She stood barefoot in a pale-yellow floral dress with scalloped sleeves.

"Hello," she said, rising on her toes to kiss his lips.

"You look bonny," he said quietly.

She smiled and motioned to the open door behind her, inviting him in.

He deposited the bags on the kitchen counter as she clicked the door shut. He looked around, taking in the stack of books on the side table, the soft couch big enough for two people only, a hooked rug on the tile floor and the long lines of the kitchen, a box of tea on the counter next to the electric kettle. No dirty dishes in the sink. No half-eaten wrapped foods on the counter. Neat and tidy.

"It's not a big place, but it's enough for me," she said, her voice cottony quiet and slow. He moved through the room and down the hall, uninvited, but she didn't object. She followed at his heels as the wind whistled through a cracked window, the tall stands of pine and birch that surrounded the home dancing in the wind. The hall was dark, lit only by a single lamp through the open bedroom door at far the end of the long hallway.

He reached a hand toward her behind him, not turning to look at her, just waiting for her fingers to lace in his. When she took his hand, the electricity of her touch shot through his arm, increasing the rapid beat of his heart. When they reached the bedroom, he stopped in the doorway and waited for her to come close. He pulled her into the room, her hand still in his grasp, her breath audible and quick. He turned to look at her, but he didn't speak. He only reached his hand up to her face, trailing a single finger along the lines of her cheek, along her neck, down to her collarbone, where he bent and planted a single kiss.

He was slow with his movements, taking his time, exploring her, trailing his hand up and over her arm, down the slope of her back, until it landed on her hip. He pulled her closer, if that was even possible, and pressed his body into hers, his head bent and tasting the skin of her neck. She tilted her head back and closed her eyes.

His mouth was on her skin, his breath hot. He wanted her more than he had wanted anyone in a long time, or maybe ever.

She tugged his shirt over his head. He pulled his mouth away from her skin for only the second needed to do so. He unbuttoned the front of her dress and pressed the fabric open but didn't remove the garment, only peeled it away from her skin, keeping his exploration of her slow and measured. He was intent on taking his time. The grain of the wood beneath his feet was smooth and cold. The window was open, and the cool of the night came in easily. It prickled his skin, a contrast with his desire. She tugged at the buckle of his belt, but he pushed her hands away then slid her dress fully to the floor in a pool around her feet.

"No fair," she whispered into his ear.

"In time," he said, pushing her gently to the bed and lowering to his knees. His mouth dipped and tugged and kissed and licked at every inch of her skin until he made his way between her legs, pulled her panties down and off, settled his face between the warmth that pulsated at her core, lifted her hips and settled in. She made a guttural sound, more animalistic than human, as he tasted her, pressed his face closer to her body, worked his fingers and his tongue in and around. He kept going until she was shuddering and making sounds he couldn't describe. He didn't stop until she pushed him away.

He stood and smiled down at her, but she was turned onto her side, her eyes closed. He unbuckled his belt, dropped his jeans to the floor and lay beside her on the bed, his body cupping hers.

Finally, she turned to face him.

"I thought you were going to make me dinner," she whispered.

"I will," he said. "But I couldn't wait."

"Mmmm."

She reached down between his legs and ran her hand up along the insides of his thighs. He was ready for her, aching, hungry to feel the heat of her. He palmed her hips, but she pulled his hands away, and when he looked at her with a question, she just shook her head. She prodded him onto his back and swung a leg over him, hovering above him.

A sigh whispered from his lips as he arched his head back and squeezed his eyes shut. He reached for her once more, but she pushed his hands away. She lowered herself almost on top of him but then lifted off as soon as their bodies made contact.

"You're killing me," he growled.

"I know."

He clawed the quilt, bit hard enough on his bottom lip to draw blood. He pressed his eyes closed. He wanted her more than he'd ever wanted anything, to feel her hot and wet, to know her closer than any two people could get. When finally she lowered down onto him, he cried out, an animal in the night, his growl fierce and guttural. His eyes shot open, and he looked at her golden face, smiling in a cunning grin, and he knew that she would always control his heart, as long as she wanted to. She was moving now, faster and deeper, bringing him to the edge of awareness, and then she was in chorus with him as they rode the waves together, calling into the night, as if someone might answer, as if they were calling for home.

"Well, that was, something," Mac said as he nosed into Eve's bare shoulder. Night sounds clicked through the open window, the wisp of bats winging through the low sky, the skitter of squirrels, the woosh of a passing car. She was smiling but didn't respond. There was no need, nothing to say.

"I'm famished…" She poked at his ribs and he buckled under her touch, an arm snaking around her naked body and pulling her on top of him. "You can have more later, but now I must eat." She pressed her nose against his and sucked on his lip. "You're bleeding," she said as she sat upright, licking her lip and wincing.

"I couldn't help myself," he said. "You got me so riled up, you've caused injury." He was laughing and he flipped her onto her back and hovered over her, drawing her into a long, biting kiss which burst open the slight cut on his lip once again. "Now we're really connected," he said. "The Highlanders used to take a swipe of blood from the wrists of the bride and groom during a wedding ceremony and bind their wrists together, tied with a cloth. Now we've done it, too."

"So we're married now because your bleeding lip seeped into mine?" She was sitting up, trying to be playful but looked scared by what he'd said.

"Ach, no, I'm just playing with you," he said, reaching for his jeans. "Scared the lights out of you?"

She scowled. "I'm fine, you fool. Now cook for me. I get cranky when I'm hungry."

"I can see that," he said, pulling on his shirt.

"Get started in the kitchen, and I'll dress and be there in a minute," she said, opening a drawer and pulling out navy blue sweatpants and a ribbed white tank top. He padded barefoot down the hall while she ducked into the bathroom.

Mac unpacked the ingredients from the grocery bags, laying two thick steaks, vegetables, potatoes, a stick of butter and a flask of oil on the counter. He drew out a bottle of Glen Grant 10-year single malt whiskey and rummaged in the cupboard to find glasses, into which he poured the amber liquid an inch deep.

Hair spilling from a topknot, Eve arrived quietly, thick wool socks muffling her approach. She sidled up beside him and pressed her lips to his shoulder.

He grunted, never lifting his eyes from his hands, which were busy chopping vegetables on a wooden board.

Finally, he laid the knife on the cutting board and handed her a glass. "*Slàinte Mhath.*" He tilted his glass toward hers.

Eve tapped her glass to his and sipped. The skillet hissed as Mac threw chopped veggies into the warmed oil. He cracked pepper over it and rained salt from his fingertips. Eve reached across and flipped the switch for the oven fan, then hopped onto the counter to tilt open a high window.

"I could've done that for you," he said, cornering her as she perched on the counter. He nibbled on her chin, then slid a finger of raw carrot between her lips. She bit down and smiled as she chewed, then hopped off the counter, grabbed her glass and perched on a chair to face him. She refilled her glass, two inches deep with whiskey. He lifted his glass, and she brought the bottle to splash more into his.

"Tell me about your family," she said.

Mac turned the heat low under the vegetables and peered into the oven at the potatoes. He tossed back a throatful of whiskey.

"My family owns the land around the Monteith. Quite a lot of land, actually. For generations."

"How many?"

He sprinkled salt over the steaks then pulled a griddle from the cupboard and laid it over two burners. He flicked on the fire and set two chunks of butter to bubble in the heat. When they were fully melted, he laid the meat on top and turned the heat to low.

"At least six, but likely more. The Monteith itself has been there in some form since just after the Rising."

"The '45?"

He nodded.

"I can only guess which side your family was on."

He drained his glass, turned off the heat under the vegetables and scraped them into a bowl, which he covered with a dish towel. Then he flipped the steaks to sear on the other side before sliding them into the oven.

"Well, that's a funny thing," he said, turning to her. Her cheeks were pink, her eyelids heavy. He stroked the side of her face. She closed her eyes as his fingers drew on her skin.

"I come from Clan MacAlister, but my ancestors switched sides around the time of the Rising to align with the English," he said. "They changed the spelling of our name to Macalaster. At some point, a few generations back, they did away with that surname and just called themselves the Monteiths. And here I am. I feel kind of funny about it, if I'm honest."

The smell of cooking meat and bubbling fat filled the kitchen. Mac pulled the sheet pan from the oven and cascaded the golden, soft potatoes into a bowl.

"I don't know much about the Battle of Culloden or Highland history, so forgive me if my questions are simple," she said. "But why do you feel conflicted about a decision your ancestors made centuries ago?"

Mac sighed and brushed his fingers back from his forehead.

"It's hard to explain. I know it must seem like ancient history to an American."

Eve rolled her eyes.

"I mean, this all happened before there was even a United States of America," he added.

She nodded.

"There's a tremor running through Scotland, especially once you leave the cities," he explained. "It's this feeling of...we've had enough of being controlled by foreign powers. We just want to live the way we've always lived, in these hills, with our music and our food and our language. All of it was forbidden when the English defeated the Highlanders at Culloden, which is why there's such a devoted Scottish diaspora around the world. The Scots have been lamenting the English incursion for centuries."

Mac poured a glass of wine, took a long sip, then continued. "To think someone in my family made a choice to abandon our culture, our heritage, all that our friends and family fought for, fiercely, to side with the English for money. It just feels wrong."

She was nodding as he handed her a glass of wine.

"Two minutes for the steaks," he said.

Eve pulled plates from the cupboard, forks and knives from a drawer. She set them on the table in the middle of the room and started a fire in the iron stove. The night was purple and twinkling, casting the cottage in shadows. The fire crackled and sparked, and the room grew warm. She filled glasses with water and set one by each plate. By then, Mac had turned off the oven and plated the steaks. He carried the steaming bowls to the table then returned with the juicy steaks.

He scooped vegetables and potatoes onto her plate, small, neat mounds of each, then slid a steak beside them, tiny rivers of juices oozing from the meat and flavoring the vegetables. She pierced the meat with her fork and sawed her knife into it, depositing a juicy bite onto her tongue. She closed her eyes as she chewed, emitting little sounds of satisfaction as she ate.

"I guess you like it?"

She nodded and cut another bite.

"If you keep moaning like that, I might have to skip dinner and initiate round two back in that bedroom," he said.

"Well then, I'll have to chew quietly because I am not going anywhere until I've eaten," she said. "I was hungry before, and I'm ravenous now. That was quite a workout." She winked as she popped another bite of meat and a soft potato into her mouth.

Mac ate his food slowly, watching Eve as he chewed. "Siblings?"

She shook her head. "I'm an only. A lonely only."

"I can't even imagine how quiet that must be," he said, gulping wine. It was smooth and tart and warmed his insides almost as much as the whiskey. "I'm one of four, and there was so much noise when I was kid. That's why I went to uni in Manchester—far enough away to find my footing without tripping over expectations or rivalries."

"I would've liked that bustle." She smiled. "It was just my father and me, no chance of a sibling."

"He never remarried?"

Her eyes lost their smile for a minute. It was quick, but he saw it. Then it was back, and she said, "I guess he never found the right person." Then she changed the subject. "I went away to school, too. Columbia. In New York."

"Ah, a bright lass. Hope I'm not too pedestrian for you."

She huffed. "You might be," she said. "We'll just have to see."

He smirked. "What did you study?"

"History and writing." She slid the last vegetables onto her fork and clamped her mouth around them. "I've always wanted to know where I came from, and I learned from a young age that stories were a key to the past. You might call it an obsession."

His raised eyebrows prodded her to go on, so she did.

"I just want to know who I am, where I come from, who I'm connected to," she said. "It's always been just my father and me. No grandparents around, or aunts or uncles or cousins. It's hard to know anything about myself without a sense of history or roots."

"No family at all? Not even stories about who they were or where they went?"

She shook her head.

"Just a few. No pictures, though, no photo albums. Just the wedding portrait of him and my mother and he tells me about their wedding. Never about her. He changes the subject whenever I ask about her or his family. All I know is she died, and then my grandparents ganged up on him and tried to take me away from him when I was four." She shuddered.

He reached a hand out to steady her. "And here I'm telling you about my family going back hundreds of years. I'm so sorry. You must think me heartless."

"How could you know?" She shook her head. "My father is incredible. He's worked at a newspaper all my life, and he supports everything I do. When I was a journalist, he never claimed credit for my career path, and now that I'm heading into archives, he says he admires me for going after my interests and is glad I don't seek anyone's approval before taking a leap. We've always been close."

Mac nodded. When he'd told his parents he wanted to run the pub, they tried to talk him out of it. The offspring of aristocratic families didn't work menial jobs, his mother insisted. But Mac did it anyway, absorbing snarky jibes at family gatherings. That's why he stopped attending Sunday breakfasts. Margaret said nothing about Collin's lollygagging and gave Emma and Shona a wide berth—Shona to her art and Emma to her bank job. Collin was the heir, Mac the golden boy, her beautiful athletic superstar son who had a brief flash of glory on the pitch. A football star was glamorous, a pub manager an embarrassment.

"Tell me about your father," Mac said, leading Eve away from the table and over to the couch. He sat in the corner and pulled her back against him, leaving enough room for her to stretch her legs along the cushions. He stroked her hair as she talked.

"My father is a selfless man. He worked his career around me, attended every dance recital, school play, debate competition. He never missed a minute of my life. We talk all the time."

What must that be like, Mac wondered. Outside, the wind picked up, whistling through the cracked-open kitchen window.

They made love again in the quiet of the dawn. Eve was up before him, getting ready for work. She looked formidable in tailored pants and a silk blouse, her hair in a bun, a gold necklace clasped around her neck. For a minute, he had a vision of his mother in her proper clothes, but he shook it off, shuddering at the thought of this lovely girl in any way mirroring his cold and distant mother.

"I don't want to leave you," he said, kissing the hollow at the base of her neck.

She smiled. "I'm sorry! I have a lot to do today. I have to get to the office by nine."

He glanced at the clock. It was just past seven. He whistled. She'd barely make it to Edinburgh in time.

"Don't you have work, too?" She fastened her watch, slipped her feet into ballet flats and strung a messenger bag across her body.

He shook his head. "My team runs the place just fine. They don't need me."

He followed her down the hall, watched her search for her keys, then slide them into her pocket after she spotted them on the kitchen counter.

"I wanted to be there when I had nowhere else to be," he said, turning her to face him and cupping her chin. He lifted her face and kissed her deep and full.

"Well, today you have nowhere else to be, my dear," she said, patting his shoulder. "Best be on your way."

***

Eve

After a week of digging in the cave with David and unearthing a second trove of letters, she was treading softly with Mac, hesitantly, wanting to know more and yet afraid of what she might hear. She'd proceed as if it were any normal early part of a relationship, continue her work properly and hope one didn't make the other impossible.

As she drove to the train station, she thought about the prior night—his beautiful face, all the details of his deep, rich history and the meager details of hers. How could a historic battle influence identity for generations to come? There was nothing like that in her family history. At least, from what she knew of it. All the Scottish battles from several centuries earlier were so long in the past, but she wanted to understand him and this place that she was beginning to call home.

How had she ended up here? She'd never known anyone of Scottish descent. At least not that she knew of. When Mac had mentioned a Scottish diaspora, the only thing she could think of was the same word in connection to the Jewish community, meaning Jews outside the land of Israel. Even so, the concept had never resonated with her, as she had yet to visit the Jewish state. She couldn't see the allure. Geography and land weren't part of her Jewish identity. Being Jewish was merely one facet of her identity, not the whole thing. From the way Mac described Scots, identity consumed them. It was everything, from food to music to language and more. She was trying, but it was all so hard to relate to.

They'd had so much to drink—she could almost still smell the cinnamon scent of the wine and the way the whiskey had radiated warmth through her body. She was fascinated with how deeply he felt about these questions of identity and how much thought he'd given to it.

It all felt so good! But it was early days, and she didn't want to trust this growing connection quite yet. Too many men had been turned off by her intelligence and her strong personality that she had become wary of any guy who insisted that what he liked best about her was her strength, her voice, her intelligence. It always seemed too good to be true and usually was. She was thirty years old and had never had a deep, enduring relationship. Deep down, she was afraid to get close, lest someone she really liked reject her when he knew her fully.

So why had she opened up so much to Mac? This was the first time she'd shared such deep yearning with a man. She hadn't even opened up like this to her three close girlfriends from childhood. Eve had spent most of her life withdrawing into herself, quiet alongside her father.

Although she loved her father more than anything, one doting parent was just not enough. She'd known it since middle school, when she saw how different they were from her friends' families. No big gatherings at holidays, no grandparents to visit in Florida. She'd wanted to know where she came from for the longest time, but when, in her freshman year of high school, he admitted that her grandparents were not part of her life because of the way they'd taken him to court to take her away from him, she couldn't bear to ask for more details.

It would be easy to let Mac distract her. But she couldn't. She wouldn't let herself get lost in love when she needed to be grounded by a budding career that gave her purpose.

It was all happening so fast. She pictured him from that morning, loping off toward his car, her stomach tumbling with excitement and fear. She couldn't admit it to him, but she'd wanted to stay home with him, too. But she'd come all this way to Scotland, quit a promising career, left everything behind. She had to prove to herself, and everyone back home who had doubted her decision, that she knew what she was doing. And that she did not fly across an ocean to fall in love.

Chapter Fifteen

*E*ve, *2014*

Eve strode into the office fifteen minutes past nine, her face glistening with the sweat of walking fast from the train station to the offices, all up steep hills.

"I swear," she muttered, dropping her bag on her desk chair and plucking a tissue from a box on her desk to dot sweat from her face.

"You're the one who chose to live far away," David chided.

She smirked, trying to still the fast pace of her heartbeat.

"I've set us up in conference room A," he said. "Let's be quick about it, and quiet. I'm not ready to share this find with anyone."

On their second day of digging on Conic Hill, they'd found a trunk buried deep in the earth. David had hit it with the shovel, the metal on hard wood ringing with reverberations, the hard jolt shuddering up his arms. They'd peered down into the dirt with a flashlight to see what he'd hit.

"This would have taken effort, and the woman wouldn't have done it alone," David said. "From all I've read, Shira was petite. I can't imagine her lugging a trunk up a mountainside. Now we

have paths cleared and steps for the steep bits, but then? She'd be climbing through wilderness. She'd have to have had help."

"Who?"

David combed his fingers through his thinning hair. "One of her children?" He shook his head. "No, they would've asked questions."

"A servant?"

David was nodding. "Spot on! Someone she could pay to guarantee silence."

Now, back in the office, it was time to see what the trunk held. Eve followed him down the hall. Still caked with dried soil, the trunk sat on a thin towel spread beneath it to collect dirt that flecked off when it opened. Farther down the table, individual letters they'd also unearthed were laid flat and held in place by brass weights, strategically placed at each corner so as not to cover the writing or crease the pages.

Eve traced the ridges of the box with her fingers. Leather strapping held it closed. From a distance, the wood looked intact, but up close, Eve could see tiny indentations along the edges, evidence of wear from moisture or critters crawling through the dark. It was not a large trunk and could easily have been hefted up the mountain by a strong servant. She said as much to David, who was reading a letter between gloved hands.

"I think the individual letters were buried separately from the trunk, at another time. The trunk must've been an afterthought or a later decision. Let's see what's in it."

With two fingers, she lifted the latch. It came open easily. The pages inside bore elegant script less faded than the ones buried directly in the dirt. She eased a pair of gloves over her hands and slid them under the stack of papers, lifting them out as if they were an infant. She backed away from the trunk until she could lower the stack to the tabletop.

David had figured out the man from the love letters was Benjamin Belzer, Scotland's first Jewish doctor, who brought health care to poor Jewish communities. His travels had been funded by the Levenson Foundation, as mentioned in that first letter they'd found.

"I accessed the Foundation minutes, read through the recipients of the many grants they disbursed. His name came up again and again. He was the only Benjamin I could find. A pillar in the London Jewish community."

"You said he was from Scotland."

David nodded. "Born in Glasgow and earned a medical degree at the University of Edinburgh. Jews weren't allowed in English universities then. We're talking the 1850s. He worked in Scotland for six years, then moved to London, where he helped build the Jewish community and sat on its governing board for the rest of his life."

In her research, Eve had discovered that Shira was born in 1842 and died a mere fifty years later. Her youngest child was born in 1875, the year the doctor died at sea.

David sifted his gloved fingers through the stack of birth records for Shira's children, ownership certificates for jewels, heirlooms, artifacts, property and land. The birth certificate for Aaron Macalaster was written in a different hand than the other children and enclosed in a silk handkerchief. There were three letters and a pair of silver candlesticks wrapped in velvet, a silver chalice with Hebrew etched into the stem, also protected by cloth, and a delicate, colorful Fabergé egg in a satin-lined box. Tipped open, the egg displayed a delicate gold star of David.

"Aha! This gives us our timeline," David exclaimed, lifting the gold star with two fingers and laying it on a cloth he'd laid on the table. Eve leaned in to look at the delicate lines of the tiny piece of jewelry.

"The star?"

David shook his head. "The egg. Fabergé eggs didn't come into being until 1885. This narrows our timeline to the last seven years of her life."

Eve was nodding. "I'll look for staff lists for the Monteiths during those years."

"It's a start," David said. "And we'll want to look at this birth certificate, why it's different from the others." He held the parchment to the light then laid it carefully on the table.

"Do you think the Jewish ritual items mean anything?"

"Don't know yet, lass," he said. "The egg raises many questions. First, how did she have connections to Mother Russia? The Levensons came to England from Germany in the seventeenth century. We know Benjamin traveled widely, but I've found no evidence that Shira ever left Britain. And Benjamin was long gone by the time this egg would've been acquired."

"It must be worth a fortune."

David's eyes went wide as he nodded. "Hoo boy! If the Monteiths hear of it, they'll want it for sure."

Eve pretended not to hear him. She was not one to keep secrets, though her father lived in them. She admired most things about her only parent, but his tendency to keep things to himself was not one of them. She refused to begin a relationship by hiding. How would she keep this from Mac? They'd been growing so close. She knew all too well how secrets could ruin a person for life.

She lifted one of the letters and scanned its contents. "The letters in the trunk are the juicier ones! The word adultery actually appears on the page here."

David peered over her shoulder. "Benjamin is asking for forgiveness, for tempting her into the affair."

There was a letter detailing Hugh's extramarital activities minus the names of offending parties. Cryptic, as if written in code. "This is more than just affairs," Eve said, pointing to a particularly confusing passage. "Something about retreating to the gardener's cottage and not emerging for days. With whom? Why so much detail?" The last letter spoke more blatantly of Hugh's affairs but again didn't mention names. Who had written the last two? It didn't look like Benjamin's handwriting, and both were addressed to Shira.

By mid-morning, they'd inspected all the items and swept out the inside of the trunk in search of hidden compartments, finding none. It was a simple trunk, well-built and solid, and had served its purpose: to protect the letters and other items for nearly two centuries. "I don't understand why she'd bury individual letters in the dirt and protect some in a trunk," Eve said. "Why not protect them all?"

"Unless she did this over time, thinking she'd hide one trove of letters, then another, then maybe something happened to make her gather all the rest and do it in one swift move," David said.

"Why are they all so cryptic about Hugh's affairs?"

"That's our next project."

He lined a felt box with generous sheaths of archival paper then placed each letter inside, one at a time, laying a protective layer of paper between them, until the box held the entire collection. He'd brought extra cloth-lined boxes for the ritual items.

"I think it's time to share this with my superiors," he said.

"What will they do?"

"Hopefully let us continue with this project," he said. "We've uncovered enough to lay claim to it, even if it falls more appropriately in the realm of one of the staff archivists. But I'll make a good argument for keeping us on it. Don't you worry." He winked as she followed him out of the conference room.

Chapter Sixteen

Eve, August 2014

"I was wondering when you were going to call."

The soft cadence of her father's voice sparked a fit of guilt. It had been too long since they last spoke, especially considering that before she came to Scotland, and even in her first weeks here, they'd spoken nearly every day.

"I'm sorry, Daddy, I should've called sooner."

He laughed. "Don't worry, sweetheart. I know you love me, even if I don't hear you say it every day."

"I do! You know I do! Team Waldman forever."

The cottage was cool this morning. Eve had cracked a window in the night to feel the cool air while she burrowed under the blankets. She didn't bother to close the window when morning came because she loved the fresh scent lingering in the small house. Outside, a squirrel scratched against a tree, clawing its trunk as it climbed.

"So, what's been keeping you so busy?"

It was ten in the morning on a Sunday, five a.m. in Michigan, but her father didn't sound sleepy. He'd always been an early riser. When she was small, no matter how early she awoke, he was already up, fully dressed, with a half-drunk cup of coffee and a newspaper or magazine spread open on the table. He'd scoop her into his arms, perch her on his lap, stroke her knotted hair and kiss her cheek as he whispered *good morning, my girl*. As he sent her to brush her teeth, he'd make breakfast—pancakes, French toast, scrambled eggs with cheddar cheese. Eve had never left for school without a full belly and a cloud of fatherly love hovering around her.

"I don't know if I should start with the work or the man," she said.

"Oooo, the man first," her father said. "It's been a long time since you've told me about a love interest."

"It's been a long time since I've had a love interest."

"So...how'd you meet him, who is he, will I like him? Will I meet him?"

She laughed. "His name is Mac. He owns a pub. It's a restaurant and an inn that's always busy, in an old building on his family's estate, which I don't know much about because he doesn't like to talk about his family."

"Red flag," her father said.

"Yeah." She paused. "The thing is, I'm not sure I want to press it. Because the work I'm doing involves his family."

"Intrigue," he said.

Some secrets needed their own time to come out, Eve knew too well. She was fourteen when she learned her father was gay. She'd been asking him for years to tell her anything about her history. Finally, one weekend, she'd brought out the diary she'd been writing questions in since elementary school and laid it open on the table for her father to see.

***

"Pick one—any one! I'll be happy learning the answer to any single question in this book." She slammed her fist on the open page, and her father jumped. "I've been writing these questions here for years because you refuse to tell me anything about who I am. Well, I'm sick of waiting. I'm old enough to know why you won't tell me about my family."

Eve looked up and saw tears trailing down her father's cheeks. She ran to his side, her cheeks warm with regret.

"I'm sorry, Daddy," she said, petting his hand. "Please forgive me. I didn't mean to upset you."

Her father sat on the couch and spoke slowly, carefully. He told her everything—how he'd grown up in an Orthodox family in a Detroit suburb called Oak Park. How he'd known he was gay at eleven years old but never admitted it until he was married to her mother and Eve was on the way. How Shaindie had told him that if he ever breathed a word of his "demented" state, she'd leave, take their baby, and oust him from the only community he'd ever known. And how, when Eve was born and Shaindie died, he'd been set free. He'd taken her and fled the religious world for a place where he could raise her without the encroaching eyes and judgment of the people and the community that had raised him.

He told her more about why her grandparents had fought for custody in the early years of her life and how they'd lost because he lived quietly, without a male partner. He hadn't wanted to tell her about his true identity because he didn't believe children should know about their parents' sexual lives, and also, he worried that she'd reject him, find him as disgusting as her mother had.

***

Eve remembered the feeling that spread throughout her body as she learned her father was gay. It was like ants marching along every limb, a trickle of discomfort, and she felt bad about it. She'd tried to shake off the feelings of guilt and anger and wonder that engulfed her, but it had been so overwhelming that she had started to cry.

Her father had reached for her, but she'd shrunk into the couch.

It had taken months for Eve to process the information, and by then, she'd feared she'd pushed her father too far away to ever regain the closeness they'd had. She'd felt like the worst child, but she'd also resented him for forcing her to act like a grown-up. She'd thought, *I'm only fourteen years old!* A few friends at school had joked about being gay, and she'd known one boy who wore skirts, drew dark eyeliner under his eyes and painted his nails black, but she'd never been kissed and hadn't been sure how she felt about it anyway.

It was her father who'd brought them back to closeness in that reassuring way he had. After so many months of awkward tension between them, they'd been back to being buddies. By the time she'd turned sixteen, Eve had been embarrassed by how she'd reacted, and she'd written a long, poetic apology to her father in a handmade card, thanking him for being the best father in the world. One of her best friends, Molly, had come out to her that year, and she'd realized how harsh her response to her father had been, how much she'd likely hurt him. She'd have done anything to repair the damage and reassure him that nothing could ever break their bond.

When Eve graduated college and went to work in Detroit, a good hour's drive from her childhood home, she insisted on living with her father for the first two years. She told herself it was because she wanted to be in a familiar setting and get her bearings before she found a place of her own in Detroit, an unfamiliar city far from home. But really, Eve had stayed with her father to make sure he was okay on his own.

He was. More than okay, in fact. By then, he'd rekindled his friendship with Simon and had told Eve about their early love when she was small. She'd wanted her father to finally have a partner. He'd been alone too long. But something was keeping him rooted in Ann Arbor, while Simon remained in New York. She'd tried to ask about it in most of their calls, but Sam had been cagey. Still, she kept bringing it up, hoping that one day he'd finally open up to her and reveal what was holding him back.

***

"How's Simon?" Eve asked.

"Don't change the subject," her father replied. "I need a lengthy update on my daughter's life."

"Fine, but we will come back to this. You're not off the hook." She snickered.

"I met Mac when I stumbled into his pub, hungry after a hike during a terrific thunderstorm. You remember that day—I called you after I found the letter? It was a momentous day in so many ways, Daddy."

She took a sip of milky tea.

"Right," he said. "I can't believe you're only just now telling me about him."

"Move on, Daddy! I showed David what I found, and we went back to see what else we could find. And boy, have we found a literal treasure trove!"

She couldn't help the excitement in her voice.

"We've figured out the identities of the people and some of their stories. Shira Levenson Macalaster and Benjamin Belzer, the first Jewish doctor in Scotland. She, well, she was a Levenson, the wealthiest woman in Britain, also Jewish. She married Hugh Macalaster, the Earl of Monteith, for access to the royal court. But it seems to have been a marriage of convenience because she was in love with Benjamin. Who died at sea, by the way."

"Is this real life or fiction?" He laughed. "And it was on the same day you found the letter that you met Mac?"

"Yep. I was tired and hungry and needed somewhere to warm up and eat, and Monteith House appeared on the road I was driving. I went in and sat at the bar and started talking to the guy I thought was the bartender. Turns out, he owns the place."

"Monteith. Didn't you just say Earl of Monteith?"

"Yep." The pieces were coalescing for her father as they had for her.

"Ahhh...I see the potential conflict now," he said.

"Right. I only told him of the first letter, when I first met him and knew nothing about anything. I haven't talked about the project with him since."

"Sounds like you're keeping some secrets." Outside, the wind ruffled the trees. The rain began slowly then picked up its pace, falling on a slant along the ground. Eve watched the ground darken under the pelting downpour. She added a log to the stove and closed the kitchen window.

She sighed deeply. "I know. I'm not happy about it. It's not the best way to begin a relationship."

"It's a relationship already?"

"Daddy! It's been two months."

"We need to talk more often," he said. "And it sounds like a Greek tragedy waiting to happen."

"Or a Scottish one." Eve snorted. The rain was slower now, and a slice of sun whitened the sky. The clouds drifted overhead.

"To very obviously change the subject, what are you doing for the High Holidays?"

"Um, I have no idea. I hadn't thought that far ahead. There aren't so many Jews in Scotland, Daddy."

"It's next month! And there are synagogues in Edinburgh, Glasgow and Aberdeen. I checked."

"Of course you did."

Throughout her childhood, her father had grown increasingly more comfortable observing Judaism. Every year, it seemed they did more for the holidays, invited friends for Shabbat meals more often. Her father insisted he'd never be religious again and that however she chose to weave Judaism into her life was fine with him. But recently, he'd seemed more interested in guiding her to be involved in a Jewish community. She wondered if he was doing it to distract himself from always being alone.

"Can we go back to talking about Simon, Daddy?"

"In a minute, honey. I'm not pushing, just offering. But if you're interested, all the synagogues are within driving distance from you. Relatively. Aberdeen is a bit far. But I'll email you the details, and you can reach out to the rabbis. It's just nice to be in a community at this time of year."

Was he speaking for Eve or for himself?

Eve leaned into the phone. "Okay, thank you. Now, how are you doing? And can I ask about Simon now, please?" She wandered into her bedroom and lifted the picture of her father in a silver, heart-shaped frame that she'd brought with her to Scotland. His sweet face, his kind eyes. Her anchor. All alone across the Atlantic.

She'd brought this photo, a stash of reporter's notebooks she'd swiped from the *Free Press* supply closet before she quit—and felt guilty for stealing but still used to journal most mornings—and a plush bunny she'd had since she was five. It had been a gift, her father said, from a family friend on her birthday. She'd learned as a teenager that it had been a gift from Simon.

"Honey, I learned long ago to be content with myself."

"I know, Daddy." A swell of love washed over her, and she wished she could hug him. She hadn't been homesick since she'd met Mac, but the familiar longing came back to her now, and she felt a hollow in the pit of her belly. "I'd just feel better if I knew you weren't alone all the time."

"I miss you too," he said. "And Simon's fine. We talk every day, and we're planning a trip to visit you actually."

"Really?"

"I think I just agreed to move to New York. The trip is a trial—a few weeks together, a chance to see you and Simon can trace his ancestral roots. We'll see if we can live together. If the chemistry is still there."

"I'm sure you can," she said. "Do you have any doubt?"

The rain began again in earnest, pelting the roof of the cottage. Eve slid the bedroom window closed and latched it. She strode back to the kitchen and fed another log into the stove plus some crumpled newspaper to encourage the fire.

"Well, it's not easy to live with someone, honey, and it has been a very long time since we were even in the same city," he said.

"When are you coming?"

"October, I think. Simon is taking care of the details. I'll let you know when we've firmed it up."

"And when are you moving?"

Her father was quiet for a minute. When he spoke, his voice was softer, less certain.

"Spring?"

"Are you asking me or telling me," she said.

"I'm honestly not sure, honey."

By the time the call ended, it was 10:45, and Eve had fallen into a melancholy brought on by the sound of her father's voice. Homesickness for the one person who had been her lifelong tether. She had been in Scotland for three months and wouldn't return home until May—and by then, her father might not even live in Ann Arbor. There might be no home to return to. Ever. It was one thing for her to leave and pursue adventures, and another to have to set down roots of her own. While she was happy for her father, Eve felt anxious about where her own life was headed now that her childhood home might not be there for her to return to.

Spend the day with me? She whipped off the text to Mac, then turned on the shower until steam filled the bathroom, dropped her clothes and stepped into the pelting spray. Would she observe the holidays this fall? Would Mac join her? Did she want him to? Religion might be a distraction here, but it might also introduce her to a community that she could call her own. Find her place, gain a sense of belonging to feel more at home in this foreign place. No, she would not invite him. If she went—and that was a big *if*—she would go alone. It was too soon to explore questions of identity with Mac, especially as she dug deeper into his ancestral drama. And she wanted to be sure what was growing between them was solid.

How many times had she mused that a particular guy was her everything, her forever-and-happily-ever-after, convinced they were compatible and deeply connected, and then, mere months into the relationship, Eve would find herself alone once again, wondering what she'd missed, how she could be so naïve. She hoped this relationship didn't face a similar fate, but she wanted to be prepared if it did. Let herself fall for him, fine, but retain as much independence as possible just in case.

Eve was bad at relationships, and it seemed quite obvious why. The only successful long-term relationship she'd witnessed had been the one she had with her father. He'd been a wonderful role model of independence and love. She'd seen other couples in their community be easy together and endure over the years, but hadn't been close enough to learn how, or why. And there had been no family relationships to learn from. She learned from her father how to be kind, how not to judge, how to welcome strangers and be open to new people and how to know yourself so fully that no one could ever talk you out of your identity or convince you to change to suit their own desires. But she'd also learned from him how to live perpetually and always alone.

What did it take to build a deep, lasting, loving partnership? How would she know when a potential partner was a good candidate?

Even though Sam had met Simon when Eve was little, their relationship happened under cover of secrecy. He'd only ever been introduced to Eve as her father's friend. And when Simon left for New York, the romantic part of their relationship ended. They wrote letters and spoke on the phone late at night, after Eve was asleep. She'd never even heard of him until high school, when Sam had opened the floodgates of information and shown his true self to his daughter. She had yet to even meet Simon.

Eve had learned to keep people at a distance and only rely on herself. For all she knew, her father's love with Simon could be true and lasting, but she'd never seen them together to know. Besides, she and Mac were at the very early stages of a relationship. And she had only come to Scotland for a year—what would they do when she returned to America?

Eve's phone pinged. *I'd love to spend the day with you.*

The phone trilled, and she answered.

"How do you feel about a mellow day indoors?"

"Sounds perfect," she said.

Chapter Seventeen

argaret, September 2014

The mist hovered over the green, sloping fields, furry trees cottoned in gray. The land was a vibrant green under the sky like a gentle wool blanket. Margaret stuck the soft ground with a walking stick and pushed her way up, up over the top of the hill to look out at all that lay before her. Monteith land, as far as the eye could see.

Blasted Mac! Her second-born son, her favorite, though she'd never admit to it if questioned. She insisted, always, that she had no favorites among her children. Whether they believed her or not was their business. Publicly, she had to support Collin the most, for he was the heir to the family estate, and she wanted to ensure that the Monteith legacy lived on well into future generations. But Collin was a spoiled fool who'd need all the help he could get to not lose everything. And he wasn't close to settling down and producing a new generation of Monteiths. She had work ahead of her.

But Mac. Sweet Mac, who lived deep in the moments. He was as intense as his stubborn mother, and he knew it, even if he didn't want to cop to it. Perhaps that was why he put such distance between them, avoided Sunday breakfasts. That's what she told herself, for there was no better reason, no rationalization she could stomach.

Margaret climbed higher, higher, careful steps over slick rocks. It had rained in the night, and she was out before the house was fully awake, as was her custom. Greet the day in the fresh air and fierce wind. She understood her second son all too well. They both lived intensely. Voices were louder, nights darker, eyes blazing brighter, laughter ringing for minutes after it actually stopped. It meant they could see the extremes of life, the very good and the very bad, and take them in, fully, in ways that no one else could. The only difference was that she held it all within, and Mac displayed his emotions and his energy for all to see. She envied him.

Margaret had been at the match where his knee cracked. He'd slid to score on an angle, and an opponent's boot collided hard with the bone of his bended knee, and the crack was as loud as the crowd's roar, at least that's how Mac had described it later. She couldn't hear it from the stands, but she watched her son go down, watched him cry out, wince, head tilted back, eyes squeezed shut, his right hand like a magnet to his knee but unable to touch it as the coach and the medic ran to the field and all the players took a knee, watching for the outcome. Mac had described the pain as hot as scalding tea, and he said he went blind for the moment as the pain vibrated along his leg and he knew, instantly, that life as he knew it, the life he'd hoped for, was over.

She'd let him cry into her shoulder, though she'd remained stiff and dignified, wanting nothing more than to fold into him, to hold him as he wept, to be the consoling island in a sea of propriety. But she hadn't given in to the urge. No one had done it for her, and look how far she'd come. She'd sworn when she agreed to marry Alex that she'd devote her life to furthering his family's legacy and footprint on this indelible land, and that had been her sole focus ever since.

The wind whipped her dark hair around her face. She pulled a hair tie from her pocket and clumped her thick mane into a smooth, tight bun at the base of her neck. Even now, even on the top of a hill, even as she climbed higher on the land that she'd grown to love, despite the hard bed of slate beneath the green that reminded her too well of the cold, lonely place she'd come from, she would maintain a public face. She would be fierce, proud, strong. No one would see her as weak, ever. No one would ever again ridicule the way she spoke or the way she dressed. She'd stand tall before all.

Today, Margaret would reach the summit. She'd worn proper hiking boots and thick wool socks but couldn't bow to family pressure to don athletic wear outside the house. So she'd dressed in wool slacks and a wool sweater, flat to her slim frame, both top and bottom in acceptable shades of gray, mirroring the heavy clouds and the slate of the ground. She looked up at the snaking trail. She'd have to scramble near the top, but she could manage it. It wasn't her first time on the mountain, and Margaret Monteith was made of tough stock. She patted her pocket, where her phone was fully charged and ready should she need help, but she didn't plan to.

Overhead, a golden eagle circled. Scotland was the only part of the United Kingdom that these beautiful birds called home, soaring over forest, moor and mountain, monarchs of the wild. From where she stood, it looked elegant, delicate, but she knew the monogamous predator was fierce, shameless. There had to be a nest not far from here, where a partner waited, and perhaps some young. She watched the great bird coast beneath the clouds, winging gracefully in the wind. Then, spotting unsuspecting prey, it dove, picking up speed, the wind pushing at its tail.

She had a vision of her family rising to renown, with her at the helm, envied, whatever was needed or desired easily within reach. The Monteiths may be aristocrats with generations of privilege and a trail of wealth, but no one knew them. They were just another Scottish family with means and history hidden in the bend of a mountain ridge, the belly of a quiet valley. Alex didn't care much for reputation or celebrity. She wanted to live exceptionally, while he and their children just wanted to live. It was partly her fault. If only she'd snugged her children in her arms when they were young, turned a tender face to her puppy of a husband. All could be fixed with a flannel blanket before a blazing fire on a cold, dark night. But Margaret was not a hugger. She admired the proper posture of the royals, aspired to their flawless, measured smiles and stiff waves. It was Alex who had huddled by the hearth with their children until Margaret's stern gaze pulled him away.

The grade of the path rose steeper, and she leaned into the shoulder of the mountain to move with the land, rather than against it. Sweat dotted her neck, dripped down between her breasts and along the ridge of her spine. She had left the trees long ago and now climbed over hard shrubs immune to the fierce winds. She leaned on the poles with each step. Her thighs burned, her breathing heavy, her lungs afire. When she reached the top, she could do, say, be anything. She could scream, she could cry, she could beat her fists on the hardened ground, she could feel sorry for her lonely self. No one would see. No one would know. She could let out all the pent-up emotions, misgivings, yearnings, and passions that she had pushed so far down she didn't know how to extract them in the safety of daylight or the proximity of another person.

Why had Alex chosen her? She'd often wondered, as their family grew and she settled into her role as the Lady of Monteith. In the early years, they had passion and partnership. Occasional fun. But it had been so long since they'd shared a bed, let alone a room or a life. He was busy with his own pursuits, pecking a kiss into her hair as he passed by at the breakfast table and smiling across the divide at the long, polished table when they ate supper together. Some nights, he took a tray to the parlor or met mates in the pub, and she retreated to her dressing room with a book and a bowl of soup. It was her fault, for choosing the role over the man. She'd been too focused on the family's legacy to put energy toward the people behind it.

On the steep incline of the mountain, she allowed herself to miss his touch. They'd had laughs and tender moments in those early years. From this elevation, she could grow soft and melancholy and have enough time on the climb down to resurrect her icy exterior. Which was the only way she felt in control.

She wished she could ask him how he felt about her now, but that would mean breaking down the stone walls she'd erected around herself. He might say he loved her for her belief in him and his family. Perhaps he admired her intensity and her drive. Her steely beauty drew him like a fire. He once said he knew the flames could singe his skin, but the way they danced mesmerized him and he could not look away. In their early years together, he'd believed she'd make him better, shore him up as the backbone his father said he lacked. But the elder Earl was long gone, asleep in his grave, and all that remained was the stern portrait in the main hall, his lake-blue judgmental eyes watching his son's every step. No wonder Alex avoided the formal rooms of their home. Margaret gave Alex what he didn't have on his own. She made him whole. She knew, early on, that he'd hoped she would soften in the glow of his love and attention. When that didn't happen, he made a life separate from her.

Was he faithful? She wasn't sure if she hoped he was or not. She had only ever slept with Alexander Monteith, but only because she had no choice. She'd never tarnish the family name by playing about. But she cared enough about her husband to want him to find solace in the soft and loving arms of a woman who could be emotional, open, not as guarded as Margaret. Because deep down, she was still a woman with a heart where love grew like a small but steady flower, clutching at the soil to survive.

Finally, she reached the top of the hill. The breath in her chest heaved, burned. At this elevation, the wind screeched, whipped at her skin. She'd pulled a down fleece over her head during the climb and burrowed into its soft hood to drown out the endless sound, the fierce gales.

It was a clear day, warm at ground level, cool up here. Not quite cold and no snow at the top, not even a saturated cloud draining its contents on the pointed land. The clouds were closer, but white, ambling across the sky, which seemed bluer, reachable. Margaret lifted a hand skyward, blinked back the brightness. She was alone on the mountaintop, but it was early, and other walkers would arrive in time. She wouldn't stay long.

Margaret settled onto a flat stone, watching the clouds move, listening to the dance of the wind. She brought a hand to her brow to see if she could spot the eagles' nest. She scanned the sky, followed the contours of hills and valleys. Finally, she spotted a pair of great winged beasts soaring high in the sky. Mates for life. Was one partner stronger than the other? Or were they matched in strength and vision? Did they retreat to their roles? Did a burn of desire smolder or dim? Did they, like most animals, do what was necessary, from instinct and not thought?

From her perch, she couldn't make out the details, and she didn't want to. She'd seen close photos of an eagle, and their fierce gaze frightened her. Better to watch the synergy from a distance, imagine the story behind the great birds.

She slowed her breath, listened to the unfettered movement of the land and the elements. From here, the loch was glassy and deep blue. The islands that dotted its surface were furred with broadleaf, conifer, oak and beech. The sun was golden at this elevation, streaming rays like jewels highlighting the yellowed brush under her feet. Although she had climbed to the top to let everything go, Margaret felt only contentment once she reached the summit and no need for any big release. She was peaceful. She wished she could carry the feeling down with her, but she had a hunch that it would be impossible.

Chapter Eighteen

*E**ve, 2014*

The sun was bright and the air warm, so Eve rolled the window down halfway as the car sped along. She looked at Mac in the driver's seat. They'd been inseparable for two months, and this first weekend away felt natural, expected, nothing special and yet deeply symbolic. She brushed her hand along his arm. He smiled and glanced in her direction.

"Excited?"

She nodded and turned to feel the breeze on her skin. The first weekend in September, and they were headed three hours northeast for the Braemar.

"They've held this gathering for nine hundred years, you know," Mac said.

"I can't even comprehend what nine hundred years of something feels like," Eve laughed. "My country isn't even three hundred years old."

"Bloody Americans," Mac muttered. "Babies of civilization."

"And yet we rule the world," she huffed. "Is that British snobbery I hear?"

He turned to her with piercing eyes and an open mouth. "How dare you! I'm a Scot."

When he'd asked her to go away for the weekend, Eve agreed without knowing where or what they'd be doing. She didn't care. She just wanted more of Mac.

"Not that I'm a loyalist, but the crowds roar as the monarch stands to claim the role of chieftain," he said.

She wrinkled her nose. "How can you support a monarchy? After all the devastation they've ignited? And continue to! A little old lady in a colorful hat and dress, her purse dangling over her wrist, as chieftain." She rolled her eyes. "Thank God my people slipped the noose of monarchy long ago." He snorted and drove faster.

They wound along narrow roads north and east, around mountain bends and through dense forests. Mac had booked a room at an inn in Strathdon. They'd spent so many quiet nights cooking, strolling through the village or naked in bed, and Eve was glad for the boisterous activity promised by the Gathering to take them out of their bubble and into the real world. She'd never experienced hordes of fans cheering as bulky men in kilts and white tank tops swung heavy metal balls around and out as far as they could fling them. Never seen couples in matching plaids hopping and stepping in precise choreography nor pipe and drum bands marching across an emerald field.

"It's an all-day thing," Mac had said. "With food and drink tents, bands parading as they play, dancing contests and track races. You'll love it."

Mac signed the guest book and offered his credit card at the registration desk. In the room, they dropped their bags and fell onto the bed. "Shall we make sure the accommodations are comfortable?" Mac stroked Eve's hair off her face and kissed her eyelids, her cheeks, her chin, and finally her lips.

Later, they wandered into shops on the High Street and settled into a pub for a dinner of fish and chips, dark beer and chocolate cake. Saturday morning, they woke early, ate quickly and headed to the games.

Eve was not prepared for the thunder of the crowds nor the unbridled enthusiasm on the pitch. Little girls in plaid skirts and matching vests, knee socks and hair in tight buns, danced in the youth division. Fiddlers played under tents to eager audiences seated on hay bales or standing behind them, and vendors sold rich cookies, handheld pies and greasy sandwiches heavy with cheese and meat and jam. The morning sun was cool but promising, and Eve burrowed into her jacket.

Mac wrapped an arm around her. "I've got you," he whispered, nipping at her ear.

She glanced around to see if anyone noticed, shivered as he nibbled on her ear lobe. "You're evil," she said. He bit harder. "Watch it," she cautioned but didn't pull away.

They walked along the vendor tents, browsing art and apparel and jewelry, creams and candles for sale. Finally, they found seats in the stands and waited for the opening ceremonies to launch the games. Sure enough, the queen sat on a raised platform at the center of the field, protected from the massing crowds but in full view so all could see her. She waved, and the crowds roared.

But Eve had seen the Saltire, the blue flags with the white crisscrossed lines going through them, outside houses and cafes, especially along quiet village lanes. Who was on the side of independence, and who preferred the monarchy? Was it an even split? Mac seemed in favor of independence, but was he really? His family was old and storied and aristocratic, even if their beginnings traced to Highland clans. He beamed as he stared at the queen. He'd said he wasn't a loyalist, but the shine in his eyes said something different. Identity wasn't linear, though Eve could never support a monarchy as her preferred form of government. They'd have to revisit the conversation because the more she loved this man, the more their politics and beliefs would matter—especially if she stayed in Scotland.

Which she was beginning to consider. Quietly, unspoken and unprompted. It wasn't like Mac had suggested such a move. They hadn't even said "I love you" yet, and she had no idea what he was thinking about the future of their relationship. And...there was the big elephant between them—her research project that involved his ancestors—which she still hadn't told him much about.

The queen sat, and a gun fired to start the games. Big burly men marched onto the field, stretching their thick arms and broad chests as they prepared to hurl heavy metal balls and blocks across the grass.

"Why are you shaking your head?" Mac asked.

Around them, the crowd tittered and buzzed.

"I'm thinking how masculine and toxic this whole thing is. Do you know where American football came from?"

He shook his head.

"It was to stop men from killing each other in duels," she said. "No joke. And it's the most popular sport in America.

Everything stops for Monday Night Football. I don't think it's a coincidence that there are more guns than people in America."

"Seriously?"

She nodded. "It's hilarious and horrifying. Just like this." She pointed to the field.

"Just let it be fun, you bloody feminist," he muttered, nuzzling her face. "I thought you liked all this masculinity."

"On you, yes." She elbowed him. "But on this field? Or draped over society as a whole?" She shook her head. "I swear, I'm waiting for them to grunt like gorillas and pound their chests."

"Well, the dancers and pipe bands are real Highland culture and great fun. You'll be swept up in it, I promise. I don't think there's anything toxically masculine there."

Hours later, when the dancers skipped onto the field and twirled, bobbed and bounced in and out of formation, and later still, when formally adorned pipe bands drummed their way in, playing and stepping in time, Eve melted into the moment and the sound and the landscape. She was entranced, just as Mac had promised.

"I told you it was special," he chirped.

By midafternoon, they were starving and parched. They left the stands, freed from being pressed shoulder to shoulder with other fans, their faces red from hours of direct sun. Eve and Mac headed for the drinks tent, where they stood in line for a good half hour before reaching the bar and ordering whiskies and dark beers.

"I'll need food if I'm to walk out of here," Eve said, double-fisting her drinks and trying not to slosh them onto the people she slipped through in the crowd.

Outside, they settled at a picnic table. "I'll get us some sandwiches," Mac offered, leaving Eve alone in the breeze. She tilted her head to the sun. September in Scotland might just be the most beautiful time, she thought.

The afternoon wind picked up. Would the closing ceremonies, with their fiery torches and drumming, be dangerous in a fierce wind? This was a country of extremes. A pendulum of experiences, all in the normal course of life in the far north. Could she live here permanently? Would Mac consider coming to America? Were they at a point to even think these things? Or was she getting ahead of herself?

Mac slapped two paper plates on the wooden table. Thick, greasy sandwiches layered with thin-sliced ham, gooey cheese, sharp mustard and strawberry preserves. Eve sank her teeth in for a big bite and moaned at the combination of salty, sweet and greasy griddled bread.

Mac was chewing quietly, watching her. "You don't do anything halfway."

She took another big bite and chewed slowly, then chased it with a deep swallow of cold beer.

"It's part of what I love about you," he whispered.

She stopped chewing.

A smile played on his lips. "Yes," he said, nodding. "I love you."

She swallowed and put down the sandwich, wiping her fingers on a crumpled napkin. She licked her lips to remove any lingering crumbs. Around her, the noise of the crowds dimmed to a buzz. People were moving in a blur. All she could see was Mac's sparkling blue eyes and his dark curls and his radiant smile.

"I haven't said that to anyone in a long time. And I didn't expect to say it to a bold, bossy American with a heartier appetite than me. But I have never felt like this."

He came over to sit beside her on the bench. She took his face in her hands, wanting to speak but her throat was clogged, her breathing heavy. The sting of tears pricked at her eyes.

She traced his face with her thumbs "Oh, Mac…" She leaned her forehead to his. "I love you, too." She heard the words as if someone else was saying them. She listened to the cadence of their softness, the intensity that pulsed between them, and she said it again, waves of relief and excitement and fear rushing over her. "I love you, too."

And then he was kissing her as the crowds roared and children skipped on the lawn and the vendor tents swelled with hungry fans experiencing everything there was to experience in a single day.

Chapter Nineteen

am, 1993

When Sam met Simon at Washtenaw Community College, he had no idea he'd become the love of his life. Although he first felt the zing of attraction to other boys in middle school, he had been raised in such a sheltered community that he didn't believe a man could love another man, much less act on it.

They started out as friends—two young men from fundamentalist religious homes, Sam from the Orthodox Jewish Detroit suburbs and Simon from a Baptist community in Okemos, a town near the Michigan state capitol of Lansing. They were both trying to learn how to live in a secular world without the support, or control, of their families. Simon was eighteen, Sam twenty-two, but both were like teenagers rebelling against the unyielding institutions that had shaped their lives. And both struggled to understand the nuances and language of secular American life.

Simon's childhood had been filled with prayer groups, Bible studies and purity promises, which weren't hard to make, as he had little interest in the sweet, wheat-haired girls that lived in Michigan's flat farm towns. He fled to Ann Arbor as soon as he could summon the courage to leave his parents' house, working in restaurants and bars and renting a tattered, damp bed in an apartment on the city's outskirts, which he shared with four other men. He followed his roommates to sports bars and nightclubs and enrolled in community college to work toward an associate degree, having no idea what he wanted to do, only that he needed some education to make it in the wider world. He heard rumors of the 80s gay cruising scene and was admittedly curious, but he was afraid to come out to his fiercely masculine roommates for fear of being rejected, or worse. And what he heard about the gay bars scared him as much as it excited him, especially in the age of AIDS, so he kept his head down and focused on his studies to get his bearings in this new and different place.

Sam had more direction, if only because he'd graduated from a yeshiva high school, trained as a bookkeeper under the guidance of an accounting firm in the Jewish community. He didn't have the courage to be out—plus, as a father, his responsibility to his young daughter was his top priority. He had no idea how to truly be intimate with another person. Would he hate himself after? And where would his baby girl be while he was off in the arms of a strong, lean man? His role as Eve's father felt like the most important part of his young life and the singular motivation to work hard and build a good life, so he couldn't bring home a stranger, and he wasn't sure he even wanted to. It was all so scary, even as the prospect was exciting.

Many nights as he slept, Sam's unconscious mind replayed the events of his youth, most notably the matchmaker meetings his parents and his rebbe had arranged. He hadn't wanted to marry, hadn't wanted to be alone with a woman, but he didn't know how to live in his community without doing so. At a certain age, the people who were tasked with raising you searched for a well-suited spouse on your behalf—someone from a compatible family with shared values and observances, appropriately religious and with no "black marks" against their ancestry. There could be no relatives with mental health issues or inherited disabilities and certainly no relations who'd left the community. The person they chose would be someone you could grow to love, they said. Someone you could build a life with, they said. Someone to start a family with, they said. It's what made a man a man and a woman a woman, this role of marriage and parenthood. It was the backbone of the Jewish community, the way to bring more Jewish souls to the world and to Torah. Everybody did it. Even if they didn't want to.

Sam knew whichever demure girl in long skirts and long sleeves they introduced him to would never be the love of his life. How could she, when all he wanted was to run his hands over the long, lean body of a man, explore his touch and watch his reactions? Resigned to living according to the only way he'd ever been shown, Sam met Shaindie Kaplan in the living room of his rebbe's house, with his parents and her parents making nervous conversation at the dining room table over cups of tea and chalky bakery *kichel*, while they made small talk in the watchful shadows of the all-knowing adults in their lives. He initiated tepid conversation. She offered lukewarm answers. They glanced under heavy gazes at each other, barely seeing the full picture of the other person. She was short and pale, hands clasped in her lap. She wore a navy-blue skirt, thick navy tights and navy flats with rounded toes. A fuzzy angora sweater in the palest shade of pink was her only spark of creativity, and it made her cheeks look rosy. She wore no makeup, and her honeyed chestnut hair fell to her shoulders. She was pretty enough. Sweet enough. Quiet enough. Sam figured she'd never hurt him, never raise her voice or a hand in anger, and so he said he'd like to move forward, and his parents and his rebbe whooped with joy and celebration, cheering *l'chaim*, over sweet kosher wine after the Kaplan family had left.

But years later, as a single father in a liberal city that didn't care whom he loved, Sam's nightly dreams turned to nightmares, replaying the years before Shaindie and the years after. First, the relentless bullying in his stark, echoing yeshiva for being too quiet, the other pasty-faced boys calling him a fag and playing tricks on him—leaving frogs in his bed, dousing him with water as he slept, tapping him as he sat in class, then hiding their torment from stern teachers, feigning innocence. He'd spent so much of his childhood quiet and alone, always wondering why no one—not his mother, nor his father—ever noticed or came to his rescue.

The memories of his marriage taunted him, too, though his waking self knew nothing could take away his newfound freedom. Shaindie came to him in those dreams, waving a stern finger, eyes narrowed in accusation. A month after the wedding, she missed a period, and by the time she was two months pregnant, Sam thought he could confide in her. A marriage was sacred. He could say anything to his wife, show his true self. At least that's what the rabbis said. And when he didn't seem interested in her the way a husband was supposed to be, when she asked, time after time, why he didn't touch her, he believed he could be honest. So he told her about his secret wanting, about the feelings he couldn't chase away since the age of eleven, feelings he'd never admitted aloud. Of course, she didn't understand. She was hurt and horrified, and she railed and cried and screamed and threw what few breakable objects they had in their little apartment, and he shook with fear that she'd tell everyone who he really was and he'd have no one—not his wife, not his baby, not his family.

He fell to his knees and grabbed her hands and begged and pleaded for her to keep his secret, in the sanctity of their marriage. She spat the word marriage at him, tried to wrest her hands free of his, but he was bigger and stronger and he held on for dear life, and finally her screams quieted to sobs and she fell to the floor and wept on his shoulder. He was shaking but not as scared as he had been. "I'll do anything," he whispered into her bony shoulder. "Just don't tell anyone."

"I would never," Shaindie said. Her eyes hardened as she swiped a hand across her nose to wipe away snot. "And neither will you. If you tell another soul this disgusting secret, I will take your child and leave you and you will never see her again."

In the dreams, Sam waved a hand and Shaindie was gone. He stood alone with a baby in his arms, like an offering. In the dreams, all the faces of all the people who were disappointed in him were bodiless ghosts taunting, calling him sick and evil and twisted and disgusting. They all had Shaindie's voice, and they hammered at him and tried to reach for the baby, but they were always just out of reach. He woke up in a sweat, his heart racing, his breathing labored. So many nights, Eve padded into his bed and curled against his body in the darkness, and on those nights, if he had a nightmare, he bit his tongue to keep his terror quiet so as not to scare his tiny daughter. He never wanted her to know the details of his wretched past lest she, too, turn against him for hiding her family from her.

In time, the dreams faded, and Sam grew more confident. Simon became a friend he could talk to. Until he was more. But even that Sam hid from his daughter because he was so used to hiding that he didn't know how not to. He feared that one day, the past would catch up with him. If no one had evidence of his inclinations, they couldn't use it against him.

Simon was happy to be out of the closet. But he loved Sam, so he honored his requests to keep their love from public view, until he no longer could. They were deeply in love when Simon took a job in New York, mostly to get away from the pain of having to hide. "I want to throw my arms around you in front of everyone, all the time," he told a teary Sam. "I spent the first two decades of my life hiding. I won't do it anymore. I moved here to start fresh. To do things on my terms. You did, too, remember?"

Sam was weeping. "But I have a daughter," he said. "And if they ever find out about me, they'll take her from me. I can't let that happen."

"You won the court case," Simon said. "You're free. They can't take her from you."

Sam cried as Simon packed his clothes into two suitcases.

"You're always going to be chased by ghosts," Simon said. "Shaindie died nine years ago. Everyone knows. They have no power over you. You're free." He brushed his lips across Sam's. "I just wish you could act like it."

"What did I win? We have no family," Sam said, gripping Simon's arms and clinging to him as if to keep him from leaving.

"You could have a family," Simon said. "With me."

Sam collapsed in sobs at his feet. Simon knelt to stroke his hair.

"I have to go," he said as quietly as a door closing in the dead of night. "I'll always love you. And if you ever start to believe it's safe to be out with me, I'll come running with open arms."

***

Sam, 2014

Now, Sam's dreams were not of the nightmare variety, but rather of the yearning kind. By the time he was ready to contemplate being openly out, Eve was in high school, and he didn't want to uproot her from her friends and community. And he was scarred by her reaction when he came out. He didn't want to be—she was just a teenager, after all! He told himself when she left for college, he'd go to Simon, but that time came and went, and he did nothing.

They kept writing letters. They spoke on the phone. He considered Simon his best and truest friend. He'd dated a few men, slept with all of them, but no one came close to what he felt for Simon. He no longer knew what was real or what was imagined. Was his love for Simon as good as he thought? What if he uprooted his life and went to New York and they were no good together?

Sam fingered the photo that he kept in his nightstand drawer. The edges were gnarled from touching, and the image had grown soft. He walked through the rooms of his mid-century bungalow, listening to the creaks of the oak floors, running his fingers over the old brown couch, the mahogany end tables, the angled Danish console and matching bookshelf. Light poured in from wide windows. He'd loved this house when he first saw it. Eve had been ten, and it was time to finally have a house of their own. It took nearly a decade of being a key reporter at the *Ann Arbor News* to save enough for a down payment. It was the best day of his life, signing those documents to own a piece of property where he could raise his daughter.

He'd lived in the Burns Park house for twenty years, and the house had appreciated in value astronomically. He was fifty, his dark, thick hair feathered with gray. The skin around his dark eyes was softer, finely lined. His daughter was grown. He didn't want to be alone any longer.

He would move to New York, be with the man he'd always loved. Simon was waiting with open arms. And Sam was ready to invite love into his life and keep it close.

Chapter Twenty

ve, 2014

Eve and David stayed late at the office, long after the sky darkened from blue to lavender to monarch-purple, a dark canvas with pinpoints of starlight. David called for Chinese takeaway. Eve scrolled and searched and printed and paced. And finally, near on ten o'clock, after Mac had texted three times asking when she'd be back and could he come over to see her that night, even if it was late, they unearthed what Shira had wanted to keep hidden.

Before Shira married Hugh, the Levensons married cousins to keep wealth in the family. None of Shira's family attended her nuptials. They cut her off from social events and holidays, and she spent the rest of her life in quiet contemplation, hiding her Jewish identity out of respect for her husband's stipulation that they build a Christian home and raise their children in his faith. He agreed to allow Shira to quietly observe alone, and she insisted that her money would go to Jewish causes through her family foundation, which she'd continue to administer and which he could not touch.

They had five children—William, Thomas, Mary, Margaret and Aaron. Hugh admired Shira's simple beauty—golden-brown hair in ringlets around her face and sparkling blue eyes. She didn't look like a Jew, he often said. She was quiet and courteous, graceful and poetic. And generous. Her family was connected. While Hugh gave her access, her money and connections let him live more easily than his meager inheritance would allow. She devoted the bulk of her fortune to England's Jewish community, while still leaving plenty for Hugh and their children. He didn't necessarily mind her Jewishness; he just didn't want it to be too public. She was open and honest and kind, and Hugh loved those qualities, especially since he harbored his own dark secret.

Hugh preferred men in his bedroom. Shira knew this from the start and kept her husband's secret on the condition that he allow her the freedom to worship in synagogue, light Shabbat candles on their 50,000-acre estate near Loch Lomond and maintain her London home. As long as she managed the raising of the children and left him to his own activities, Hugh stayed out of her way, and they created a companionable friendship that allowed their marriage to endure. And he fulfilled his husbandly duty by giving her children.

But were the children Hugh's? Now that she knew about Shira's affair with Benjamin and had read in that first letter mention of a child they had conceived, Eve wondered if there might be more.

In the wake of their admissions of love at the Braemar, Eve had grown less comfortable keeping the information of her work from Mac. It was time to share the truth of what she'd found. At least one of his ancestors was a full-on Jew—perhaps all of them. Love meant sharing all of yourself, even the hard parts, and if this news caused Mac to leave her, she'd have to face it sooner or later. It wasn't a rational fear. Why would he leave her because she'd unearthed a possibly uncomfortable truth about his ancestry? But as well as she knew him, she really didn't know him at all, and she'd never met his family.

She whipped off a text. *Leaving now. Meet me at my cottage.*

Her stomach flipped. How would he react?

That late at night, the trains came sporadically, and it took Eve longer than usual to get to her car at the Stirling station. Nights were cold now, and dark came early. But the drive from the station was fast, with no traffic on the quiet country roads. It was eerily quiet this late. The vibration of the car lulled Eve. She was tired. She rolled the windows down so the cool air could keep her focused and awake. David had encouraged her to take the next day off, since they'd stayed so late researching. Nothing was urgent in the world of archives, he insisted, and she was grateful.

On the drive, she sifted through the details of what they'd found. Jews in Scotland had a relative ease under the monarchy during Shira's life, but they weren't fully accepted. The more they tried to blend in, the better they were received. Eve remembered a plaque at the Braemar about how the queen at that time had anointed this annual gathering with her royal approval in 1866 and had a presence there every year after until her death. *Could I really live here,* she wondered. A place with history fringed by antisemitism. *What place isn't? I'm making a problem where there is none.* She turned the radio louder and pressed the pedal faster.

Even now, there were synagogue shootings and antisemitic attacks everywhere there were Jews. Every few decades, the old tropes reared their ugly heads, usually in conservative political circles and among far-left apologists. She'd read an article in *The Guardian* recently about how antisemitism was rising in Europe at an alarming rate. The article called it the "worst times since the Nazi era." She was kidding herself to think she was any safer than Shira had been nearly two centuries earlier. Eve wasn't sure she'd be any safer as a Jew in America amid growing right-wing extremism than in mostly Protestant Scotland.

It was half past midnight by the time she parked on the gravel outside the cottage. One lamp was lit in the main room, but the bedroom was dark. Mac sat up in the bed, pillows stacked behind him, gazing at the moonlight out the window, a half-drunk dram of whiskey balanced in his palm.

"Late night," he said, his voice husky.

She nodded, though she was sure he could barely make out her silhouette in the darkened room. She pulled her sweater over her head and dropped it on the floor, stepped out of her jeans and crawled into the bed.

"Worth the wait." He placed the glass on the nightstand and leaned into her warm body.

She closed her eyes and let his arms wrap around her. She wouldn't say anything tonight. It was too much to drop on a person, too long a story to tell in the wee hours after a long day. She'd wait until they were fresh and then see what he knew. But she felt empty.

She had so much hope pinned on this relationship. She thought he was The One. But she was so nervous about how he'd respond to the information. Could she be with someone who came from a family that hated the very core of who she was?

By the time Eve awoke, the sun was bright, and from the towel she could see hanging in the bathroom, and the fact that his clothes were gone from the chair, Mac had obviously showered and dressed. She smelled the enticing aroma of sausages frying. Outside, birds twittered in eager conversation. There was no wind, the trees tall and resolute. She peeled back the covers and sat at the edge of the bed.

"Wait!" Mac called from the kitchen. "I wanted to bring you breakfast on a tray."

She threaded her fingers through her tangled hair and smiled. He was lovely.

But then she remembered all that she needed to say, and the smile left as quickly as it had come.

She scuttled into the bathroom to wash up. After her teeth were clean and her face washed, Eve pulled on sweatpants and a long-sleeved T-shirt and then climbed back into bed to nestle against the pillows in exactly the position she'd found Mac in the night before. Minutes later, he swooped in with a plate of hot food and a mug of tea.

"Thank you," she said. "I'm ravenous."

He settled the tray over her legs. On it sat a plate of glistening eggs and juicy sausages. She dug in. "Hmmmm," she said. "Delicious."

He climbed into bed and sat close. "You got back so late." Concern embedded in his furrowed brows. "What kept you there? Scots don't slave over work like Americans. We know when to quit."

Eve ignored his comment and inhaled the food. She would tell him what she'd found when she was ready.

Finally, she placed the tray on the nightstand and cupped the mug in her hands. As she'd eaten, she had played over how the conversation might go and finally felt ready to dive in.

"So we found the identity of the people in the letters."

"Grand!"

He was close to her ear as he said it, the heat of his breath sending chills through her body. *Not now*, she thought. She turned to face him.

"It turns out, the letters are from your ancestors. Shira Macalaster. The wife of Hugh Macalaster, Earl of Monteith."

He nodded. "Yep, a great-great-great-grand-something. How cool!"

"Did you know she was Jewish?"

His eyebrows knit together. "I guess Mum left that part out. If she even knows. Not surprising, though. I can't imagine my family wanting to admit they're Jews."

She froze, a shiver rippling along her spine.

He bit back his words. "I didn't mean... I'm sorry."

"So your family are hostile toward Jews." Her voice was icy, sharp.

"Well, they're stuffy aristocrats," he said, running his hand over her arm. "They're not bad people. Just head-in-the-sand types. It's almost posh to be antisemitic in some circles." He tried to laugh.

Eve bristled. "Not funny."

She didn't want to date someone from a family that wouldn't like her. But that wasn't the problem she'd imagined when she thought of telling Mac about Shira and Hugh and Benjamin. She'd thought the hard part was yet to come.

"That's one secret. There's another. Hugh was gay."

Mac stared out at the trees and heaved a big sigh. "There were rumors. It was illegal to be gay of course. Every family had someone closeted. I don't see why that's a big deal." He traced the lines of her fingers, but she didn't respond, still numb from what he'd said earlier.

"Right," she said, wanting to stroke his hand, to feel the smoothness of his skin, the strength in his sinews. She would miss him, so much.

"The letters I found were love letters. Between Shira and a man named Benjamin Belzer. First Jewish doctor in Scotland. They had quite a love. Hugh knew about it. They kept each other's secrets. At least one of their children was Benjamin's."

Mac didn't look surprised. He cupped a hand against her face.

"Love, if you only knew how many ancestral webs there are in the UK," he said. "Aristocratic families are too tangled to uncoil. None of us knows the true lineage because there was so much playing around, so many secrets."

Relief rushed through Eve's body. Mac was nodding, pulling her closer.

"Really," he whispered against her cheek, his hot breath sending tingles along her limbs.

She leaned in, closing her eyes and letting herself believe this could work, despite the inevitable ending she'd imagined on the long journey home the night before. She could have no secrets from this man because nothing would shake them. This could be real. Lasting.

As long as his family could overcome their antisemitism.

She laid her head against his chest. "I was worried you'd leave me."

"Why?" He lifted her face, so she was looking at him and kissed her hard. "I can't imagine anything that would take me away from you."

"Even the idea that you might be Jewish?"

"That would make us even better suited, wouldn't it?"

And with that, she set herself free from worry, released the little birds of anxiety that had been fluttering within her, watched them wing off into the white autumn sky.

Chapter Twenty-One

Mac, 2014

Although the news didn't bother Mac, he was agitated as he left Eve's cottage. His family—mostly his mother—would not like her poking into their history, and though he didn't plan to tell them, it would come out eventually. And then what?

Damn, he loved this woman, and he could see trouble ahead for them. As long as she pursued this project, it could be a wedge between them. They'd be under scrutiny anyway when he finally brought her home. For being American. And Jewish. He loved his mother as a dutiful son does, though he didn't like her much, and she wouldn't approve of anyone who wasn't of the same stock as the Monteiths. They wore their long history like a badge of honor, as important as the family tartan—which had flecks of purple against a deep Scottish green.

The family crest had at its center a red heart, small but identifiable. Eve had said something about Shira's family coat of arms having a red shield at its center. Did Hugh Macalaster alter the Monteith crest to include his wife's heritage? They'd always joked that the tiny red heart represented all the bloody battles his family had fought in. If he traced his lineage, he'd find proud Highlanders chafing against English incursion before the Monteiths crossed lines.

And…he'd find Jews, too.

Soon, they'd hunker in for the long and cold winter. The season when Monteith House reverted to a local crowd, and Mac was happier. Familiar faces, easier conversation, late nights with old friends, fire licking at the hearth.

He poured a tall glass of Traquair Jacobite Ale. *In keeping with history*, he thought as he gulped a long, cool swig.

CHAPTER TWENTY-TWO

*E*ve, *2014*

If she hadn't already decided to attend Rosh Hashanah services at the egalitarian Edinburgh Jewish Congregation, Eve would be certain to go now, in the aftermath of Mac's revelation about his family. Nothing like good old-fashioned antisemitism to ignite Jewish pride. The small congregation met in an old building on the University of Edinburgh campus. She'd emailed the rabbi, a young man called Stephen Raimi, to ask about the community because she didn't want anything too religious, and he assured her that the service was accessible and welcoming. She wondered how Jews got to Scotland in the first place and what made them stay in a fiercely Catholic country. Of course, now it was more Protestant than Catholic, since the Catholics had been run off or shut down during the Highland Clearances of the 18th century.

The rabbi had offered to find Eve a place to stay so she didn't have to travel back and forth each night, but she felt weird staying in a stranger's home, so she politely declined. She was used to the commute and wasn't sure how immersed she wanted to be in the Jewish community anyway.

She skipped services on the first night and arrived at half past nine on the first day of the two-day holiday. Edinburgh was a city of steep, sloping sidewalks, crisscrossing streets and severe elevations, framed by gray stone. Dirt-stained, rain-streaked, the streets carried the scent of damp. The train was late, so Eve trudged up the ten flights of urine-soaked Scotsman's Steps across from Waverley Station instead of taking a more round-about and less lung-burning route. She quickened her pace toward campus, grateful for the cool autumn air and cloudy skies so she wouldn't stink of sweat by the time she slid into the quiet room where the rabbi was already facilitating the service.

The holy Ark was a wooden box on wheels with a red velvet curtain hiding the Torah scrolls from view. Fifty parishioners gathered in a half-circle where chairs had been set up, a prayer book on each seat. Many wore prayer shawls, and some of the women even had yarmulkes pinned atop their heads. Eve wasn't the youngest person there, as she had feared. The congregation was made up mostly of college students and faculty and their families. She found a seat in the last row.

Three hours later, the service finished, and a few parishioners draped a white cloth over a folding table along the wall, upon which they set bottles of whiskey and paper plates of brownies and cookies and little apple tarts, in honor of the Jewish New Year. The rabbi wound through the crowd, shaking hands, patting children's heads, smiling and talking to the people. "Join us for a *l'chaim*?" he said when he reached Eve.

She nodded. He couldn't be more than five years older than her. "Nice service. Like nothing I've experienced."

"It's a nice community," he said, tilting one of the bottles to fill two plastic shot glasses and handing one to Eve. They tapped the glasses together, and he muttered a prayer, one she hadn't heard.

"*Shehakol*," he explained. "The prayer you say when there's no other prayer to say over food."

The whiskey burned her throat and warmed her chest. "I didn't know there was such a prayer."

"It literally says, Blessed are You God, who creates everything through His Words."

She chuckled. "How long have you been in Scotland?"

"Three years." His lips fluttered in another prayer before he popped a bite-sized brownie into his mouth. "Before that, Aberdeen." He laughed. "You wouldn't think there would be many Jews that far north, but a lot of the men working the oil rigs in the North Sea use it as a landing spot. Lotta night life there, a university and two Jewish congregations."

"I haven't been that far north. I got as far as the Braemar."

"Good taste of Scottish culture," the rabbi said.

"Forgive me, but are you Scottish? I don't hear an accent."

"Right. No," he said. "I was raised in Israel to American parents. The throaty r's of Gaelic are similar to the hard consonants in Hebrew, which I've got down, but I'm no good at the Gaelic. I'm reminded of this all the time. Scots aren't shy." He chuckled.

A petite woman in a gray silk dress approached them and placed a hand on the rabbi's arm. He leaned down to kiss her. "Meet my wife. Eve Waldman, an American working at the National Archives for the year. My wife, Sadie."

She smiled. "You'll come for lunch?"

"Oh, um, I hadn't planned on it."

"Please," she said, her brown eyes shining with warmth. "I've cooked for an army, and we only have a half-dozen guests confirmed."

"Well, if it's not an imposition, sure, I'd love to," Eve said. "Thank you."

She nodded and drifted away to talk to the remaining parishioners. Only about twenty were left in the room.

"That was my cue to wrap things up," the rabbi said. "I'm glad you're joining us. Sadie wasn't kidding. She makes all the symbolic foods for the holiday—sweet, honeyed challahs, carrot tzimmes, whole fish, pomegranate seeds in the salad and of course, apple and honey desserts. The meals might be my favorite part of being a rabbi." He winked as he folded his tallit and slid it into a zippered bag, motioning for her to follow him out the door.

It was already dark when Eve got back to the cottage that night, though it was only seven o'clock. The days were growing shorter, the light fleeting. She was exhausted from all the food and the intensity of the long, interesting day. She slept alone, despite several texts from Mac asking about her day. She wished she had taken the rabbi up on his offer to stay close to campus.

It was late when she noticed the figure at the edge of the bed. She sat up, startled, scouring the dark for an object to use as a weapon.

"Mac?" she whispered. It didn't look like him, and besides, he wouldn't come into her home without warning. And if he had, he'd slip into the bed and pull her to him, and she'd know who it was by his scent and his touch and feel safe.

The figure hovered, small and hesitant. It was a woman, no taller than five feet. She watched Eve but didn't speak, didn't move closer.

Eve tried to make out the woman's features in the moonlight through the windows. Her golden hair hung in ringlets around an angelic face, with sparkling blue eyes. She had small lips and smooth skin. Eve peered closer. She was surprised how unafraid she was.

The woman wore a dark chiffon floor-length dress that silhouetted her hips. At her neck, jewels gleamed—perfectly round rubies encased in gold.

The room pulsed with silence. Eve smoothed the blankets and licked her lips.

Then the woman sat on the bed and reached toward her.

"Darling," she said in a light voice barely louder than a whisper. "I've been waiting to meet you."

Eve breathed slowly through her nose. Her heart thumped madly, and she wondered if the woman could hear it. It thundered like a waterfall over a cliff, until the sound becomes something you no longer hear, only feel.

"You're the first person to discover my letters. I've waited for nearly two centuries to share my story. To tell the truth."

"Shira?" Eve croaked.

The woman nodded.

"How...! You died in 1889...you...died. You can't be here."

Sweat dotted her face and trailed down her back. She gulped in air but couldn't get enough.

The woman settled a hand on Eve's leg, which sent warmth through her body and slowed her heart to a more normal pace.

She could breathe more easily now. Eve closed her eyes, half-expecting that when she opened them, the image would be gone and she'd know it had been a dream. But when she lifted her lids once again, the woman was still there, and Eve could feel her hand heavy on her leg.

"You're real."

The woman nodded.

"You're the one to tell my story. I lived for so long in silence. I was so lonely without Benjamin. So many generations of my family kept secrets. It's time to stop hiding, stop pretending. The world is different now. We must live in truth."

"I'm not sure what you're asking me," Eve said.

The room felt bright, though it was shrouded in darkness. Had the moon grown lighter?

"You know what I'm asking."

"I really don't," Eve said. "I'm just here for a year, to work in the archives."

"You were looking for history, to find the family you never had. Telling my story will lead you to your own. Write this story. Tell the world the truth."

"What am I to tell them? And who's going to care? I'm no one," Eve stammered.

"You are the exact right person. This is your story to tell."

"I don't see how." Eve was growing impatient, panicked. "This has nothing to do with me. I'm not a Scot. I'm not English. I'm sure there is someone better to do this for you."

The woman shook her head but kept smiling.

"I had one great love, and he died at sea. But that isn't the story. There's Jewish blood running through British aristocracy.

That's the secret no one wants revealed. With my letters, you can tell a story no one wants to hear. But everyone needs to. The world is getting colder, angrier. The time will come, in the not-too-distant future, when Jews will feel as unsafe as they've felt at our worst times in the past. This story can be a forewarning of what happens when we don't claim our identity with pride."

The woman patted Eve's leg. Then she stood and gazed into Eve's eyes. "Please. You're all I have."

And with that, she was gone.

Eve blinked. Had she been dreaming? She'd felt the hand on her leg. She'd heard the voice. A cool breeze shivered her arms. She draped the blanket over her body and glanced to the window to see if she'd left it open, but it was shut tight.

She walked into the kitchen, opened the tap and filled a glass with water and chugged it down. She scanned the rooms she'd been living in for the past four months. They had become familiar, filled with her clothing and books and shoes by the door. The iron stove had gone cold. The bucket of ashes needed emptying in the shed behind the house. Yesterday's coffee mug sat in the sink, awaiting washing.

She returned to her room, where the clock read 5:16. Too early to be awake. She climbed into bed and pulled the blankets to her chin. She gazed out the window at the trees backlit by the fading moon and sank into sleep.

CHAPTER TWENTY-THREE

Mac, 2014

"Hello, Mum." Mac air-kissed his mother. Like a swan, she was elegant and erect, but also like the great white birds, she was fierce. It was Sunday breakfast and months since Mac had been to the family estate.

"Mac! You came." Her smile was bright, her eyes sparkling. She squeezed his elbow, though he wished she'd give him a kiss or, one day, a hug. He'd been yearning for warmth or affection from his mother for as long as he could remember.

"Your siblings are already here." It was less a statement than an admonishment. He followed his mother into the dining room, her pleated gray wool pants, burgundy cashmere sweater, and single strand of pearls the refined air he remembered. Her dark hair framed her face. While he resembled his mother, Mac's eyes twinkled with a lightness that he could never find in hers. Her cheeks pulled taut, bearing a seriousness that bordered on severe. All his life, he'd tried to crack her hard shell and at twenty-eight, he was no closer to succeeding.

She'd surveyed his outfit, her scrunched nose evidence that she found it wanting. Well-loved jeans baggy at the knees and fraying at the ankles, a cable knit sweater and Chelsea boots, the dark leather faded with wear at the toes and heels. He'd known when he'd dressed that morning that his clothing would not meet his mother's standards, but it was enough that he was going to breakfast; she'd have to be satisfied with that. And he was nervous. His siblings knew about Eve—Collin and Emma had met her, liked her, and sworn not to say a word about his American girlfriend to their parents. He wasn't consciously keeping her from Shona, his other sister. He just hadn't had the chance to bring her round. But with the research project Eve was knee-deep into, he'd need to tell them about her before they found out through other channels.

The long table was set with silver and China, each setting a good few feet from the next. On a buffet, chafing dishes steamed with poached eggs, stewed tomatoes, sausages and toast. A porcelain teapot steeped loose leaves of black tea, beside glass carafes of orange and cranberry juices. Pots of butter and jam featured gooseberry, cranberry and strawberry, all harvested from family lands.

Alex occupied the far end of the table with Mac's sisters on either side. Collin sat nearest their mother. Shona's boyfriend hadn't been invited—no significant others were welcome at Sunday breakfast, Margaret's rule, until there was an engagement. This was family time, even if there was too much space between each of them to have a real conversation. But no one dared bring anyone to Sunday breakfast until the relationship was official—meaning, a ring and a wedding date.

He took a plate and slid two eggs, two sausages and a scoop of tomatoes onto it. Polished cutlery lay on the table beside cloth napkins embroidered with the family crest. Mac sat to his mother's right, sons doting on the matriarch, daughters focused on their father. Mac forked a scoop of soft egg and speared a chunk of sausage, taking it into his mouth at once.

"How's business?" his father droned from the end of the table.

He gulped some juice. "Brisk, Dad." He forked another mouthful to avoid going into detail.

Alex nodded, shoveling food into his own mouth.

"That's not all he's been busy with," Collin teased, eyes glimmering.

Fuckin' Collin. Mac inhaled another bite.

His mother's eyes were wide, her eyebrows raised.

"Who?" Margaret's face was steely.

"Shona, tell us about your burly lad." Mac shot a pleading glance at his sister, hoping she'd bail him out.

"Ach, they all know about Andrew. He's old news."

"Any closer to an engagement?" Margaret pressed.

"Mum!" Shona huffed, crunching into a piece of toast.

The conversation moved on, and Mac was relieved. He'd get Collin later.

When breakfast finished, Mac planned a quick departure, prepared to cite a full day of work, but his mother had other ideas.

"We so rarely gather all together," she said, a hand on Mac's arm as the family retreated from the dining room and the maids swept in to clear away the dishes. "Why don't we go for a hike on the lands?" She peered out at the gray sky as Mac searched on his phone for the day's weather forecast.

Sure enough, rain was projected within the hour, and he showed his phone to his mother, shaking his head. "Wish we could, Mum. Besides, I don't have my boots or my parka."

"Then a games day." She waved her children into the sitting room.

"Mum, I can't stay," Mac pressed.

"But we don't get time with you every week, like your siblings."

"Ach, let the boy be," Alex said.

Margaret shot him a look.

"He wants his time. Let him have it."

Margaret seethed. "A mother wants her son around. Whatever happened to *honor thy mother*?"

Mac chortled. "I came for breakfast, and I'll come again. And now, I'm leaving."

"Let him go," Collin called. "It's more fun without him anyway."

Mac shot a deadly look at his brother as he ducked out.

As much as he cringed at his mother's demands, Mac couldn't escape the feeling of contentment that had overcome him when he'd stepped into the familiar rooms. Although he lived more simply now by choice, there was a comfort in the place that raised him, and the people, too. He hadn't missed his mother's stern gaze, but his father was sweet and he loved his siblings and wished he saw at least his sisters more frequently. Collin...well he could take or leave his brother. What was that stunt, hinting at Eve?

He hadn't seen her over the two days of the Rosh Hashanah holiday, but he thought about her constantly. What was it like?

Did she miss him like he missed her? Why hadn't she invited him? And would he have gone if she had? He was curious. He'd never known a Jew, and while she wasn't religious, he admired her devotion to the holiday. He rarely went to church even for Christmas.

He was curious about what she'd uncovered. He'd feigned knowledge when she mentioned a gay ancestor and Jewish lineage, but most of it had been a surprise to him. Especially the Jewish part. There'd always been deep, dark family secrets that no one talked about, so he didn't truly know what everyone was hiding. Or why. It was so British to hide the truth, and even though they were Scots, they'd been part of the aristocratic web for more than two centuries. It was embedded in their bones.

The countryside was a blur as raindrops pelted his windscreen. He glanced at his phone in the cupholder. Eve hadn't texted or called; it was nearly noon. Girls had always fought for his attention. He wasn't used to waiting for them to notice him. And they'd professed their love for each other. Why was she avoiding him?

Without thinking, Mac steered toward Eve's cottage, hoping she was there. Sure enough, as he pulled into the gravel drive, he spotted her car, and relief flooded through him.

As he slammed his car door, Eve appeared. She hung back from the rain, in the open door, barefoot, her hair soft and fuzzing in the mist. He sucked in his breath at the sight of her. Those slim hips, those shapely legs. She wore sweatpants and a tank top, the swell of her breasts outlined in the thin fabric, her nipples prominent in the cool air.

"I've missed you." He wrapped his arms around her as he pushed inside the house. She shut the door behind him as he rained kisses on her skin. She tilted her head back as he nuzzled her neck.

"It's only been two days."

"Three. You were gone for two. I need to make up for lost time."

"It's not a race," she said. "I'm not going anywhere."

He was relieved once again. Why was he afraid she'd leave him?

"What are you thinking about?" Eve ran a finger along the ridge in his chest.

"Nothing. Tell me about the holiday."

"It was wonderful." She closed her eyes to replay it in her mind. "The rabbi is a sweet guy, and his wife is an amazing cook! Growing up, my father and I had holiday meals with friends from this little synagogue we're a part of. It's a makeshift community of liberal hippies, and our services were short. These were not! Three hours of Hebrew I didn't understand. Daddy made chicken or brisket, bought challah from the bakery, cut up an apple to dip in honey. This was so much more."

She stroked his hair back from his face and threaded her fingers through his thick curls. She tightened her fingers in a clump of his hair, and he winced.

"Keep doing that, and I won't be listening to your story." He pulled her close to feel her warmth through his clothes. "Tell me. I want to hear it all."

"Not in this position." She kissed his neck then licked it.

"Eve." Her name was a whine, a long low moan. He walked her backwards down the hall to the bedroom then gently lowered her onto the bed. They were inches apart. Fine dots of sweat ridged her nose, and gold flecks glistened in her warm brown eyes. "Please. I want to hear. There's time enough for that later."

She leaned against the pillows and began to talk of the past two days, of the people she'd met and the singing and solemn prayer, the total exhaustion after she returned each night, and the early mornings in the university building.

"And then, the weirdest thing happened. Last night, I had this strange dream. At least I think it was a dream. I swear, she was standing there." She pointed to the foot of the bed.

"Someone was here?" His stomach clenched.

She stared at the empty space beyond her bed. "It felt so real. Shira came to me—Shira Macalaster. Your ancestor. She wants me to write her story. Reveal all the secrets—Hugh's homosexuality, Benjamin as the father of at least one of her children, everything."

Mac quirked an eyebrow. "We dream about things that are on our minds, right? You've been focused on your research. Some dreams are so vivid they feel like they're real. But they're not."

Eve shook her head. "No, this was a whole other level. Like nothing I've experienced. I swear, she was here."

Outside, the rain had quietened. It was now a light touch, velvety fingers occasional on the window. The trees dripped, leftover raindrops like tiny crystal balls on the edge of pine needles. The sun was trying to shine through the clouds.

Mac shrugged. "Okay, so what then? You're writing a story about these people? About my family?"

"I think she means for me to write a book."

Mac wrinkled his face, clawed at his hair. "Um, no offense, but who's going to want to read this? I mean, who cares about bloody aristocrats from the 19th century and their secrets? People have always been gay. Always fathered illegitimate children. So what?"

Panic quickened his heartbeat, and he felt clammy, like he had to move. He stood, walked to the window, looked out, but couldn't focus so he returned to the bed. His mother was not going to like this one bit.

"Well, I think the story is how Jewish blood runs through the aristocracy—despite all the antisemitism. You know, Hugh was a prime minister of England. Only lasted a year, but still, that's big. I don't think there's been a gay prime minister in recent times, but apparently there was one 150 years ago."

"There's probably been loads of them," Mac huffed. "Sounds like gossip." He leaned on his thighs, his hands in his hair. "And how do you even know that a publisher will want this? I mean, I'm sure you'll write a beautiful book, but someone's got to agree to publish it, right?"

She laid a hand on his back. Her voice was quiet, tender. "This could be why I came to Scotland. My path, my purpose."

"How is this yours?" He shrugged her off and stood.

She stood and went to him. "Mac, my father is gay. And he was cast out of his family because of it. They even tried to take me from him."

His eyes softened. It felt like they'd been together for so long, but they were just beginning to know each other. He reached for her hand.

"So this hits close to home." He ran his thumb over her knuckles, counting each one, feeling the softness of her satin skin. "There's so much I don't know about you."

"Well, I'm telling you now," she said, her voice rising. "In my father's community, he couldn't be out. When my mother learned the truth, she threatened to take me from him. Then she died, and he was free. But when I was young, my grandparents sued him for custody and almost won. In his mind, he's never been free. My whole childhood, he was afraid to be his true self. He's spent half a century hiding. Never had a relationship in front of me, and the only man he ever loved left him long ago because he didn't want to hide. He didn't even come out to me until I was in high school."

She laid a hand on Mac's forearm and leaned close. "I love you. I've never loved someone like I love you."

He smelled her hair, the scent of her, a faint musk and something floral all at once, and he leaned toward her. It could be that easy. He could let it be that easy.

"But I want to pursue this. I'm not religious, but my people have not had it easy. Jews have been hated and exiled and persecuted and vilified and blamed throughout history. This story, Mac, it's not about you and me. It's not about you, even. It's something I have to do."

His voice was a croak, and his eyes shined with tears. "You don't think the universe sent you to Scotland to find me?"

She swallowed. "Maybe that too." Her fingers were light on his face, her thumb lingering on his lips. "But I don't want to have to choose."

He pulled her against him and held her there. "Let's not go there," he whispered. But he thought, *If you had to choose, I hope you'd choose me.*

CHAPTER TWENTY-FOUR

*E*ve, October 2014

Every night for the next week, Shira came to Eve. It was always around three in the morning when she woke with a start and saw the figure at the end of her bed, but she was no longer scared. Shira was relentless in pleading her case.

These were the Days of Awe, the time between Rosh Hashanah and Yom Kippur, when Jews were supposed to approach people they'd wronged and ask forgiveness before God could forgive them.

Growing up, being Jewish had been more about food and friends than meaning and sin. But since she came to Scotland, Eve's Jewish identity had become more important, perhaps because there were few Jews around.

Eve and Shira sat up until the wee hours of the morning talking like old friends. The apparition always hovered near the end of the bed. Eve tried to come close, but Shira would retreat, as the cool of the night sifted through the cracked window. Eve wrapped herself in a blanket and learned to keep her distance as she listened to the woman's pleas.

"We had a rare love," Shira said. A sunny backlight shone when she spoke of Benjamin. "In my time, and in my world, you didn't marry for love. Marriage was an obligation, a transaction. You married to improve your family's standing."

"But you chose Hugh."

"He wasn't very good-looking," Shira giggled. "He was pale as the milk in my tea, but tall with beautiful blue eyes and shiny brown hair, and did I tell you he was funny? My father had died and my mother wasn't well, so I had to make my own match. Family friends helped orchestrate it and made introductions."

Shira shook her head.

"I was fond of him, but I didn't marry for love or passion. When my father died, I became the wealthiest woman in Britain. My mother was frail, and we'd been banished from the royal court. It was rare for a woman to manage family funds. I married for access and to control my assets."

Just then, a breeze blew through the open window. It was a cold night. Eve pulled the blanket up to her neck, wondering how soon the snow would come. The cold obviously didn't bother Shira, and she continued without noticing Eve huddling into the blanket.

"We met through family friends. It was as much a political match as anything." She was swaying, eyes closed.

Night after night, Eve learned more details. She told Mac not to sleep over because she wanted Shira to come to her. He respected her wishes but scoffed at the idea that a ghost was visiting her.

The more entwined she became in Shira's story, the more she withdrew from Mac. By the end of the week, she'd stopped responding to his texts.

The night before Yom Kippur, Shira delivered her final message. Eve was not going to Edinburgh for the holiday. She wanted to spend the day in the mountains, in her own quiet contemplation. It was a lot to digest. Mac wanted to join her, but she insisted on being alone. "It's not that I don't want to hike with you. I just need to process all that Shira's told me," she said. "I miss you, too, Mac. I just need this time to figure things out."

That night, Shira was the most radiant she had been—haloed by a golden light, dressed in shimmering pale pink and layers of crinoline, her eyes sparkling in her soft round face.

"Why me?" Eve said.

"You seek your own roots," Shira said. "I can trust you."

A chill rippled through Eve.

"I will never get over losing the love of my life," Shira said, pressing a pale hand to her bosom and closing her eyes.

Eve sucked her lip. Was she willing to lose her own love by taking on this woman's story? Why would Shira want her to make the same sacrifice that she regretted? Maybe Mac was right. Maybe this story wasn't as important as she'd thought. Interesting, yes. But worth upending her life over?

In those moments of doubt, Shira came close and clasped Eve's hands. It was a different touch than any she'd known—lonely and hollow and chilling.

"I kept my husband's secrets. I hid my true identity from everyone—even my children! And I died young from the heartache."

Eve rubbed her eyes. She was tired. So incredibly tired. Night after night of communing with a ghost, of being riveted to far-fetched stories from a distant past that had nothing to do with her.

She pulled her hands free from Shira's grasp. "It's a lot to take in," she said. No one would know if she did nothing with the information. A chill went up her neck.

"I'm begging you. You're the first person who has ever listened. You know it's important. I chose you for a reason."

And then, she was gone. Eve searched the darkness for a glimpse of the hallowed light that had illuminated the old floors minutes before, but there was nothing to suggest it had happened. She yawned and lay back against the pillows. *I don't have to decide anything now*, she thought as she fell into a dead sleep.

***

Mac

He ached for Eve and felt gutted as she became distant, like someone had hollowed out his stomach. Incomplete, unmoored and unbearably alone.

He wasn't satisfied with her explanations, but he had no choice, so he busied himself at the pub, becoming a bother to his staff. Until he could take it no longer.

Though she'd insisted she wanted to hike alone, he had to see her, had to know if she was done with him. She was lacing up her boots in a porch chair as he pulled up in front of the house.

She glared a questioning glance in his direction. "What are you doing here?"

He stood before her, hands deep in his pockets, his flannel shirt unbuttoned. He hadn't even combed his hair that morning, hadn't showered in days. But he was too panicked to be embarrassed by how he looked.

"You're killing me," he said. "I thought you loved me. I thought this was good, something with a future. I love you more than I've ever loved anyone, and you're shutting me out. For a ghost."

He sank to his knees in front of her, eyes rimmed with tears.

"Damn you," she muttered. "Why can't you just let me figure it out? Why can't you give me the time and space I need?"

He grabbed her hands, pressing the satin of her skin into his cheek, waiting for her next words.

"I needed today to be alone on the mountain, to not have to make a decision—can't you give me that?"

She pulled him to standing and led him inside, down the hall to the bedroom. The silence pulsed between them. It was slow this time, careful, as if every touch would be recorded. She kissed his face, tasted his dried tears. His hands were in her hair, gliding along her neck, palming her bottom. She kissed him slowly. He started to pull her shirt over her head, but she stopped him.

Eve sat on the bed and untied her hiking boots, slipped them off and the socks, too. He watched her, wordless. She unbuttoned her pants, stepped out of them, took her time folding them and placing them atop the dresser. By the time she stood naked before him, he was throbbing in every corner of his body, desperate for her. She held up a hand, telling him to wait even longer. And then she started undressing him. The power dynamics had shifted in their relationship, and she now held the reins. He would go where she directed him. For better or for worse. Finally, skin to bare skin, he laid along the length of her, the heat of their bodies momentarily cooled by the ever-open window.

***

Eve

The nerve! Why couldn't he have respected her boundaries? But he'd looked so pathetic on his knees on the porch, the cool autumn breeze raising bumps on her skin. She'd wavered between wanting to yell at him for interrupting her solitude and pulling him to her. Several days of shadow darkened his cheeks and chin. She loved him, she wanted him, but anger smoldered inside her.

He'd looked like a puppy caught rummaging in the cupboard. And you couldn't stay mad at a puppy. She didn't want to lose him, but she didn't want to lose herself either. She was just coming to understand who she was and who she wanted to be. And she had a feeling that Shira's story held a key to that.

After they made love, she was even more confused than she'd been when he arrived. The chemistry between them defied description. This was what she wanted. Wasn't it? It was so clear, as he pressed into her.

She'd never make it to the hike, and later, she'd be angry with herself for giving in to his insistence. But she would never regret the time spent in his embrace, moving as one, consuming each other in the way the hungry gulp down food, uncertain that there will be another meal.

That night, sleep eluded her. Mac stayed and fell into a deep, peaceful slumber almost instantly. Eve lay awake, thoughts and worries tumbling in her head. She got out of bed, downed a shot of whiskey, then another, and stared out the kitchen window at the moonlight. When she finally drifted off, she didn't sleep long, coming awake to a sense that there were people around her. Not the way she'd felt when Shira had come. This was different. The room felt crowded, stuffy. There were two figures in the shadows, hovering at the end of the bed. Mac was on his side, facing the other direction, in a dead sleep.

"Mama?"

Eve didn't know how she knew. She couldn't see a face, only the gleam of crystal eyes and the slope of a tentative nose. But she knew it was Shaindie.

"You can show yourself," she urged. "Please."

She'd wondered about her mother all her life, never satisfied with the wedding portrait Sam produced when asked for a story about her mother. Teeth clenched, face gray, his eyes empty of their usual fire, her father described their wedding day, not his love for her mother. "And then we made you" was always how he ended the story.

But now she was here. Eve could feel it.

The vision stepped from the shadows.

"Chava, my baby girl." She invoked Eve's Hebrew name, her voice steady as rain. "I always imagined you as beautiful. Patient. Kind."

The way she described Eve was more a reflection of Shaindie's upbringing than any real knowledge of her daughter. Suddenly, Eve pitied her. Mac shifted in the bed but didn't wake, and Eve kept her voice low. She wasn't sure if she wanted him to see that she wasn't making anything up or keep sleeping and let her have this moment alone with her mother.

"You were never able to truly live," she said. "So sheltered from real life."

"You were supposed to be my start, not my end," Shaindie said.

Was she blaming Eve?

Then, she sensed another presence. The room felt stale, like there was no air and no space to move.

"Children can't be your purpose," the other voice spoke.

Shaindie whipped around. Shira's round face and angelic curls glowed across from Shaindie's hardened gaze.

"I would know," Shira said. "They can be your legacy, but not your purpose."

Shaindie glared at Shira. Did they know each other? Was there familiarity in the spirit realm? Shaindie's eyes were wild, dark circles burning a gaze into the other woman.

"I wouldn't know. I never had the chance." Shaindie's voice was sharp.

"Maybe that was *your* legacy," Shira said, reaching a hand toward Shaindie.

"I just wanted to be loved," Shaindie gulped. "Even my husband couldn't love me."

"It wasn't Daddy's fault," Eve said. "It wasn't about you, Mama."

"It never was," she said so quietly, Eve had to draw closer to make out her words.

So many generations of women whose sole purpose was to facilitate the lives and desires of others. All the women throughout history, even so many still today. Silently, sadly, pining for a moment to matter, a time when they could take center stage. Shira, Shaindie, their lives over, Eve's just beginning. She had nothing to prove to the world and every opportunity. The proving was just to herself. She felt a weight bearing down on her, the responsibility for redeeming all the women who'd had no choices. Women like her mother, and now, Shira.

Mac stirred and sat up in the bed.

"Eve?" He reached for her; she could hear his heart pounding. Golden rays of light shimmered beyond the edge of the bed, where two visitors, soft, angelic outlines, stood, as if projected onto the wall. He stayed quiet, watching.

"You have an incredible daughter," Shira said.

"She's nothing like I imagined," Shaindie said. "If I had raised her, she'd be reserved, modest. She'd care about Yiddishkeit. She's in this *goyish* place, chasing after a Gentile man, and she doesn't know what it's like to be a Jew because of her father's twisted influence. And I'm helpless to do anything about it."

Eve felt Mac go stiff as she cycled through anger, resentment, hurt and an aching sadness. The first time her mother came to her, and this bitterness poured out? She wanted to defend her father, to explain everything. But then she saw the papery skin of her mother's face and knew it would do no good.

Her mother had died so young. Nineteen years old. What dreams had she held close, tucked into her wedding bouquet or her pregnant bosom? She had never been a person in Eve's eyes, only the mother she'd never had, the woman who threatened her father. She'd never considered her as an independent, thinking, wanting individual. Her heart ached for the sadness of it all.

"Mama," she whispered, stepping closer. "Mama." She reached for Shaindie.

Shira was smiling, glowing. For a moment, Eve felt the fragile flesh of her mother's hand, the steady pulse, the long, lean lines of the bones that mirrored her own.

"I would have loved you," she said. "I've missed you every day of my life."

Shaindie's face crinkled in a painful smile. And then, she was gone, no trace of her oval face or long, sad eyes. Gone, as she had always been, out of reach.

"Was she really here?" Eve asked, but Shira was gone too, and her voice echoed in the empty room. Eve stood alone before the wide window, the half-moon white and still through the glass.

"She was," Mac whispered, shadowing her body with his. His warmth chased away the night chill as he wrapped his arms around her. "I see now," he whispered into her ear. Eve turned and buried her face in his chest, shaking with sobs.

"Shhh," he cooed. "I'll keep you safe. You won't be alone, not as long as you have me to hold you."

She burrowed into his warmth and listened to the soothing calm of his voice, wanting desperately to believe every word.

CHAPTER TWENTY-FIVE

Sam, 2014

Sam stood naked in his bedroom, staring at his body in the full-length mirror hooked to the back of the door.

"You're an old, saggy man," he said, his voice startlingly loud in the empty room.

Long, muscular legs, white as paper, for they never saw the sun. Where he used to have a round, hard butt, it was flat, pulled down by gravity, the skin soft and creased. He'd never had a lot of chest hair, but it had been dark and glossy. Now it was sprinkled with gray and thinner. So many gay men shaved or waxed, but he hadn't want to spend money on grooming. The men he'd slept with clutched at it as if it were a novelty. The hair on his head was still dark as night and thick, and for that, he was glad. His balls, once tight and hard, were responding to gravity just like his ass, going soft and saggy. At least he had no trouble getting hard or staying that way.

Would Simon show the wear of aging, too? Or would he be as hard and shiny as he had been two decades before?

Sam would fly to New York on the third Wednesday in November, and together, they'd jet to Edinburgh. He was nervous, excited, fearful and relieved. Finally, time together. And he'd see his girl, too.

He dressed and shut the light. Sam loved early mornings, when the light was lavender, the day slow to brighten. He sat in his kitchen, sipping coffee slowly, plenty of time before he was expected at the paper. A letter had come the day before. Even as they planned to spend time together, they continued to write, something Sam loved about the tenderness of their relationship. He'd come home from work and fished the mail out of the box, but when he saw it, he dropped the bills and magazines on the foyer table and tore it open. Simon's jagged scrawl, evidence that he took the time to write his thoughts and transcribe all the happenings of his big city life, when he could be bustling about Broadway, caught up in the theater world where he'd have no shortage of options for a quick fuck or even a relationship. This letter was proof that despite all his anxiety and all the years that had passed, Simon still cared for him. Deeply.

Sam had insisted he was content, that he didn't want to shake up his life. He'd already done that at too young an age, and the memories made him shiver. He didn't want to start over again. Staying reminded him of all he'd built—a loving family, a life filled with friends and yes, the freedom to love men. Ann Arbor reminded him how far he'd come and how good life could be. If he left and it didn't work out with Simon...

But why wouldn't it?

He fingered the soft paper of the letter and sipped his coffee as he read about Simon's latest off-Broadway show that had exceeded investors' expectations. He read about late nights and after-parties and felt a twinge as he read about Simon going home alone in the middle of a raucous celebration because all the nightlife was so tiring. *This would be the moment I'd give him a reassuring hug*, Sam thought. *If I were waiting for him at our cozy apartment, or if I were draped on his arm at whatever event he needed to show his face at. He could give me a tug, signal that he was ready to leave, and I'd pull away, happy to be his excuse.*

Sam finished the last dregs of coffee, rinsed the cup and set it beside the sink. He folded the letter and left it on the table to respond to later, pulled on a burgundy fleece, grabbed his work bag and headed out.

As he backed out of the driveway, the phone rang. Eve. Three in the afternoon in Scotland. His stomach tightened. She should be at work!

"Hi, honey. Everything okay?"

His turn signal clicked rhythmically in the background.

"I don't know what to do, Daddy."

On the next block, he pulled over and parked. He'd be late to work, but he was the senior employee, so no one would mind.

He put the phone on speaker and laid it on the dash.

"I'm fine. Just confused."

"Let's talk it out."

"I love Mac. I don't want to lose him. But this story...I want to follow it. I was meant to find it, tell it, write a book. It's why I came here, I know it. But I also think I was brought to Scotland for love."

"Whoa, whoa, whoa. Slow down. Why would you lose Mac?"

She'd told him everything in earlier calls—her discoveries, the research, Shira's visits, the Monteith family's Jewish roots, Mac's suggestion at antisemitism in his family. So why was she unraveling now? Was there something new, something he didn't know about?

"I thought you worked it out?"

"He hasn't said it, but I think he'd prefer that I drop the book idea. It's going to cause trouble in his family, I think, and could cause trouble for him and then for us. I haven't met them yet. If I do this, they'll never accept me."

"You don't want that," Sam said.

Outside the car, birds twittered on the branches of an old oak. Black-capped chickadees and elegant blue jays. Sam watched them as an old woman in a quilted bathrobe dragged a trash can to the curb near his car. They made eye contact, and she shot him a questioning glance. He smiled and waved her off, pointing at his phone. Her face softened, and she nodded before retreating into the house.

"Eve, real love doesn't make you choose."

"I know."

She was silent.

"Maybe this isn't my project after all."

"Now hold on. Don't doubt yourself just to keep a man. Trust your instincts. If Mac loves you, he'll find a way to understand how much this project means to you. I'd hate for you to stay with him and give up your work and then one day have regrets. You'll end up resenting him."

"But he'll resent me if I do it. Or at least, he might."

He wished he could leave today to hold her in a tight and loving hug.

"It's not just the hidden Jewish identity of the Monteiths," she said. "It's also Hugh's hiding his homosexuality, Daddy.

This hits home. It was a crime to be gay, punishable by death, and Hugh became Prime Minister—the leader in Britain. A closeted gay man whose children were Jewish. It feels important."

"Then you have your answer," Sam said. He sighed. "It took me nearly two decades to tell you who I really was, Eve. And you are the most important person in my life. I was so scarred from a lifetime of hiding. Wouldn't we all be better off living in truth? Do you want to be part of a family that persists in hiding? Mac may be wonderful—I'm certain he is if you love him. But when you marry someone, you marry their family, too."

He thought of Shaindie's disgust once she knew his true identity. Her wrinkled face, her narrowed eyes, her cutting words. Her threats to keep his child from him if he revealed his true nature or contemplated acting on it. And then the lawsuit—family wanting to rip his daughter from him as if he were sick or tainted! He'd shut the door on toxic family and would never wish it on anyone, least of all his daughter.

Chapter Twenty-Six

E^{ve, 2014}

By the time Eve rolled up to her cottage that night, Mac was already there. Lights glowed in the kitchen. The sun set early now, and a brisk chill swept through the mountain air. She slung her bag over her shoulder and headed inside.

"Hey, love," he said, a towel tucked into his waist. He wiped his hands then kissed her.

She loved the look of him. Sweet eyes sparkling in his finely chiseled face. God, she would miss him.

The kitchen smelled of roasted meat and long-cooked onions that had turned brown and sweet. Her stomach tumbled with hunger. And nerves.

"Smells good."

"Bangers and mash."

Sausages sizzled in a cast-iron pan; onion gravy bubbled in a saucepan. Mashed potatoes were already creamy and set aside in a covered pot, and fried peas in a small skillet were as green as the evergreens outside.

Mac uncorked a bottle of red zinfandel and poured generously into two glasses, handing one to Eve. She took it and gulped.

"Hard day?"

She shook her head.

"What?" He laid the wooden spoon he'd been holding on a small plate beside the stove and turned the fire low under the sausages.

She took another gulp then set down the glass. "I wanted to at least have dinner first."

"Don't. Let's eat and make love and lie in each other's arms in the moonlight. You can tell me whatever it is in the morning."

She sucked on her lip. Could she? One last night with this man, only for her to walk away in the morning and never look back? Was there anything he could say to change this awful situation?

"Mac," she started.

He laid a hand over hers, his eyes pleading. "Please, Eve. Give us this night."

He refilled her glass and topped off his own. The sausages were apparently done, and he shut the flame and plated the potatoes, then the meat, then drizzled gravy over top. Finally, he arranged the peas in a half-moon on the rim.

The table had been set when she walked in, and they sat opposite each other. The cottage was silent, all sounds of cooking and preparation done and only a far window above the sink cracked open to let in fresh air.

Even though the dinner was delicious, Eve had a hard time eating. She cut the sausage smaller and smaller to ease it down her throat. And though she was hungry, she got to a point where she just couldn't eat another bite.

"I can't do this." She pushed away from the table. "I can't wait until morning. I can't sit here and pretend like we don't both know what I'm about to say and what's to come after that," she said, tears streaking her face.

"Ach, Eve." He reached for her. "Come to me."

He pushed back from the table, and she slid onto his lap, her arms coming round his neck as she buried her face in the soft warmth of his sweater. She sobbed, and he held her, stroked her back.

"You're going to do the book," he whispered.

She nodded but didn't lift her face, didn't loosen her grip.

"And you're going to leave me." Tears slid down his cheeks. "I wish I understood why this is so important to you. Maybe I can learn to be okay with it?"

It was more of a question than a statement, and Eve shook her head.

"You'll resent me for distancing you from your family," she said. "You'll never forgive me. And neither will they."

She wiped her eyes with her hand and pulled upright to look Mac in the eyes. "I have never loved like this," she said. She was trying to maintain composure, to not crumble. She swallowed once, and then again, breathing in slowly. "And I don't want to lose you."

"I can weather their angst," he insisted. "I've pulled away from them on my own. They know I follow my conscience, go my own way. And they always welcome me back. I promise you we can get through this. I can't lose you."

She was shaking her head.

"I want to say okay," she started. "I want to cling to you and never let go. But I really think that in time, you'll wish you weren't wrapped up in this. That you had a partner who just blended into your family. One day, I really believe you're going to want that, and if I stay around, you'll hate me for it."

"I could never hate you." His voice was soft. "I still want this night," he said. "One last night together. Will you give me that?"

She nodded.

He pulled her to him and kissed her.

She inhaled his scent, tasted him, traced the contours of his face, tangled her fingers in his dark curls. And then he was covering her body with his and moving in sync with her in the angled moonlight until they were spent and satisfied and sadness draped over them like a weighted blanket.

They drifted in and out of sleep, clinging to each other. And when dawn slowly showed its face, in lavenders and pinks, they made love again, slowly, achingly, until they reached a pinnacle together, shuddering with tears and pleasure all mixed together. Eve pulled on a robe and fastened it at her waist while Mac slowly dressed. They walked silently from the bedroom, past the dirty dishes and greasy pans from the night before.

She followed him out the door and into the cool morning. Her skin prickled in the cold. The wind was brisk, rushing through the trees and swaying them in a dance that on any other day, Eve would have loved to watch. She hugged her arms in front of her and shivered.

Mac gripped her arms and stared into her face. "I wish it didn't have to be like this."

She nodded. "Me too."

"Will you change your mind? Reconsider?"

She slowly shook her head.

"I'm going to miss you so much." She was nodding as he said, "I'll be here if you change your mind."

She rose on her toes to plant a soft, silent kiss on his lips. "I love you, Mac," she said and then walked past him into the house and shut the door behind her.

***

Mac

When Mac remembered that time, he'd think first of the sadness in her eyes when she walked in the door, and his stomach lurching. He'd remember being struck by a sense that his life would never again be the same.

It came to him at night, when he was loneliest, when the energy and noise in the pub swirled to excess, all his customers happy and well-fed. He'd watch them from behind the bar and think of the way her hair framed her pale face. The way her eyes were pools of melted chocolate with flecks of gold. He'd think of all the meals they'd shared, him watching the elegant lines of her neck meeting her sloping shoulders, the even pace of her chest rising and falling with each breath. She wasn't just beautiful; Eve was interesting and smart and funny and scrappy. Everything he wanted in a woman. And he had lost her.

Sometimes, he remembered the sweet coconut scent of her hair and could almost smell it. He remembered the scent of her skin, salty and earthy and a little bit sweet.

He wished he could have said something to change her mind. He turned it over and over in his mind, knowing he would never choose work over such a great love, but they were different and he loved her enough to let her go. Still, he hoped one day, she'd find her way back to him.

Sometimes he wondered if all this reminiscing was making him sadder, but he didn't want to stop. The sadness turned into longing, and it was if he could run his hands through her hair, feel the soft skin of her face, trace the silhouette of her body. He wanted to remember every detail, so he let the memories come, resigned to living in the sadness for as long as it took.

Chapter Twenty-Seven

argaret, 2014

Margaret stalked up the hill, stabbing the soft ground with her walking stick to steady her gait. The wind stroked her face, not winter-cold but cool enough that she shuddered into her corduroy blazer. *Should've worn something thicker*, she thought and winced. The throaty call of a mourning dove came from a nearby tree. Margaret looked up but couldn't spot the creature, only heard its persistent song.

The call this morning had been troubling. Some American researcher nosing around the family archives, looking for information about Shira and Hugh. This wasn't even her family line, and she was the only one protecting it! What was interesting about these old folks anyway? It had been decades since anyone inquired about the Monteith ancestors. The family archives existed to keep the legacy intact and in one succinct place, nothing more. They weren't the kind of family who needed to open their home to tourists as a source of income to maintain the manse. They were fine on their own, with income from inns, pubs and other real estate that Alex's father and grandfather had wisely purchased and protected. She was grateful to not have to depend on tourists to keep her home.

Margaret climbed higher, stopping to steady her breath and ease the burning in her chest. The slope grew steep quickly, and she felt almost dizzy, one leg cocked higher than the other as the land rose. Soon, the snow would come and slick the hills with ice. She'd burrow in for the winter, maybe fly off for a sunny holiday in Ibiza or Cape Town to bide the time until the sun shone longer in the day. She was hill-walking to steady her anger. She didn't want anyone nosing into the family past. It happened every decade and was quickly quashed. She'd do it now, too, to keep the family secrets hidden.

Early in her marriage, when Margaret had discovered the truth about Alex's blasted ancestors—homosexuality, infidelity, illegitimate children, Jewish roots—she was horrified to see the family's lineage as tainted with drama as a soap opera. But she wouldn't be the one to let loose the secrets that successive generations of Monteiths had artfully kept hidden. Margaret smoldered with anger.

At a plateau on the mountain, she settled onto a flat perch of slate to survey the family lands. It was impressive, breathtaking, and all theirs. All *hers*. Even though she'd married into the clan, she claimed it as her own.

When they met, she didn't know immediately that Alex came from wealth and station. Which made her feel more righteous in claiming it as her own. She hadn't known what to look for. Maybe a girl who came from his same station would have recognized the telltale signs—the way he dressed or spoke or the ease and frequency with which he took weekend ski trips or treated all the lads to drinks at the pub—but her nose had been buried so deep in books, and she'd been unschooled in the ways of the wealthy, that all she'd seen was a smiling, playful, gentle man who adored her. She loved him still. Not that she ever showed it. Poor Alex. Stuck with a cold shell of a wife.

The autumn wind stung her face. She wrapped a cashmere scarf in the family plaid around her cheeks. One more glance at the incredible view on such a rare clear day, and she turned to head down. It was early on a Sunday, and the kids would be coming. She hoped to see Mac among them. Collin had whispered that Mac's great romance was over, so perhaps a mother could nurture a broken heart and coax her son back into the fold.

At the service door, Margaret stepped out of her muddy boots and left them on the mat, entering the house in wool socks. She changed out of her walking pants into something more dignified—brown wool slacks and a soft pink cashmere crewneck. She smoothed her hair, painted on lipstick, lengthened her lashes with mascara. She dotted concealer under her eyes, hiding the fine lines there, brushed powder over wind-reddened cheeks.

Alex was already at the table, sipping coffee and reading the *Times*. "Morning, love." He smiled as she entered.

She walked to him, planted a kiss on his cheek. He squeezed her hand.

Shona and Emma came in a swirl of conversation and cheeriness.

"Girls!" Margaret chided them to tone it down. Beautiful and young, unaware of all that lay ahead. She wanted them settled, all of them. She wanted bairns to continue the family line. Young people today were so content to take their time! Her children were well past marrying age and running out the clock.

None of the Monteith children shared Margaret's concerns. Mac had once said that "class didn't matter—no one is better or worse than I am. A human is a human, and you won't make me believe anything different." Margaret shuddered at the memory. How could they not care about protecting all that the family had built over so many centuries?

Quieter now, the girls poured tea, set their cups at the table, and then returned to the buffet for food. Collin sauntered in, smiled at her and kissed her cheek. She nodded at her fine son—such a catch! And perpetually unattached. The oldest should set an example—didn't he know that?

They were all eating, utensils clinking against plates, when Mac arrived. He didn't apologize for being late, didn't kiss his mother in her seat at the head of the table. Margaret stiffened, wondering why his insolence bothered her. It was nothing new, and he was here. That's what mattered. Maybe they'd see more of him now that he was unhitched. She wouldn't say a word about the breakup, not until he broached the topic. Especially since she had no information about the girl. Must not have been important if he'd let her go.

"Mum, Dad." He nodded as he strode to the buffet to fill a plate. When he was seated and eating, Margaret set her fork and knife at angles against her half-full plate and surveyed her family. They were beautiful, all of them, and clever. She'd done her duty—produced a robust, keen next generation to carry on legacy and lineage. It was up to them to do something with it, to take it to a new and higher level. If only they cared enough to realize what they were inheriting.

She cleared her throat. "We've had a researcher poking around the family archives," Margaret announced. "Asking questions about Shira and Hugh Macalaster." She licked her lips and watched for reactions. Emma glanced up but kept eating. Shona nodded, sipped her tea. Collin waited for her to say more. Alex shifted the newspaper to look at his wife but didn't put it down. Only Mac didn't seem surprised.

"Do you know something, Mac?"

He finished chewing a bite of sausage, dabbed his mouth with his napkin, laid his cutlery on the table and folded his hands in his lap. "I might."

She looked at him with a pointed gaze that demanded, *Tell me what you know.*

He rose and paced along the long end of the table. The others stared from Mac to Margaret and back. Alex put down the newspaper.

"It's Eve," Mac said.

Collin coughed. Margaret glanced at her other son, arching her brows in question.

"Mac's girlfriend," Collin muttered.

"Ex," Mac corrected.

Collin pursed his lips. "Sorry, mate."

Mac nodded toward his brother, his eyes hollow and gray.

"When did you break up?"

"A month ago."

The whole family was watching, listening. A maid had come in to clear the table, froze in the silence, and scurried out. It was so quiet, the tick of the grandfather clock in the hall reverberated through the echoing room.

"I'm fine. But she's not going away, Mum." He turned to her. "She's a strong woman." He huffed. "You'd like her. But you won't like the project she's working on. It's why we broke up."

Margaret's stomach flipped. *What the hell was this girl doing? Good for Mac, though, for steering clear of a train wreck!*

She exhaled audibly, and everyone but Mac turned to look at her, waiting for her to speak. Mac combed his fingers through his dark hair.

"Well, don't keep us in suspense," Margaret said, twisting her hands in her lap.

"She found some letters from Shira to Benjamin Belzer, Scotland's first Jewish doctor. Found 'em in a cave up Conic Hill while hiking. She and her boss at the National Archives dug them up, and they're preserving them in a collection at the Scottish Jewish Archives Centre." He went to sit down but paused before doing so. "Oh, and she's writing a book about it."

"Excuse me?"

He cocked his head toward the ceiling. "Mother, it's a long and complicated story, and I don't feel like entertaining the whole fucking family on a Sunday morning about the reason that I can't be with the woman I love," he spat.

"Language!" Margaret reprimanded.

"Seriously? My words are the worrying part?"

She pursed her lips, narrowed her eyes into a glare. He looked away, thrust his hands into his jeans pockets.

"Let's just say the secrets this family has been hiding for centuries are now going to come out. It's all coming out."

He laughed as shiny tears glazed his eyes. "Did you know, we may actually be Jewish? Oh, and there's a long line of gays in this family. It's a right soap opera."

He tucked his chair into the table. "I've lost my appetite," he said and walked out of the room.

"Mac!" Margaret called, but all she could hear were the echo of his footsteps along the long hallway.

Chapter Twenty-Eight

S am, November 2014

The seven-hour flight seemed quick and easy. Sam gazed at Simon, whose sleeping head leaned against his shoulder. His straight sandy hair was flecked with gray now and shone in the light. Sam couldn't sleep on planes, so he'd plugged in headphones and thumbed through the movies available for viewing on the screen in the back of the seat in front of him. He didn't fly often—he had nowhere to go and rarely took a vacation. When Eve had been in college in New York, he'd driven half the time to visit, only occasionally springing for a flight. He didn't mind the long drive and actually preferred being in control of his time. Plus, years of having to count his pennies left him frugal to a fault. Which was a blessing now that he neared retirement and was warming to the idea of packing it all up and moving in with Simon, starting over in New York. He had a generous nest egg and a flush retirement fund, all because he'd never wanted to feel the desperation he'd experienced in those first years after he left home.

The lights flashed on in the cabin, and a flight attendant came over the speaker. "We'll be serving a light breakfast shortly and landing within the hour."

Simon blinked awake. He sat up, looked around and flushed when he realized he'd been napping on Sam's shoulder.

"It's alright with me," Sam said.

Simon squeezed his hand then leaned in for a kiss. "I can't believe you're really here," he said.

"When I say I'll do something, I do it," Sam said, warmth coursing through him in the aftermath of the kiss.

"Jet lag is going to hit you hard around lunchtime," Simon chided. "Wish you could've slept a bit."

Sam shrugged. "Me too. It's the excitement of being with you and the anticipation of seeing my girl. My stomach won't settle, and my heart is pounding out of my chest."

Simon patted his hand and smiled. "You must be so eager to see her."

Sam nodded. "More than you know."

The plane touched down gently on the tarmac just over an hour later and rolled to the gate. His first time overseas, Sam stared out the window for a glimpse of something different than what he knew. But it was quite the same—gray runway, massive planes, a fading green field dusted with new snow.

They collected their suitcases and ribboned through the cordoned lines for border control, showed their passports to the straight-faced agent and found a taxi to take them into town. The first sign that he was in a different place was the driver's rolling accent, his r's in the back of his throat, his vowels emphasized differently than the way Sam would say them. He listened closely to be sure he understood what the man was saying.

Simon chatted easily with the guy. "The Scotsman Hotel," he commanded, and the driver nodded, then put the car in gear and took off.

On the plane to New York, Sam had worried that it would be uncomfortable, awkward between them. But when he'd seen Simon's familiar smile, his tall, lean body, his strong open hands, he'd felt silly for worrying. It had always been easy between them, and years of letters and phone calls only drew them closer in deep and meaningful ways. Sam had walked slowly to Simon, taking him in, his heartbeat fluttering, his breath coming in shallow gulps. When he'd stood before him, Simon wrapped his long arms around Sam and pulled him close. "You're here," he'd whispered, sending tingles up Sam's spine.

The taxi deposited them across the road from the train station, popped the trunk and wheeled their suitcases to the ground-floor door that offered street-level access to the hotel. "In there and up the elevator." The driver pointed.

Simon thanked him, pressed payment into his hand and headed for the door, Sam at his heels. They'd keep Edinburgh as their base for the week, with guided day trips to the Highlands. But the main focus, as far as Sam was concerned, was time with his daughter.

He whipped off a text to Eve. *Made it to the hotel! When can I see you?*

They checked in and rode the elevator up to the eighth floor. Their room was cozy but well-appointed, a queen-sized bed under windows that looked out at the city's rooftops, a gleaming marble bathroom with a shower big enough for two and two small bottles of local whiskey, a dram each to welcome them to Scotland.

Simon came up to him, cupped Sam's face in his hands.

"Finally."

The kiss was long and deep, his taste as familiar as daylight. Sam closed his eyes and felt the softness of Simon's lips, the wet of his tongue, tasted the salt of his skin.

"Nervous?"

Sam shook his head. It was like all his life had been pointing toward this moment, and now that it was here, he let himself fall into it, trusting he'd find his footing. He wasn't even nervous to undress in front of Simon. It would be just fine—perfect, even. They were soul-connected, and their bodies would follow suit.

Chapter Twenty-Nine

Sam, 2014

The Eve who met them for dinner wasn't the daughter he'd kissed goodbye the previous spring. She was withdrawn, gray-faced, sad.

"I guess the breakup is official?"

She fell against his chest. His arms came around her in a protective hug, and he murmured into her hair, "It's going to be alright."

"This way." A woman with spiked, ink-black hair waved them into the belly of the pub, and they followed her to a heavy wood booth set against a far wall. She slapped menus on the table and left.

Eve slid in beside Sam, and Simon sat across from them.

"Sorry, Simon. I don't mean to spoil the party," she said. "And this is the first time we're meeting. I promise I'm not a basket case. I've been wanting to meet you for so long."

He shook his head. "Never you mind. Heartbreak sucks. Your dad filled me in."

She nodded. "Let's have a good meal and a lot of drinks!"

Sam narrowed his eyes. "But won't you have to drive back in the dark to your cottage tonight?"

Eve shook her head. "I'm crashing at the rabbi's house. I often stay there when I leave work late and don't want to drive all the way home to an empty house."

Sam and Simon were quiet.

"They've become friends. I like their company."

"Look at you, getting religious." He elbowed her, trying to hide the hollow feeling in his stomach as the fear of losing yet another person to religion gripped him.

She clamped a hand on his arm. "Daddy, I will never. They're just friends with an extra room close to the office." Her grip slowed his racing heart, and he breathed more evenly.

They ordered fish and chips and dark beer and talked for hours. At eight, a fiddler started to play, and the drinks kept coming, empty mugs cleared away to make room for frothy brews. By the time the man finished his set, their heads were swimming and the pall that had started the evening was gone.

They walked down the Royal Mile arm in arm, three abreast, with Eve between them. The night was brisk and sparkly, black beyond the low streetlights on the High Street. The shops were shuttered, the wide walkways empty of people except the occasional drunk or late-season tourist. A dusting of snow covered the wide stones and peaked rooftops.

"We'll escort you to the rabbi's house," Sam said. He wouldn't have his daughter walking alone at night in a foreign city, although it was only foreign to him, not to her. Nonetheless, he didn't want her wandering in the dark alone.

After, he and Simon took their time meandering back to the hotel.

"She's a lovely girl."

Sam smiled. "I know."

"You did that."

He didn't know what to say. It was true. All that she was, was due to his tireless efforts and attention, but he couldn't take credit for the person she'd become. Sam believed people came into the world wholly formed, with personalities and interests and destinies no one could alter. People tried, but in the end, they couldn't erase who a person was at the core. He breathed in the cool air and pulled his coat tighter. It had been dark for hours, and except for a brief nap at midday, he'd been awake for nearly two days. Every inch of his body ached for sleep.

Simon's arm snaked around his shoulders. "You must be exhausted."

"How do you do that? Read my mind."

Simon only smiled and hooked his arm tighter around Sam. "Thank you for coming to Scotland with me," he whispered.

Sam leaned his head toward Simon's and closed his eyes. They stopped on the empty sidewalk, and Simon edged him back against the stone wall. Sam felt the weight of Simon's body pressing into him and the cold, hard building holding him up. Simon leaned closer. Their mingled breaths puffed into the night air. Simon's mouth came down on his, hard, biting his lip, kneading it between his teeth. For a minute, Sam panicked. They were on a street in a big city. Anyone could see them together.

"Back to the hotel," Sam muttered, his stomach tight. "Not on the street."

"As you wish," Simon said. "But this is okay. It's safe to show our love to the world."

Sam nodded and slipped his hand into Simon's. They walked briskly along the pavement in the direction of the hotel.

CHAPTER THIRTY

E^{ve, 2014}

"The Monteiths put in a request for the letters to be moved to their family archives," David said the next morning as Eve walked blearily into the office.

"Remind me not to drink that much on a worknight." She dropped her work bag and went for coffee.

The collection filled two manuscript boxes that they were keeping in their office until they knew where to catalog it. It had been reviewed and put in protective cover by David's superior, an old archivist who specialized in 19th century aristocracy. They'd debated whether the letters belonged in the Levenson archives in London, the Scottish Jewish Archives Centre in Glasgow or at the National Archives, since they'd discovered and organized the collection. They didn't want it going to the Monteiths—for if it did, it would be the last anyone heard about Shira, Hugh and Benjamin. They'd made a case for keeping the entire collection at the Scottish Jewish Archives, given that Benjamin was not part of the Monteith clan and the letters mostly featured Shira and Benjamin. Everything would be safe there, they hoped. Finally, they agreed to move the collection to the Scottish Jewish Archives, and quickly, so it could be opened, giving Eve the freedom to work on the book she was mapping out in her head. She also wanted to create an exhibition that would live online.

David knew about the breakup, and he'd been cautioned not to bring it up. "For my sanity," Eve had said, "I cannot talk about Mac Monteith."

She'd called and emailed the Monteith estate for comment, additional research and interviews. There'd been only one response, to say that the family discouraged continued pursuit of the project. Then silence.

When she updated David on her lack of progress, she scowled. "Did they think I'd go away that easily? They have no idea who they're dealing with."

David smirked.

"What?"

"I've known you for half a year, lass, but I've never met such a formidable opponent."

"I stand up for what I believe is right."

"And so you do. And what will ya do when they come calling with lawyers?"

Eve's smile disappeared. "Will they?"

David nodded. "Absolutely. Americans aren't the only ones who are happy to sue. If they don't want dirt dug up on their ancestors, they'll try to stop it. The Monteiths have deep pockets. They're one of the few aristocratic families that don't need tourist traffic to keep them in carpets and paintings."

Eve clamped her lips together. It was too bad she never got to meet Mac's family or visit their home. Would things be different now if she had? Of course! Either she'd have abandoned the project out of guilt and pressure, or she'd have charmed them into submission. But there was no sense musing on what-ifs. This was where she was—alone and vested in a project that would not keep her warm in the dark night but would propel her days forward with purpose and build a career that she had grown to love.

"I can't worry about what hasn't happened. Full steam ahead until they come knocking. How did the Jewish Archives respond?"

He cocked his head. "They're fending them off. There is good ground to argue that they aren't solely Monteith property. I just hope we don't hear from the Levenson archives, too." He snorted.

"Should I go to Glasgow?"

David looked at her bright face and sighed. "Give 'em a ring. They're not open on Friday or Saturday."

"Is it a religious community?"

David nodded. He told her how his Jewish friend at uni had grown up in a fairly religious family, and he'd once gone home with the lad for a holiday. "We lit menorahs and played dreidel games, and I'd thought the community cheery and welcoming. Funny that they lived right under my nose, and I'd never known a jot about them. Bang on to them for persisting in the midst of this cold, Christian country. We've stayed friends over the decades, and I always say yes to a Passover invitation. Even my kids have loved it. Nothing like a good bowl of matzoh ball soup on a cold spring day." He laughed. "The Glasgow synagogues are quite religious. You might want to pack a skirt."

Eve winced. "That's so old-fashioned. I can't imagine not being allowed in on the basis of my clothing."

David shrugged.

She'd bring the report on the collection that she and David had put together, talk to the director about their plans for the collection and hope to build a relationship that would help her as she wrote the book.

"Good luck," he said.

CHAPTER THIRTY-ONE

*E*ve, 2014

The proprietor of the Garnethill bed and breakfast led Eve down a long hallway to a corner room, turning the key in the lock and swinging the door open. "You'll be in this room." She dangled the key toward Eve, who grabbed it and slid it into her pocket.

"It's lovely," she said. Full bed with white sheets, charcoal gray blanket pulled flat and taut, red plaid pillows. A window overlooked the garden, and a door led into a small bathroom with white fixtures.

"Full Scottish breakfast served from seven until nine thirty," the woman said as she pulled the door closed, leaving Eve alone.

Eve collapsed on the bed and tucked her hands behind her head. The ceiling was a white canvas with a solitary light fixture in the center. It was a functional, if not beautiful, space. She leapt off the bed to crack the window and let in the night air.

She pulled her phone from her backpack and dialed her father.

Sam picked up on the second ring. "Everything alright?"

"Fine, Daddy. I'm in Glasgow for the night, for work, at a B&B. I'll be visiting the Scottish Jewish Archives, and I might stay for Shabbat. You and Simon were going on that two-day trip to Skye, so I figured you wouldn't miss me. Apparently, it's quite a religious community. David even suggested I wear a skirt!"

Sam was silent.

"What is it, Daddy?"

Eve listened as he told her about his sister, Bracha, coming home from school, her face streaked with dried tears, complaining to their mother about the headmistress measuring her skirt length with a wooden ruler and finding it just shy of the required four inches below the knee, then whacking her with the ruler and sending her home to lengthen her skirts before returning to school. Eve's heart ached when he told her about Shaindie laughing at him when he asked if she'd be too hot wearing a high-collared, long-sleeved shirt under a sleeveless jumper in summer.

He said, "Her response was a mix of bafflement and anger when she said, 'Like I have any choice? Modesty is one of the most important mitzvahs for women.'" Then he sighed.

"Sorry, honey," he said. "Bad memories. But keep an open mind."

Eve fell quiet.

"Have you heard from Mac?"

"Not a word."

"The good ones are hard to let go," he said.

Eve sniffled. "I've never been like this over a guy."

"Maybe you'll find a way back together," he said.

"Enjoy Skye, Daddy. I'll see you and Simon when you get back."

And then they'd leave, and she'd be alone once again.

She should've gone with them. She hadn't been to Skye yet, and she could have come to Glasgow after they'd returned to America. Why was she always keeping her distance from people she loved?

Stop the pity party, she thought. *Deal with the choices you make. Or make different choices.*

Eve propped her suitcase on a chair and unzipped it, rooting around for the single dress she'd brought to Scotland. It was long and black, cotton and sleeveless, so she'd packed a cardigan to wear over it. She pulled on scrunchy socks and sneakers. *No way am I wearing pantyhose or fancy shoes.*

The people were nice enough. Night fell early, the darkness heavy as a cloak by four. She'd walked to the synagogue for the evening service, and after, a middle-aged woman approached her.

"Good Shabbos and welcome! You don't look familiar."

Eve explained what had brought her to Scotland and to the synagogue that evening, and the woman reached a hand and clasped it around Eve's wrist, pulling her to meet the rabbi and a few young men of the congregation.

The woman invited Eve to join her family for Shabbat dinner, but she begged off, too tired and, frankly, a tad nervous to sit around a table with a bunch of strangers. She'd never been in an Orthodox community, and she was afraid to venture in too deep after all her father had told her. Plus, she didn't want to seem naïve about her own heritage. The woman insisted she come back Saturday morning and join them for lunch after services. Eve couldn't say no. She wondered if the woman would balk at her wearing the same outfit the next day. She could blow off Saturday services if she was too worried; she'd never be back to this community anyway. She was meeting with the archivist Sunday morning then returning to Edinburgh to spend the afternoon and evening with her father and Simon.

Back at the inn, Eve peeled off her socks and settled her shoes under the chair that held her suitcase. Outside, twigs cracked under the skittering paws of squirrels in the garden. She laid the dress over the open suitcase and pulled on sweatpants and an oversize sweatshirt. After she cleaned her teeth, Eve climbed under the blanket.

She didn't remember falling asleep but awoke with a start some hours later. The room was purple with night and cold. She debated closing the window but didn't want to leave the warmth of the quilt, when she noticed a figure shuffling in the shadows.

"Who's there?"

There was a humming, and then Shira's face emerged from the dark. She hovered near the bed.

"You're back?" Eve croaked, sitting upright. "What now? What else could you want?"

"You're on the right path," Shira said, patting Eve's foot.

Eve felt the hand on her foot, but it wasn't heavy like a human hand; it was tingly, light.

"I'm nursing a broken heart for you," Eve said.

"My babies were so beautiful," Shira said. "But Hugh took one look at William and nearly spat on his face. *He looks too*

Jewish, is what he said. And then he walked out of the birth room. Never held him, not once."

She paced, twisting her hands as if reliving the memory.

"I sat at the side of the queen, long before I married Hugh. And then everything changed. Banished despite my family's wealth, which funded the bloody court. Jews are never safe. You're a Jew. This is as much your story as it is mine."

"I know who I am," Eve said, annoyed. She flexed her feet and cracked her toes. She was buzzing with wakefulness but aching with exhaustion.

"Do you?"

Eve seethed with anger. How dare this woman upend her life! And keep demanding more. She balled the blanket in her hands to keep from lashing out.

"Hugh's Protestant status opened doors for me. But I never abandoned my Judaism. He wanted me to hide it, to turn my back on my ancestors. He wouldn't let me take the children to a synagogue. I lit candles in my rooms. I went to services alone. But still I went."

"As many Jews have done throughout history," Eve said. "I'm sorry for you, but it's not like that anymore."

Although the room was dark, moonlight washed over Shira, haloing her in the light.

"That's what you think. Before World War II, some Monteiths supported, even advocated for, the Germans to take Britain. They wanted a United Kingdom freed from Jewish taint. There are some today who feel the same."

Eve yawned, and her eyes watered. "No one cares that much today."

"You'd be surprised," Shira whispered.

A cold wind fluttered the white curtains framing the open window. "Ask him," Shira said.

"Who? Ask what?"

"You know. Ask him. It's not always as you think."

And with that, she was gone.

Eve reached for the nightstand, where her phone was plugged in and charging. The clock read three. Could she call Mac? That had to be who Shira was talking about. He'd be glad to hear from her. Also, worried by a call so late at night. She laid the phone down and slithered lower in the bed but couldn't sleep. Her eyes were wide, searching the dark. *Damn you, Shira. You come with such drama, then leave in haste.*

What should she be asking Mac? Should she even call him? How would she get over him, heal her broken heart, if she kept in touch?

The clock flipped to four, and Eve turned onto her side. The night paraded on in shifts and shadows, and the cold air bit in from the open window as she turned over and over on the bed, wishing for sleep. By six, she had settled into a prone position and drifted off, only to be wakened by the smell of hot coffee and sizzling bacon. She rubbed the grainy sleep from her eyes and stretched her limbs. She swung her legs over the side of the bed and pulled herself upright. The day ahead would be long, but she had to face what would come.

CHAPTER THIRTY-TWO

E *ve, 2014*

The archives offered quite a bit about Benjamin Belzer and a fair amount about the Levenson Foundation, as it related to Benjamin's work. Little about Shira and nothing about Hugh, for obvious reasons. Eve met with the head archivist, who assured her that the new collection of letters would be safe. The Scottish Jewish Archives Centre was protective of its materials and had won many a stand-off against prominent families who made claims to move collections to private archives.

They discussed Eve's plans for the book, and she left feeling confident that she'd have easy access to the materials whenever she needed to review a letter. The archivist promised to work with her on the best way to include the letters in the book, and they agreed to partner on any future exhibits of the collection.

"One thing you should know," he cautioned. "We don't digitize most of our materials, so you'll have to be here in person if you want to look at anything. I can sometimes scan materials, if I have time, but I can't scan the entire collection. We're a small team and get a fair bit of researcher traffic."

Since the breakup, Eve had been thinking seriously about ending the internship early and heading back to America. It was too hard to be so close to Mac and not go to him. She'd be stronger in her resolve if she were far, far away.

"That might be a problem," she said. "I'm heading back to the States soon."

He shrugged. "Don't know what to say, lass," he said. "This is the collection's new home. We'll keep it safe, but we are keeping it, and you'll need to come here if you need anything from it."

She nodded and slipped on her coat. As she left the building, a cool, late-autumn wind burned her face. *Am I running away?* she wondered. *Am I nothing but a coward?* She huddled into the neck of her coat and headed for the train station, back to Edinburgh and the warm embrace of the people who loved her.

Chapter Thirty-Three

*E**ve, 2014*

The bonfire in the center of the village sparked and popped, its orange dance bright in the early dark. Vendors offered hot toddies and ham and pea soup in mugs. Eve had never seen the square this busy, not even during the height of summer.

Guy Fawkes Night. One last Scottish celebration before breaking the news to David that she'd be writing the book from her father's home in America and leaving Scotland.

For good.

Wrapped in a merino wool sweater, her feet sheathed in wool socks, Eve drew eyeliner, swirled mascara, swiped opalescent powder over her cheekbones. She brushed her hair until it shined, painted a soft gloss on her lips and surveyed the curve of her jeans over her backside. She'd surely run into Mac tonight.

She missed him terribly, even though her heart was hollow in her chest and her stomach was permanently twisted in knots. With little appetite since the breakup, she had to cinch her belt to its tightest to keep her jeans around her waist. So many nights, she'd lain awake, wondering if she'd made a mistake. So many times, she'd dialed his number and then shut off her phone entirely, hiding it in a drawer. The sadness was unbearable, which made her doubt her resolve to write a book that cost her the love of her life.

It was a short drive into the village. By the time she arrived in the dusky night, the streets were packed with vehicles in regular spaces and wedged in at angles. She drove far down the lane a good half mile to find a spot, beneath the branches of an overgrown lime tree. An extra drink might make the walk back to the car easier as the night grew colder.

People left work early to immerse in the festivities. It was five o'clock, and darkness shrouded the village, the first stars blinking in the night sky. As she walked toward the village center, the sounds grew louder: laughter, the hum of chatter, the crackle and whip of logs consumed by fire, spitting sparks as they burned to ash.

Monteith House sat at the edge of the square, which had been cleared of benches for the bonfire, a conical writhing tower of dancing flames that shined warm light onto the faces of those who surrounded it. Everyone held a warm drink—lemony-sweet whiskies steeped in cinnamon, anise and cloves, cocoa for the kiddies. A woman from the town bakery stirred a cauldron of soup, ladling it into metal mugs and offering warm, palm-sized oat cakes for dunking. The village smelled of smoke and the crisp of winter air before a snow, against a soundtrack of belly laughs and children running, their parents calling after them to stay away from the fire.

"I wondered if you'd come."

He stood in the center of the square, villagers milling around him. There were celebrations like this in every town of the countryside. She could've gone to any other village to experience this celebration. But Eve had wanted to run into Mac, to see him one last time before she left. Not to prolong the pain, just to prove to herself that she'd made the right decision.

"Mac." His name came out in a breathy whisper.

He looked her up and down. "You look bonny," he said, stepping closer. "Eve." He reached for her, and she inched toward him, her body moving while her brain screamed to hold back.

She couldn't show how much she missed him. He'd suck her back in, and she'd let him, and then all the resolve she'd built in the rationale for their breakup would dissolve. She didn't want to lead either of them down a path of resentment. She wanted a relationship that had a chance of beating the odds. She wanted a love without complications.

If such a thing existed.

She swallowed to dislodge the lump in her throat, but it refused to move. She swallowed again, more like a gulp, and nodded. "Mac."

She wanted to say, *I miss you. I love you. I want you. I'm an idiot and I was wrong and we should be together.*

But the only word that made it past her lips was his name. "Mac," she whispered again, not loud enough for him to hear, and he took a step closer. The smell of him, even outside in the cold night, drew her close.

He looked wonderful. His dark curls alive in the firelight, his blue eyes reflecting the dancing flames. His jaw was set and solid, his hands wrapped around a steaming mug.

"I've missed you," he said, his eyes serious, his lips slightly open, his breath heavy.

She swallowed again, and the flutters in her stomach kicked up their dance.

"Come back to me. Please. We can work this out."

The voices in her head were arguing. For a minute, she couldn't remember why they'd broken up, what good reason could keep this kind of love from growing. But then she remembered. She slipped two fingers into her front jeans pocket and fingered her keys to have something to focus on.

"Mac," she said softly, her voice a plea. "Nothing has changed."

"Fuck the book. Don't let us go. I'll do anything to keep us together—I'll make my family understand why it's important. I'll fight for us, Eve."

Could he really go to bat for her with his family? Could they weather whatever might come from his parents? Or would being with him soften her commitment to her work and lead her to a life of regret?

"Real love doesn't make you choose," she said.

She wouldn't touch him, though she wanted to more than anything. One touch would be like the spark that lit the bonfire that danced toward the sky in the village square. Burning without control, its flames dangerous, scorching.

"I'm not making you choose, Eve," he gulped. "I want you and everything you are. Even this book. I can deal with it. I can handle my family. I've always gone my own way, and they know it. If I had to choose between them and you, I'd choose you every time. But I don't believe it'll come to that."

"How can you know?" She stroked his hand, wondering if the soup in his mug had gone cold in the chill air. He still palmed it with both hands. She took the mug and set it down on a table. The night air swirled around them. In the square, the bonfire was like fingers pointing toward the dark sky.

He grasped her hands.

"It's my family you're outing," he said. "But I'll fight for us. I'll stand by you. Us against the world." His voice trembled, but his eyes were soft. She couldn't tell if he was sad or scared.

"Is that what you want? To fight your family to keep a lover? In time, I'd feel terrible for letting you. I know what it's like to not have family," she said. "I wouldn't wish it on anyone. Certainly not the man I love."

She laid a cheek against his shoulder, breathed in his musk—soap and woods—and the sweet mint of his breath.

"You love me," he said.

She nodded. "Of course. I wish I didn't. It would be so much easier."

"You came tonight to see me," he said. "You could've gone to any village. You must have doubts. Which means I have a chance."

She sighed. It would be easy to give in, to stay, to let the future unfold rather than trying to be mature. Her father's voice echoed in her head. *Real love doesn't make you choose. You don't want to be in a family that resents you.* Was he speaking out of concern for his daughter or from the scars of his own experiences?

"Did you know," she said, pulling back, "Hugh Macalaster ridiculed his children for looking too Jewish? He hid his gay identity, but when he was in government, he imprisoned others like him."

Her voice swelled as the fire blazed, whipped up by the wind.

"Shira was banished from the royal court because she was Jewish, even though her wealth funded the royals. Only marrying Hugh allowed her back in."

Eve's cheeks burned. Was any of this reaching him?

"There were Monteiths who sided with the Nazis," she continued. "They wanted to cleanse the United Kingdom of Jews. Even though they were Jews themselves!"

She turned his face, forcing him to look at her. "Your family isn't the only one, but it's an example of what's wrong with the aristocracy. I've been given this story. Believe me, I wish I hadn't. I wish I'd found nothing in that damn cave."

Mac's eyes were wide. She was relieved that this was all news to him, that he wasn't part of the hiding his family was so good at. At least she could continue to believe in his goodness.

"None of that is me." He pulled her closer. "And none of it is you." His eyes shimmered in the moonlight.

The swirl of the celebration was making her head spin.

"Who was Guy Fawkes, anyway?"

He drew her to him, close enough to kiss, hard and long. All the sounds of the celebration muffled into one string of sound.

"He tried to blow up Parliament because his religious beliefs weren't accepted in the kingdom," Mac whispered.

"When people aren't accepted, they do crazy things," she said. "Someone needs to speak up."

"Why does that someone have to be you?"

She knew he wasn't okay with it! She'd been right all along to walk away, despite how much it hurt.

He stepped back but kept hold of her hands, his gaze boring into hers. He looked sad, defeated. He slowly shook his head as silent tears streaked his cheeks.

"You're using my family as an example of a torrid past, and that isn't fair," he said. "We may be symbolic of some awful trends in British history, but we're not the entirety of it. I don't know why you're singling us out."

He dropped her hands and swiped the tears from his face.

Feeling anger and disappointment radiate from his body, Eve bore a pang of regret. It *wasn't* fair.

A little voice chastised her. *You're letting go of the best thing that has ever happened to you, your first chance at real love. You're a fool.*

She blinked. Who'd said that? She was tired of voices appearing and telling her what to do. She shook it off and looked at Mac.

"I'm an American and a Jew," she said. "Born of rebellion and endurance. It's in my blood. My father's family rejected him because he's gay. The kindest man I know, and his family believes he has no value. I'm sorry, Mac, but I won't let it go."

She stood tall in the cold night as the party swirled around her. She could not remember why she'd come to the village square, what rationale had urged her to confront him. The dance of the fire had whipped up a ferocity in Eve that felt otherworldly. Some force was pulling strings, and she was the puppet. Even if she wanted to back down now, she couldn't.

He turned his face toward the fire. She shivered, took his hand and rubbed it against her cheek. She tried to imprint his scent on her memory. Most people didn't know when it was the last time they would see someone, couldn't trap tactile memories to carry with them on the long, lonely road beyond. But she would.

She closed her eyes to remember the rhythm of this night. She threaded her fingers into the silky curls at the base of his head. She fit perfectly into the cleft of his chest. He let her lean in, though the fight had gone out of him. She focused on remembering how perfectly they fit together. She'd need it on the long journey home.

Chapter Thirty-Four

Eve, February 2015

It took two months of writing every morning to hash out a first draft. Eve spent afternoons hiking in the snow along the Huron River, wearing wool socks, winter boots and lined pants. She'd moved back to her father's house while he was still there, but the house sold quickly so she didn't have long.

David hadn't seemed mad when she quit the internship, only disappointed to lose her, but she was sure she'd burned a bridge and ruined any chance at an archival career. Everything rode on this book. It had to be good, for all she'd given up to do it. Most days, she wondered if it had been worth it.

"You have to stop making me dinner every night, or I'll never want to move," her father said that evening over bloody steaks, roasted potatoes and a salad with homemade lemon vinaigrette. After Scotland, he'd given Simon the green light to look for a place in New York that would be their shared home. It hadn't taken long to find a brownstone with potential in Brooklyn Heights. He was moving in May, and he kept saying it couldn't come soon enough. Simon came to Michigan for long weekends, and Eve was enjoying getting to know him. Late at night, alone in her room, hearing their muffled voices through the wall, she longed for Mac and hated herself for leaving Scotland. The book's storyline was interesting but not compelling enough. She lost focus, lost passion for the topic. She was just lost.

And she was sad about her father's impending move. She knew it was time for him to go, and she was happy that he finally had love. But it was the end of her childhood, the loss of her home base.

"The place stays with you," her father had said. "The relationships are the anchors. I'll always be home for you, wherever I am and wherever you go. And you're my home, too, honey."

Nice words, but Eve felt the pang of loss so deeply that she moped around the house, wishing Mac would call, knowing he never would. She went to bed early each night in the winter dark and wrapped herself in layers of blankets. But she slept fitfully, often waking in the wee hours of morning to stare out at the old tree in the backyard and feel the loneliness in the hollow of her throat.

She'd left Scotland at the new year, Hogmanay as it was known in the village. It had been a cold white morning with bells ringing in 2015. The tinny whine and clang called over the distance. She had packed up the cottage she had loved living in and driven slowly through the village that had become home to her.

The night of the fire, she'd torn away from him and run to the car. At home, she'd wept until there were no more tears to shed. And then, she was numb. She'd spent the remainder of her days in Scotland making copies of letters so she'd have them to work with once she started writing the book. She didn't want to have to go back to Scotland, go anywhere close to Mac.

That resolve turned into regret the minute she touched down on American soil. She *was* a fool! That voice by the bonfire, the voice of her conscience she'd decided, had been right. Making a problem where there wasn't one, inventing a reason to not get close, to not risk getting hurt. What a coward! But her ego had prevented her from calling Mac, so she'd gone forward with her plan and headed home in shame.

Chapter Thirty-Five

S *am, 2015*

"Morning," Sam said as he strode into the kitchen and kissed Eve on the cheek. She smiled but didn't look up.

She cradled a mug between her hands and stared out the kitchen window at the old oak in the backyard where a lone, red-breasted robin balanced on a sturdy branch. The sky was white with cold, the windows rimmed with the lace of condensation.

"We need new windows," she said, pointing at the sweating glass.

"Someone else's problem." Sam smiled. "Old houses need constant love and attention. And this one is not mine for long."

He poured coffee into a mug with a sunflower painted onto the ceramic and slid two slices of bread into the toaster.

"Have you eaten?"

She shook her head.

"Did you not sleep well?"

Her eyebrows lifted.

Sam had been trying to break Eve's melancholy since she'd arrived home, but nothing worked. She spent most days writing at a small table in the living room. Sam had always liked how cozy this house was, sufficient but not overwhelming and easy to clean. When he was a boy, he hadn't been included in the household chores that his mother had insisted his sister take part in. As a boy, he hadn't learned how to cook or clean or even make a bed. There had been strong delineations between women's work and men's work—which was to say that the women did all the housework and the men showed up to enjoy it. He couldn't remember his father or brothers fixing or building anything like he later learned to do as a single father. In his religious childhood, Sam's obligations centered around public prayers in synagogue with the men, studying Torah and letting the women care for him by working, raising children, cooking and cleaning. He'd never imagined he'd be the one to brush his daughter's hair and coerce it into a ponytail before sending her off to school.

But he'd embraced the life he ended up in and kept a neat and tidy home. There was always food in the refrigerator and nourishing meals on the table. Three cookbooks rested on a shelf above the stove—*The Best Slow Cooker Cookbook Ever, Family Circle Encyclopedia of Cooking* and, wanting to give his daughter a taste of their heritage, *The Complete American Jewish Cookbook.* Most nights, he'd opted for a breaded chicken schnitzel recipe with rice and steamed broccoli or spaghetti with store-bought meatballs. The first time he'd sprinkled Parmesan cheese over his noodles, he'd waited for some great calamity to come as he mixed dairy with meat, violating the kosher laws. He'd only done it because Eve had asked, having learned from her friends that Parmesan cheese made a pasta dish better.

Sam bit back his instinct to say no and sprinkled the soft cheese over the dish. Eve swirled the spaghetti onto her fork and slurped it into her mouth. Sam did the same. The taste exploded on his tongue—the sweet acid of the tomato sauce, the soft velvet of the noodles, the tang of the Parmesan and the heartiness of a chunk of seasoned meat, all in one bite. When no lightning bolt appeared, he wondered why he'd been so zealous in his observance of the kosher food laws. To stay in the good graces of the community? Well, that ship had sailed, he chuckled as he consumed another delicious bite.

"How's the book coming?" Sam sipped coffee and surveyed his daughter's gaunt face.

Eve shrugged and gulped her own coffee. "I've finished the draft."

She didn't seem excited or relieved or accomplished as she said it. Just stated it as if she were reporting on the weather. He wished he could erase the sadness from her face and body.

Sam sighed. "I hate to see you like this. What will it take to break your mood?"

"I don't know, Daddy." Her eyes glistened with sudden tears. "I miss him so much."

Sam chewed slowly, swallowing a bite of toast as if it were glue. He chased it with a swig of coffee. Had he given her bad advice that night in Edinburgh? Was he wrong about encouraging her to choose the project over the relationship?

"Maybe I was wrong, honey." He gulped. Parenting was so hard. Just when he thought he'd gotten the hang of it, he led her astray. "Maybe you *can* have both."

She looked up with wide eyes, her jaw set. "Are you kidding me?"

He sat back in his chair. "Are you mad at me?"

"Um, well, if you're saying you gave me bad advice and I listened to you as I always do, then hell yeah, I'm mad."

He breathed in and counted to three before letting the air out and finding the words. He kept his voice even and low.

"I'm only human, Eve," he said. "I can't know everything and certainly not about relationships. We both know I haven't been the best example in that department."

She slammed her hand onto the table and pushed her chair back, scraping it against the floor. "I'm an idiot," she said a little too loudly for the small kitchen. "I shouldn't have listened to you! You're right. You suck at relationships. Why the hell didn't I see that?"

His face stung with heat. Even in her teenage years, they hadn't fought much. There'd always been an ease between them, even when his parenting wasn't perfect. She forgave him, and he forgave himself.

Where was this rage coming from?

He cleared his throat and flattened his palm on the tabletop. Another slow breath in, to calm his racing heart.

"You're an adult, capable of making your own decisions," he said. "Although it might be easier, you can't blame me if you regret your choice."

"That's rich," she said.

"I'm going to work now, and we can talk later, when you've calmed down," Sam said. "I love you."

He left the kitchen, grabbed his coat and his work bag and fled the house, trying to coax his heart to slow its pace. In the car, as he buckled his seat belt and started the engine, he closed his eyes to calm himself. He was shaking.

They'd get through this. They had to. Except for the distance when he came out to her, they'd never had distance between them. Sam took careful breaths until he felt his heartbeat ease, and then he backed onto the street and headed for work.

*****

Eve

Why did I do that? Eve kicked herself for yelling at her father. *I'm thirty-one fucking years old. I should take responsibility for my own life. Even if it's a total wreck.*

She dialed her father's cell.

"I'm sorry," she said when he answered. "When Shira was coming to me at night, I felt like I had an important mission. Riding high on a cloud of purpose. Now, it seems ridiculous. A piece of a dark past long gone."

He didn't say anything, just listened.

By the time her father returned from work that night, Eve was calm and clear. She had other things to be angry about.

She waved a piece of paper in his face. "The nerve!"

He examined the return address on a torn envelope on the coffee table. *Campbell and Stewart Solicitors, Edinburgh.*

"Can I see?" Her father reached for the letter, scanned the words on the ivory page of fine linen. A law firm logo in the upper corner, a list of solicitors laddering down its left side. The typed words said the Monteith estate would sue Eve if she didn't stop the book project. They gave thirty days from the date the letter had been sent—a week prior—to drop it, or they'd pursue legal action.

"Do you think Mac's behind this?"

Eve shook her head. "I doubt it."

"I wonder if they have any standing," he said. "I mean, it's another country, and all of this information is readily available, right? In a public collection at the archives. Maybe they're just trying to scare you."

Eve dropped into a tufted chair and cradled her face between her hands.

"Is it even worth it?"

Sam patted her knee. "Only you can answer that."

That night, Eve tossed in her bed, staring at the ceiling as moonlight angled in through the window. She hadn't pulled the curtains closed or lowered the shades. She went from angry to listless. Her stomach churned with hunger and regret, and her heart ached.

As dawn neared, Eve texted Mac. *How dare you! Do you really think a lawsuit can scare me off this book? After all we've been through?*

She laid the phone on her nightstand and curled into a pillow, exhaling almost into sleep. But the phone buzzed, and she grabbed it.

"What are you talking about?"

He was angry, but his voice sounded like honey and she wanted it to cover her. She sat up in bed.

"Eve, what's this about?"

"You don't know?"

"I wouldn't ask if I did. I've been hoping to hear from you, but not like this."

Her stomach lurched. He'd been missing her? But of course he wouldn't reach out, because she broke up with him and left Scotland. *Dummy.*

"You don't know anything about the lawyer's letter that I received from a posh Edinburgh firm, threatening to sue me?"

"It wasn't from me. How could you think that?"

His voice was steely and cold, but she was elated. Thank God he'd had no part in this!

Adrenaline buzzed in her limbs; her head vibrated. God, how she'd missed his voice. Its Scots curl and roll, the thunderous depth of it.

"I'm glad." She slid beneath the blanket, relief washing over her.

"Eve." His voice was softer. "I would never take action against you. And I'm hurt that you thought I would."

"I didn't really," she whispered, fighting against the sleep that was overtaking her. "I'm sorry." She wanted to soften into his voice, let it wrap around her and comfort her and finally find rest. She clicked off the call and closed her eyes.

Chapter Thirty-Six

Margaret, 2015

"You've made a right mess of everything!"

Mac stormed into the family home the next evening. Margaret was alone in the small study, reading. Alex was out. She hadn't asked where, and he hadn't specified. The lights were low, reflecting in the leaded-glass windows that steamed from the heat inside against the cold of the winter night.

Margaret looked at her son, knowing full well what he was ranting about.

"Control yourself, son," she said in a steady voice. "Monteiths don't behave this way."

"I'll bloody behave however I want."

"Stop carrying on like a child."

She didn't move from the chaise, where her manicured toes glowed in the light of the hearth. Even at night, even at home alone, Margaret was impeccably attired: slim black pants, a warm red crewneck sweater and the ever-present single strand of Scotch pearls. Her fingernails matched her toes, and her lips shimmered with gloss.

Mac fumed.

"Someone had to put a stop to this nonsense," Margaret said, reaching for her cut-crystal tumbler of whiskey and swallowing it in one gulp. "I won't have some nosy American rummaging in the attic of our ancestors and writing a book about it for all the world to read. I won't have it."

Mac sat on the end of the chaise and leaned in close.

"Eve is the love of my life, and because of this family, I can't be with her."

"We never even met her, so I don't see how we can be the cause of your relationship's demise," his mother said. "And if she was the love of your life, why aren't you with her now?"

She walked to the fireplace to watch the licking flames.

"Don't play games with me, Mother. You know what you're doing. And you know that your voice in my head is what ended this relationship."

"I didn't realize I had such influence over you," she said. "I'm relieved, actually. I thought I had no impact on my children."

While she remained calm on the outside, inside her heart pounded.

"Withdraw the lawsuit immediately," Mac demanded.

She shook her head. "It isn't in the best interests of this family to have our long-hidden secrets exposed."

"Withdraw it."

She stared at him.

"Or what?"

"Or you'll lose me...forever."

She kept smiling, even though she didn't really feel it. She stared at her son, wondering if he meant it. Scots were so damn hot-blooded. They said things in the heat of a moment but didn't always follow through. But if he were serious… She couldn't lose her golden boy. Collin might be the heir apparent, but Mac was the wunderkind, her silent favorite. She hadn't worked this hard to build up the family line to let it all go. And he would do it. Her son never said a word he didn't mean.

While all these thoughts pinged inside her head, Margaret kept her even gaze and held her son's eyes with her own. She would not show weakness. She would leave him thinking that this was the best stance for the family and he'd better fall in line. Except inside, she was quaking.

This is not the moment to grow weak, Margaret reprimanded herself. Not the time to show heart.

Or love.

She waited until he stormed out to release her breath in a woosh of air. She crumpled to the floor, heaving with silent sobs. She'd worked so hard to build her family, but in the end, she was all alone.

***

Eve

A friend of her father referred them to an attorney who practiced international law and could find out if the Monteith family had a legitimate claim. They faxed him the letter, and he phoned by the end of the next day. Eve put the call on speaker so her father could listen in.

"I'm not sure they have standing," he confirmed. "You discovered the letters, and they're safely ensconced at the Scottish

Jewish Archives, so it's for a Scottish court to decide who owns the collection."

He paused.

"I'm not sure a court would even take up the case," he said. "The family is trying to strong-arm you to scare you off the project."

Eve felt the freedom of release coursing through her. She might not have to battle anyone, and she could go ahead as planned. Suddenly, she felt a renewed passion for the project.

"It's going to be pretty hard to prove that anything you write today about people who lived more than 150 years ago will do real damage to their living descendants," he added.

Eve sighed, and Sam patted her hand. "I have an agent who likes the project but no commitment yet from a publisher. Could this complicate my chances of landing one?"

"Yep, yep. It could. Look, it's my job to be straight with you. I'm coming at this from a legal perspective, not a creative one. There isn't standing here, but there is always a risk that they oppose something you write and tie you up in lawsuits that could cost you time and money. You want my advice? Write a different book just to make your life easier."

"Thanks, but that's not an option."

"I figured," he said. "But you asked for my legal advice, so now you have it. Do you want me to respond to the letter?"

"Sure," Eve said. "What will you say?"

"Exactly what we've discussed. No standing, the book goes on as planned, back off."

***

Sam

Later that night, Sam huddled into the phone in his room behind a closed door. "You'd think the lawyer's call would boost her mood," he said to Simon.

"How did you feel when I left?"

"What?"

"All those years ago. When I left, how'd you feel?"

Sam thought back to the second worst time of his life, after the nightmare of leaving his family and community. He'd pushed the memories so deep into the recesses of his mind that it was hard to pull them out now.

"Hollowed out."

"That's where she is now. A legal win won't erase it."

How could Simon be so beautiful, so attractive and so smart all at once?

"I love you."

Simon chuckled. "I might be good at this parenting thing after all."

"Not that a thirty-one-year-old daughter needs parenting," Sam said.

"You always need parents," Simon said. "I still remember how alone I felt when I left home. How I missed my mother's soft hand. I yearned for someone to care about my well-being."

"Yep," Sam agreed, awash in his own memories. "You never stop needing a parent."

Chapter Thirty-Seven

*E*ve, 2015

After a shower, Eve pulled on sweats, a T-shirt and scrunchy socks and made her way to the kitchen. Sam stood over the stove, steam wafting toward the hood, the fan whirring beneath it.

"Smells good." She rose on her toes to kiss her father's cheek.

He nodded and smiled as he stirred the pot. "Beef stew. A cold winter night calls for hearty food."

She peered into the bubbling pot. Bits of carrot bobbed alongside chunks of meat and potato. "When will it be ready?"

"Soon."

She sat at the table, scrolling on her phone. There were several texts in a group conversation including her childhood friends Kate, Melissa and Molly. The foursome had been inseparable from middle school onwards, all returning to Ann Arbor after college. They'd been Eve's social circle until she left for Scotland. Maybe reconnecting with them would lift her mood.

This weekend—get the band back together? read Kate's text. She was a marketing manager at General Motors, always dating someone new.

"Best way to get over an old flame is to get under a new one," Kate had joked when they'd met for drinks shortly after Eve returned home from Scotland. "Besides, I need a wingwoman as a buffer on some of these dates."

Eve had smiled and begged off, pleading for time to nurse her broken heart before jumping into the dating scene. Ann Arbor was a small town, and she didn't want to get caught up in its web before she was ready to give someone an honest try.

But now, two months in, she typed a hasty, *Yes, let's do this!* and immediately received a thumbs-up and goofy face emoji from Kate, followed by a heart from Melissa and a flurry of fruit emojis from Molly.

"Dinner is served." Sam placed a steaming ceramic crock on the table with a matching ladle sticking out of it. He brought two bowls and forks. "The meat is tender enough to fall apart. Water? Beer?"

"Something dark," she said.

Sam pulled a Guinness from the fridge for her and a Luciernaga from Jolly Pumpkin—a new-to-him pale ale—for himself and placed them on the table with glasses to pour them into. He'd told Eve he was expanding his taste for beer beyond Killian's, exploring Ann Arbor craft beers from an impressive array of small-label breweries.

Eve spooned stew into her bowl, steam rising to her face. She opened her beer and poured it slowly into a glass. Sam scooped stew into his own bowl.

"How are you feeling about the attorney's call?"

"It's always a risk when you publish something," she said, forking a hefty bite into her mouth and savoring the flavors—sage and rosemary and tomatoey thickness and the soft pliant sinews of long-cooked meat.

Sam nodded. "Did you mention it to Lucy?"

Lucy Thompson was Eve's agent, an aggressive New Yorker who was the second person Eve had queried with her book proposal and the first to jump at the chance to represent her. She wasn't sure she liked Lucy, but she loved that it had been so easy to land an agent. Lucy liked Eve's writing and the book's premise. She was shopping the proposal around to publishers, with some early interest from an editor at KGR, a major New York house. But they had yet to receive a firm offer.

"I will," Eve said, heaping a second helping into her bowl.

"You're going to have to be honest when you land a publisher," Sam said. "Up front. Don't hide anything."

"Touché." Eve smiled then took a healthy swig of beer. "To change the subject, I'm going out with the girls this weekend."

"KMM?" Her father's shorthand for the trio of friends.

She rolled her eyes. "Honestly, Daddy."

He laughed. "Old habits. Glad to hear you're going out. Getting back to normal." He cringed and turned to her. "Sorry. That word—what is normal anyway?"

That weekend, Eve joined her friends at Seva. The food was comforting and creative and the place large enough that they could sit and talk for hours. After, they walked to Main Street, to the Ravens Club.

"What Scottish whiskey do you have?" Eve shouted to the bartender.

"Glenlivet and Oban," he said, tipping the tap to fill a beer glass and not looking up as Eve considered what to order.

"You're a whiskey drinker now?" Molly elbowed her.

Eve grinned. "I guess I'm missing Scotland." She nodded to the bartender. "Glenlivet with one big rock."

"Fancy," said Melissa. "Chasing after a two-year-old, I can't remember the last time I had a drink."

"I'd be drinking all day if I were home with a toddler," Kate said.

Melissa shot her a glare. "Just you wait. One day, you'll want all this, too."

Kate snorted. "Never gonna happen, my friend." She spent long days in the GM marketing department and was often away on business trips to all points of the globe. Eve couldn't imagine her career-minded friend ever settling down, let alone having children. And maybe that was a good thing. Kate was the least nurturing person she knew. She told it straight, whether you wanted to hear it or not, and liked her late nights and a revolving door of sleepover guests. Eve admired and pitied her equally.

She took the tumbler with amber liquid from the bartender and laid a ten-dollar bill on the bar. "Keep the change."

"Generous," sniffed Melissa, who lived on a tight budget. She ran a tutoring business from home in the odd hours that her daughter napped or her husband was home from the garage where he worked as a mechanic on classic cars.

Molly was the most laid-back among them. She lived in Dexter with her partner, Alice, on a five-acre farm where they grew produce, raised chickens and goats and had cultivated a devoted audience that flocked to their table at local farmers markets.

The whiskey burned her throat and warmed her chest.

Kate grabbed her elbow, turning her away from the bar to survey the crowd. Clumps of twenty- and thirtysomethings stood around high-tops or milled in the middle of the room. There were a few square tables in the center, and booths lined the far wall. "Who looks good?"

"I'm not interested in hooking up."

"You've got to shake off this funk," Kate proclaimed.

Molly shook her head, and Melissa gasped.

"Since when did you two get so prudish?" Kate barked. "We've all been there." She nodded, pointing at each of her friends in turn. "Just because you're old and boring and married now doesn't mean you can forget all our crazy escapades!"

Her voice rose when Melissa crossed her arms and pouted. "Don't give me that. Remember how you met Charlie, Mel? I mean, you might be stodgy parents now, but you used to be fun and racy like the rest of us."

"Not me," Molly said. "I've been with Alice for a decade."

"Yeah, and even that was crazy when it started," Kate said. "You slept with her the night you met and moved in together after a hot minute."

Molly's eyes narrowed, but she smirked. "Fair," she said, sipping her Jack and Coke.

"You've become the friend group archivist," Eve joked. "I guess we all need to watch what we say and do, for fear of Kate chronicling it for future use."

There were plenty of cute guys in the bar. Behind the din of chatter, Bruno Mars and The Weeknd played from speakers high up on the wall.

After the recent call with Mac, she'd been missing him more. In a way, the call gave her hope, but what could really happen from this far away? The lawyer's letter cemented the distance. She should move on. Maybe they'd find a way back to each other in time, after the heat of this moment blew over. But she couldn't wait for that.

"Okay, who are we eyeing?" she said, gulping the last of the whiskey.

"That's my girl!" Kate proclaimed.

"That guy?" Melissa pointed at a tall man with thick red hair wearing a checked button-down tucked into dark jeans that were rolled at the ankles.

"I've never been one for gingers, but he is cute," Eve said.

"We're going over," Kate said, grabbing her arm and pulling her across the room. The man stood at a high-top with two other guys. Molly and Melissa hung back, watching and snickering.

"Hello." Kate elbowed her way into the trio. "I'm Kate, this is Eve, and you are?"

The guys looked at one another and back to Kate. "Well, hello," said a tall, beefy guy with a blond ponytail. "Pat," he said, extending a hand, which Kate shook.

"James." The redhead smiled and tipped his beer in their direction.

"Paul," said the third guy.

Kate chattered between Paul and Pat, while James turned to Eve. "So your friend's not shy," he chuckled.

"No," Eve laughed, wishing she had something to busy herself with—a drink to nurse, a bowl of peanuts to swipe from.

Instead, she stood awkwardly, looking everywhere but at the man before her, suddenly nervous.

"What do you do?"

"Small talk not your thing?"

James blushed, and Eve immediately regretted her snark. "Sorry. I don't do this often."

"Do what?"

"Meet guys in bars. Make small talk with strangers. Go out in Ann Arbor. Take your pick."

He nodded but didn't respond. The bar was near capacity, and the temperature had risen at least five degrees since they'd arrived. Eve's armpits were sticky inside her sweater. She wanted another whiskey.

"Let's get me a drink," she said, grabbing his hand and pulling him to the bar.

Kate gawped as the pair left, then returned to her three-way conversation. Eve couldn't see where Molly or Melissa had gone. Maybe they'd left.

James followed and paid for her whiskey, then led her to the perimeter of the room, where he leaned in close to be heard above the din. She sipped the burning liquid.

"So are you going to tell me what you do?"

She laughed. "I'm a writer studying to become an archivist."

"What do you write? And what is an archivist?"

The sounds in the bar beat a steady pulse that Eve felt in her body. She gulped the last of the whiskey, then set the glass on a table full of empties.

"I was a journalist before I went to Scotland on a fellowship with the National Archives, and now I'm writing a book about some historical figures from there."

"Wow," James said. He finished his beer and set it beside her empty glass on the table. "Wanna walk outside?"

She nodded and followed him out, shrugging into her coat.

His breath puffed in visible clouds. "My family is Scottish. Carrollton. Not sure what clan, but Scots through and through."

"Of course you are."

"What does that mean?"

"I was in love with a man in Scotland, and it ended, so I came home. Figures I'd meet a guy here who's Scottish."

The night grew darker as they strode away from the downtown. Houses shouldered together on quiet streets, and parked cars lined the curbs. Eve dug her hands into her pockets, fishing for her gloves. The night was growing colder, stars switching on in an inky sky. She slipped the soft wool over her fingers.

"Broken heart?" His shoes scraped the concrete as they walked.

Eve shrugged. "I'll get over it."

They circled back toward Main Street, awash in streetlights and neon restaurant signs. It was quiet, the click of footsteps along concrete punctuating the rush of night air. They settled on a bench three doors down from the bar. Eve inhaled the smoky scent of human sweat, wet pavement and the residual mint of a waning winter.

"Probably not smart of me to get involved with someone nursing a broken heart," James muttered.

"Probably not," Eve joked. "Maybe just a one-night stand?"

A couple of university students skittered by in sweatshirts and leggings. It had been a decade since Eve had had gone without a coat on a cold night. *Older and wiser?* She huffed and hunched into her jacket as she looked at James. The streetlight reflected in his light eyes. Freckles dotted his nose. He had wide lips that suddenly looked kissable. She glanced at his hands—long, strong fingers and perfectly oval nails. He was a nice guy, nice-looking, patient and a good listener. Easy to be with.

"Maybe we can get a coffee?" she suggested.

"Sure." He was a good head taller than her. She caught his eye and lifted a gloved hand from her pocket, snaked it behind his neck and pulled his lips down to hers.

"This just took an interesting turn," James said.

"Shhh." Eve brushed her lips against his and closed her eyes. Soft, satin, light pressure, the salty taste of saliva as his lips pushed against her teeth. She pulled his head closer, pressed her body against his and lifted up on her tiptoes. *Best way to forget is to move forward.* She heard Kate's voice and plinky laughter as she erased the space between them. If only she could close her eyes and see anything other than Mac.

Chapter Thirty-Eight

*E*ve, *March 2015*

"So what do you think?"

Eve gnawed on a fingertip as she watched her father's face. He held the printed manuscript and stared at it. When he looked up, his dark eyes shimmered with unshed tears in the low light of evening.

"It's a powerful and beautiful work, honey. Important. And brave. I'm so proud of you."

He set the manuscript on the table and rubbed her arm. She closed her eyes, breathing in his praise.

"I am so relieved. I've been second-guessing myself."

Sam shook his head. "Every writer does that. Have you sent it to Lucy?"

"First the father, then the agent." She smiled. "You'd be honest, wouldn't you, Daddy? You'd tell me if it's uninteresting or poorly written or boring?"

His gaze was serious as he nodded. "Of course. I wouldn't want you putting out an inferior work and having to bear the onslaught of criticism."

Eve sighed with relief. Night had fallen, and the darkness was a wall outside the wide windows. She could barely make out the outlines of old oaks and thick maples in the yard. Sam drained the last of his tea.

"What are you up to tonight? I know it's just a Tuesday, but we should celebrate!" The hiss of the sink faucet sprayed over his hands. He scrubbed the dishes and stacked them in the drying rack.

"James wants to meet up, but I'm tired."

"You're not into him."

"I miss Mac." She slumped. "I thought being with someone new would make it easier."

"It takes time," he said, drying his hands on a towel.

Lit lamps cast a warm glow over the small space.

"Come to the couch." He waved her away from the kitchen.

He pulled a photo album from under the coffee table and spread it open on his lap.

"You were little when I fell in love with him," Sam said, thumbing through the pages and lingering long enough on each for Eve to scan the images of him and Simon, in full smile, hands locked, arms slung around each other's shoulders. "Whenever I look at these pictures, my stomach clenches and I feel the emptiness of loss. I was a fool to let Simon go back then."

"Oh, Daddy. Look how young you are! How happy."

She fingered a photograph of the two men, foreheads touching, eyes closed. Who had taken that picture? It held all of their love in a tender moment, the complete release into each other's safe embrace. It was the kind of love that came rarely and, when it did, deserved holding on to. She felt sad that he'd let Simon go.

He swiped at the corners of his eyes.

"This kind of love comes along once in a lifetime," he said. "And I let it go. Because I was afraid."

"And you're showing this to me because of my feelings for Mac?"

Sam nodded.

"I didn't realize at the time how deep my love for Simon was. And how rare our connection was. When he moved away, I thought I could move on. But I never really did."

"But you've written letters all these years. And you're back together now," Eve said.

Sam nodded and pulled out a box from a cupboard.

"I've saved them all," he said, sifting through the letters and showing them to Eve. "Over the years, I'd reread them just to hear his voice."

He closed the box and turned to her. "I wasted decades that we could've had together, honey." He laid a hand on her thigh. "Don't be like me."

Eve hugged her father. The warmth from his body radiated into her. He stroked her hair.

"I'm just saying, you can change your mind. Don't be afraid to," he said. "I was. And I'll regret it for the rest of my life. If James isn't the guy, that's okay. And if Mac is, that's okay, too. You've written a gorgeous and important work. But life is not made of professional pursuits alone. They can't define us. And you don't want to live with regrets."

Chapter Thirty-Nine

*M*argaret, 2015

Margaret was furious. The solicitor had sent an email—coward!—saying that the American writer would not back down. The letter had done nothing to push her off, and the book was going forward as planned. The letters she'd dug out of the cave on Conic Hill were firmly ensconced at the Scottish Jewish Archives—the nerve!—out of reach of the family archivist, and no amount of legal muscle or money would change that.

Alex swept into the house after a night away, unexplained. She turned her rage on him.

"The least you could do is pretend to hide your affairs!"

He stared at her, stopping mid-stride in the parlor, where she paced and fumed.

"I wouldn't be off with other women if you showed the least bit of interest in me." His voice was calm, even.

There it was! Proof of what she'd feared, but he was right. She willed her lip not to tremble, her eyes to remain dry. She stopped pacing.

"I didn't think you had it in you," she said, her voice lower. "I've wondered. I didn't know if I wished you to be faithful or to have someone to keep you warm, show you affection."

He stared at her.

"When did you get so cold?" He came closer but didn't touch her, didn't raise a hand, just stared. "I've always wanted you, Margaret, from the day we met. I don't want other women. But I also don't want to be alone. It's you who doesn't want you. And that story has gotten very boring."

She was shaking, whether with rage or sadness, she didn't know. She counted her breaths—one, two, three, four—and watched him. Her husband. The tall, happy-go-lucky pushover of a man she'd married, with his Scottish red hair and jeweled green eyes. Beautiful in his own way, jovial and easy to be around, the complete opposite of her. And, it turned out, he wasn't such a pushover after all.

Suddenly, she didn't want him to be with anyone else. She saw a scene unfolding where she lost everything she'd been fighting to hold on to. Losing it because of how hard she held on. If she kept this up, Alex would leave her one day. Her sense of propriety and entitlement would be her undoing.

He turned to go, but she grabbed his arm.

"Wait."

He stopped and turned, waiting for her words.

"I'm sorry."

His eyes crinkled. "For what?"

"All of it."

Her voice was breaking, and she was doing everything in her power not to collapse.

"I don't know how to protect the family legacy and let myself love you," she said. "It's always been one or the other, and I did what I thought was more important."

"See, that's where you've gone wrong," he said. "Loving me protects the family."

Chapter Forty

*E*ve, 2015

Eve sent the manuscript to Lucy, then fell into bed and slept long and hard through the dark night. Two days later, she had a response, full of exclamation points.

"Love it!! Love it!! Such great writing, such a great story. But I want YOU in this book."

Eve dialed her number.

"I've got a few minutes, so talk fast," Lucy barked.

"What do you mean you want me in the book?"

"I want the story of you finding the letters, you researching the identity of the people, the whole connection with Mac's family—I mean, what are the odds? And then, of course, the dreams. There's nothing about the dreams here, and my God, that's the best part!"

Eve's mouth went dry. *No way. No fucking way.*

"It's not a memoir, Lucy."

"Well, not this version, but it should be. You discovered the story—finding the letters in the cave would make a great scene! What about a mirror trope, parallels—your time in Scotland, the love you found and had to let go of, opposite Shira and

Benjamin's tragic love story? Mirror images of love and loss? Plus, the irony of learning that Mac's family descends from them—I mean, you can't make this stuff up! And breaking up with Mac after you realize the connection to his family—it's too good! I could sell the film rights for that version, easy."

Eve was shaking her head. No way was she making this about her. If Mac didn't hate her now, he surely would if she changed the book. And his family!

"I'm sorry, but no," Eve said calmly.

Inside, she was fuming. She'd written a good book, and she would not sensationalize it just to land a generous deal. The book would become theirs, lose its purpose and, most certainly, its message.

"I hear you, I really do, but I worry an editor won't go for it unless it has some currency." Lucy's voice had softened as she tried to soothe and persuade Eve. "Marketability is essential, and this twist will sell heaps of books. Trust me."

If Lucy knew about the deeper personal connections—Eve's family history, her father's sexual identity—she'd want that, too. Better to keep quiet and hold her ground.

"I'm not looking to write a book about me, and I don't want to betray Mac's privacy," she insisted. "It's done historically or not at all."

There was silence on the phone.

"Well, those are some stark terms," Lucy finally said in a sharp voice. "I'll have to think about it and get back to you."

The line went dead.

Eve's hands were shaking. Was this the end, after all she'd sacrificed? She massaged her face with her hands. *She's not the only agent in the world.*

Out the window, a blue jay hopped along a tree branch. Its tail feathers were a mosaic of blues and blacks and whites, its crest sharp and angled, a perfect balance to its pointed, dark beak. It was one of the most beautiful birds that flitted about their yard. Its white barrel chest pulsed, and Eve imagined its little heart pumping fiercely, keeping the small body going.

Birds followed their instincts, without thought or debate, without reasoning or argument or drama. Humans were supposed to be the most evolved species on the planet, but it was the animals who weren't burdened with worry or despair, depression or fear. They had one purpose—survival—and went about it with meticulous precision because there was no other choice.

The bird lifted off the branch and fluttered away.

Chapter Forty-One

argaret, 2015

Margaret didn't expect Mac to come to breakfast the next Sunday, so she was surprised when he walked in without ceremony and on time. He glanced around, nodded in her direction, filled a plate with food and sat. As she sipped her tea, she noticed a pointed look between him and Emma.

"I have some news," Shona announced, laying her fork and knife across her empty plate. "I'm moving in with Andrew."

Emma didn't look up, evidence that she already knew. Neither Mac nor Collin looked surprised either. Was Margaret the only one not in the know?

"Did he propose?"

Shona winced. "No, Mum, and I don't expect him to. I'm not even sure I want to marry."

Margaret's heart raced. "It's not proper."

"We are just fine without legal or religious acknowledgement of our relationship," her daughter said, green-gold eyes blazing.

"Well, we are not," Margaret said, crunching into her toast.

Across the table, Alex shot her a look. In the aftermath of their conversation the other day, he'd kept his distance, and she'd replayed his words over and over. She wanted to go to him but hadn't been able to. His look right now told her to stand down.

"If you're happy, we're happy, darling," he said, smiling at their daughter.

"Thanks, Dad," Shona said, jumping up and striding to the end of the table to throw her arms around her father's neck. He smiled as she nuzzled close.

"Glad you've found a good lad." He looked across to Margaret, weighing the words before he said them. "I think it's time to invite him for Sunday breakfasts."

The floor fell out from under Margaret. She was losing control of her family, becoming the odd person out. She looked around the table at her four gorgeous bairns—*her* children, dammit!

But they were his, too. She had to repair this rift before it became an irreparable rupture. Alex's steady gaze—stronger, more confident than he'd appeared in a long, long time—told her to get with the program or get out. Her hands shook. She thrust them under the table onto her lap. But even as she seethed, she admired this stronger version of her husband. It reminded her of the man she'd fallen in love with at uni. She needed to figure out how to return to the woman she'd been back then.

"That would be fine," she said in a measured voice, surprising even herself.

Heads whipped around to stare at her. She read disbelief, shock and, finally, relief on their faces. She laid her hands flat on her lap to still the quivering and gain calm. From his seat opposite her along the length of the fine table, Alex smiled and gave a slight nod of approval.

Emma cleared her throat. "I have some news of my own."

Margaret pressed her hands into her thighs to keep still. Mac reached to his sister, patted her shoulder and nodded.

"I'd like to bring someone to Sunday breakfast, too." Emma's voice was slow, hesitant. "Her name is Finlay. We've been seeing each other for over a year."

So that's why Mac had come to breakfast. Moral support for his sister. They'd always been close. Margaret fumed silently. The alliances in this family excluded her and evaded propriety. The nerve! But at the far end of the table, smiling like a beacon, her husband presided over his family like the strong man she'd always wanted him to be. He got up from his chair and went over to their daughter and laid a hand on her shoulder, offer reassuring, accepting words.

"We will love whomever you love," he said as Emma dabbed at her eye, the first time Margaret had seen her daughter break down in a very long time. She got that steely exterior from her mother.

I'm sorry, darling, Margaret thought.

She didn't want her children to be as hard as she'd become. It was a lonely existence, and she was sick of it. She unclenched her fists and breathed deeply.

"I'd like to meet her." The words were so quiet, she wasn't sure she'd spoken them aloud. But when the heads of her family turned in her direction, she knew she had.

"Really, Mum?"

The look on Emma's face was so hopeful and eager. Margaret immediately felt her heart break at how hard she'd been with her children for too many years. And how easy it was to change the tenor of their relationship! Warmth flushed through her.

"Yes, dear." Margaret nodded, her voice soft and encouraging.

Alex looked at her across the distance, his eyes softer than she'd seen them in a long time, his smile genuine.

"Any other big news today? Or is that enough for one Sunday morning?"

When they all shook their heads and smiled, she swallowed the lump in her throat, broke out a feeble smile, stood and strode out of the room before they could see her crack.

CHAPTER FORTY-TWO

*E*ve, 2015

Eve glanced at the red numbers on the nightstand clock. Four twelve. She'd been awake for hours. *Just after nine in Scotland.* Mac would be brewing coffee, burrowing into a thick flannel or corded sweater. He'd be staring out at snow-dotted trees, basking in the sunrise that was slow in coming at this point in the year.

Or maybe he was naked in bed with someone new.

By five, she had given up on trying to sleep. She peeled back the covers, pulled on a pair of blue wool socks and a cardigan sweater over her flannel pajama bottoms and ratty T-shirt and padded into the kitchen. She trod lightly so as not to wake her father.

"Honey?" he called from his bed.

Eve peeked in the slightly open door. "Daddy, go back to sleep. I'm just making coffee."

"At this hour?"

She shrugged. "Couldn't sleep. We'll talk when the sun is up."

He fell back on the pillows as she walked away. By the time the coffee was brewed, he was in the kitchen in his flannel robe and slippers.

"It's the first day of spring," he said. "Why don't we go for a hike?"

Eve looked up and nodded as her father poured steaming coffee into a mug with the words *What Deadline?* painted on its side.

"I discovered a few new trails along the west side of the city," he added.

Hours later, dressed in old jeans, a sweater and hiking boots, she filled a water bottle and waited for her father in the car.

They drove past students huddling into heavy backpacks as they trudged toward libraries and classroom buildings. They passed the heart of the university and the M-14 overpass into the wooded neighborhoods on the other side of the river.

The trails were coming alive after days of steady, cold rain had melted the snow and saturated the ground. Budding trees shadowed their walking as squirrels loped over matted leaves left behind from the fall. Eve squelched into sucking mud, gazing at the treetops. The gulping rush of the river competed with the sounds of swaying trees and birds in conversation. She grabbed her father's arm and pointed at an elegant blue heron in the water. They watched as the magnificent bird spread its wings and lifted into the air, pumping up over the river and away. They smiled at each other.

"This is what I was hoping for," he said.

"You always know what I need."

They resumed walking, their steps snapping sticks on the path, echoing the creatures leaping along the forest floor. The river was high and fast with snow melt, its gray waters mirroring an overcast sky.

The trail was wide enough for them to walk side by side, Sam staking a walking stick into the mud every few feet to gain purchase.

"Fire the agent," he said.

Eve picked up pace to meet his stride.

"Go directly to the editor and see if she wants it," he said. "You have nothing to lose."

"I don't know if you can do that," she said.

A swarm of starlings dipped and soared over the river. The trail wound to a break in the trees, and suddenly they were at the riverbank. They continued alongside the rapid river. The sky a canvas of clouds, five ducks—a brown mama and four fuzzy chicks—wagged along in the current, spinning in an eddy and kicking their way to an alcove of frothing water.

"I'm not in the industry, but I know that you should do the book the way you want it done," he said. They'd been on-trail for an hour and a half, and the sheen of sweat glistened on his nose.

"Thanks, Daddy." She leaned against his chest, and an arm came around her, stroking her hair.

Chapter Forty-Three

*E*ve, 2015

There was no response to her short email to Lucy thanking her for her support and asserting that it was time to part ways. She wasn't surprised. After Lucy had hung up on her, Eve had assumed she was no longer her agent.

She then called Pearl Ashley at KGR, the New York publisher that had dangled a contract with a healthy advance in front of Lucy when she'd brought Eve's proposal. Nervous to contact the curt, middle-aged woman directly, she didn't want to leave a paper trail. When the call went to voicemail, Eve left a brief, vague message. She clicked on the imprint's website and scrolled around until she found Pearl's picture—gray-streaked black hair and pale skin a perfect and formidable contrast to the bright-red lipstick that outlined her full mouth. She epitomized what Eve had imagined about New York publishing people—more comfortable with written words than spoken, assertive and no nonsense, eager to work with the stories that moved them and no patience for those that didn't.

She hoped her father was right in his advice, but she was nervous that going around the agent would blacklist her in the industry. Pearl had liked the premise of the book—without any of Lucy's love-gone-wrong suggestions.

Or so she thought.

But she never returned the call. Instead, Pearl sent an email, nearly as short as the one Eve had sent to Lucy, confirming her worst fears: *I'm sure your book is fantastic, but this isn't how the publishing industry works. We respect the agents we work with too much to work around them, and you should, too.*

Eve burned with shame. She wished she'd trusted her instincts. The hope that had begun to take up residence inside her turned to stone, pressing her down.

***

"It's not over," her father assured her that night at dinner. He slow-poured Guinness into two glasses and waited for the foam to settle before taking a sip.

He'd made rosemary-garlic pizza dough in the morning and left it to rise all day. When he'd returned home from the newspaper, Eve had watched as he'd punched and stretched it flat, spooning tomato sauce over and sprinkling handfuls of shredded cheese and fingerfuls of diced green pepper, mushroom and onion on top. The finished pie was bubbly with a crunchy crust.

"Daddy, I appreciate your support, but I shouldn't have listened to you," she said. "No offense. I knew it wasn't right to go around Lucy. I'm pretty sure I'm blackballed by all the big publishers now. I knifed my agent in the back and went over her head. I didn't play by their rules."

"Why should you?" He wiped the froth from his lip before tearing into a pizza slice. Eve noticed he chewed to the rhythm of the music on the kitchen radio, the local station playing an indie band that squawked more than sang.

"There are many ways to get published," he said, swirling a string of cheese from the slice to his mouth and sucking it off his finger like a young boy. "I'm having a few friends over this weekend for a little dinner party, including Delta McGuinn. You've met her. Publisher at University of Michigan Press. Why don't you tell her about the book?"

Eve shrugged and pulled a slice from the stone in the center of the table. "I have nothing to lose," she said, chomping into the gooey piece. "But I think I'm learning that I need to start trusting my instincts. I need to stand on my own two feet."

Now that she was invited to the party, Eve offered to help prepare. Planning a menu, grocery shopping, chopping, cooking and baking would fill her days. Since she'd blown off James, Eve had avoided Kate, Melissa and Molly, too. They called and texted, inviting her for lunches and dinners and nights out at the bar, but she'd declined all their invitations, focused only on finding a way to publish her book. If she hadn't left Scotland early, she'd be well on her way to an archival career. Busy, interested, not floundering in her childhood home. The home she was about to lose.

The night of the party, the house smelled of smoked meat and sizzling onions.

"This is so much better than if I had cooked," her father laughed, peering into pots and sliding a fork into bubbling dishes to sample the flavors.

Eve shooed her father away. "Easy, Daddy. You'll taste it all when the guests arrive. I made a modern cassoulet; a salad with grapefruit, fennel and hearts of palm; and garlic-thyme fondant potatoes."

"And for dessert ... " She swept her hands toward the refrigerator and opened it wide. "Individual chocolate mousse cups with homemade whipped cream and a single raspberry on each."

His eyes popped. "Literally, no words. Who taught you to cook like this?" He winked at her.

The doorbell dinged, and Eve pointed her father toward the front hall while she untied the apron from her waist, folded it and placed it in a drawer. She turned off the burners and dimmed the kitchen lights.

Voices swelled from the foyer. The closet door slid open and clicked shut as he hung coats.

"Eve, you remember Delta, Calvin and Marty?" Her father's face was flushed. She smiled as she shook hands with each guest. He uncorked a bottle of Cabernet on the maple buffet, pouring the gemmy liquid into goblets. The bottle emptied after the fourth glass, so he opened another and filled the fifth.

The group settled around the table as Eve brought in salad, the platter of potatoes and, finally, a crock with the cassoulet, which she set on a trivet in the center of the table. Her father had arranged the seating, with Delta to Eve's right.

Delta wasn't one to dance around, so minutes into the dinner, she turned to Eve. "I hear you've written a book that I might want to publish?" Delta forked a hefty bite of cassoulet into her mouth as Eve shot her father a look.

"It's a story of aristocratic antisemitism, hidden homosexuality and secrets from British high society," she said.

"Nice elevator pitch," Delta said. Her wide eyes nudged Eve to continue.

"I found letters in a cave near Loch Lomond when I was in Scotland on a fellowship last year," she continued. "Written between Scotland's first Jewish doctor and the wealthy Jewish patron who funded his world travels bringing modern health care to the poor."

Delta scooped food into her mouth as she listened.

"She was married to a Scottish Earl who was secretly gay. Years later, he became Prime Minister, hiding his identity and his liaisons. Meanwhile, she had an affair with the doctor, who fathered at least one of her children."

"You've verified everything?"

Eve nodded. "I was a fellow at the National Archives of Scotland. The collection is open at the Scottish Jewish Archives in Glasgow."

She paused.

"And I've received letters from living descendants demanding that I halt the project, which I take as further verification of its truth."

Delta tilted her head as she thought.

"Why hasn't a publisher scooped this up?" She looked pointedly at Eve as she speared a potato and popped it into her mouth.

Eve sipped some wine.

"Well ... " The word hung between them as she considered how to explain. "I had an agent who brought it to KGR. They wanted it, but my agent insisted that I add my personal story to the book, and I didn't want to."

The skin of her face and neck felt hot. She put down the wineglass and sipped some water.

"Why not?" Delta asked.

"It's a long story," Eve replied. "I fired the agent and went directly to KGR. They were pissed that I went over her head and turned me away."

"As they should be," Delta said. "That was not a cool move."

She cut into a potato, chewed a bite, swallowed, then took another bite.

"I've known your father for decades," she said. "He's a dear friend and a good man. Great writer, too, so you're probably not half-bad. I'm intrigued ... but my gut tells me your agent might've been right."

Eve's stomach clenched.

"Tell me why you didn't want to add your story to the book," Delta said.

"I fell in love in Scotland," Eve said. "As luck would have it, he's a descendant of Shira and Hugh, or Benjamin. It's his family that wants to string me up on legal details and prevent the book from happening."

Delta's smile widened, and her face flushed.

"I love this," she said, draining her glass. "I get why the agent wanted it included. It's too good!"

Eve nodded, feeling the hope that had been bubbling up now draining away. "So you'd want that in the book, too?"

"I mean, yes, but I'm not saying I won't publish it without," Delta said. "I'd have to see the manuscript first."

Eve was back to hope, a seesaw of emotions that left her breathless.

Delta pressed a hand over her forearm. "No promises. We can discuss the details later. Just send me the manuscript."

Eve grinned. She looked to her father at the far end of the table. He smiled in her direction, then winked at Delta.

Chapter Forty-Four

Margaret, 2015

That night, Margaret crept into Alex's room. They'd slept apart for nearly a decade, their rooms connected by a shared closet and matching bathrooms. It had taken a week for her to muster the courage, during which she'd visited the hair salon, had a facial, manicure and pedicure, and whisked into Edinburgh for a shopping spree at her favorite lingerie boutique. In a white satin negligee with thin straps and a curl of lace over her bosom, Margaret had glossed her lips and pinched her cheeks to add color.

Alex was reading on the loveseat. A low guitar hummed from the speaker, his favorite jazz music that she'd long ago told him to play without her. What an idiot she'd been. And how close she was coming to losing everything she cherished!

She tapped at his door and peered into the room. "Knock, knock."

The lights were low, as rain spattered the tall, leaded-glass windows.

"Margaret."

His voice held surprise. He didn't rise, but he put down his book and folded his reading glasses on the side table.

He gazed at her in a way she hadn't seen in a long time—warmly, slowly, his eyes taking their time up and down her body. It sent tingles through her limbs, a lovely surprise.

"I'd like to come in," she said, entering the room and settling on the edge of the bed.

"Sit here." He patted the couch beside him.

She nodded and moved closer.

Alex laughed.

"Why are you nervous to sit with me? Jesus, we've been married for more than thirty years, lass!"

Margaret shook with nerves. It had been so long since they'd shared a bed, since anyone other than a paid masseuse had run their hands over her skin. It shouldn't be so hard to reconnect with one's spouse.

"I've made a real mess of things, haven't I?" It took all her strength to keep her voice even.

He reached a hand over and laid it on her thigh. "You look lovely."

Her whole body warmed under his touch. "What say we forget all that and start anew?"

She smiled as he leaned in to brush his lips along hers.

"Darling, that sounds lovely," he said.

She hesitated before continuing, her heart pounding but wanting to finally let down all the guardrails and come home to herself.

"And from now on," she said, "please call me Mags."

In the days that followed, they were like the young lovers they'd once been, tentatively reaching out, then waiting for responses in kind to prove that their interest was shared, their love deepening. It was better than it had been at uni. Maybe you had to come close to losing everything to see how valuable it all was.

Mags felt lighter each day, catching herself when a judgmental thought fluttered into her mind. Alex stayed home more nights in a row until he was there every night, or if he went out, it was with her at his side. They fell into an even, choreographed dance, and the big house didn't feel quite so echoing and not at all lonely.

She took to calling the children, one at a time, and inquiring about their lives. The first tries were met with voicemail, but she kept at it, and before long, they were answering when they saw her number come up on their phones. And then it wasn't long before they were sharing details from their lives and waiting for her interested response. Margaret wondered why she'd kept her distance for so long, lamented all that she'd missed. But at the same time, Alex reminded her that it was never too late to let love in.

On Sundays, the kids plus two significant others were warmed by the new dynamic between their parents, a thawing of the ice that had covered the family for as long as they could remember. She took to wearing pink and lavender and soft blue sweaters instead of the grays and browns she'd favored over the last many years. She found that she didn't mind Shona and Andrew's unorthodox arrangement quite so much, and she actually liked Finlay and was warming to the idea of her involvement with her daughter. Things were good for a time.

Chapter Forty-Five

*E*ve, *April 2015*

Delta was over the moon about Eve's manuscript and offered a publishing contract within days of reading it.

"I'm going to need all the research so my team can double- and triple-check everything," she said. "It's to protect our own hides. And send the lawyer's letters, too. We'll be on the hook if they have a chance in hell of winning a defamation suit. Which I doubt. But I'll need legal to take a look."

Eve was relieved, elated and excited to finally move forward. "So I don't need to add in anything personal?"

"I'd love it if you did, but it's not a deal-breaker," Delta said. "The only catch is that in your book talks, I want you to mention your personal angle. In whatever way is comfortable for you. It's interesting and timely. Makes the story more cur-rent. You can handle it delicately, and respectfully, but I want some personal details and experiences in your talks. It's a fair compromise. Can you live with that?"

She wouldn't get a better deal. If she said no, it would be over and she'd have wasted a year of her life with nothing to show for it. At least this way she'd have control over how and what to share. She agreed, and Delta whooped for joy.

She wanted to text Mac the good news. She missed him desperately, and telling his family story over and over again would only keep him alive and present in her mind.

And in her heart.

They'd hammer out contract details later, Delta had said. There would be a meager advance and decent royalties, and the press would spearhead a book tour.

"There'll be more interest in the UK," Delta warned. "We'll book some US big cities—New York, Washington, maybe LA, but the bulk of your signings will be in England and Scotland. And we'll be doing a full-scale press campaign, especially to British media. The tabloids will go crazy."

Which meant she could see Mac again.

It would be at least six months before the book launched. What would she do in the meantime? Sam was paying the new owners a rental fee to stay until May, and she had nowhere to go.

That night, over a dinner of lasagna, crusty bread and salad, Eve said, "I'll be busy once the book comes out, but what to do until then? I probably have no chance at archival work after leaving before the fellowship was over."

"Get a job in town to bide your time—coffee shop, Zingerman's—until the book comes out," her father said. "Stay with one of your friends. Or find a short-term rental."

"Doesn't seem fair to take a job for only six months," she said.

"Can your advance hold you?"

She shook her head.

They ate in silence for a while.

"I've been wondering, Daddy—do you think my grandparents miss me?"

He'd taken a bite of food but froze at the question, his eyes a blank question. He coughed and gulped water before answering.

"Where's this coming from?"

"This book is all about family, even a messed-up one with secrets," she said. "Mac and I broke up because of his family. You have Simon. And I'm all alone."

He looked at her with concern, his brow bent and his eyes serious.

"I'm just saying, I've lost the love of my life because of family ties, and I don't have any of my own."

"Let's clean up and sit outside and talk about it," Sam said.

Later, when the dishwasher hummed and the food was packed into containers in the fridge, they sat on the deck, holding glasses of wine. Night draped the trees in a cloak of progressive darkness, lavenders and dusky pinks descending into periwinkle and navy hues. The sky glittered with stars.

"If I couldn't be with you, honey, I'd think about you every day," Sam said. "It's been so long since I've known my family, but I'm sure your grandparents think about you."

"I want to meet them," she said. "I have a right to know them."

He closed his eyes, the cool night air steadying his racing heart.

"Yes, you do," he said.

Chapter Forty-Six

Sam, May 2015

On the first of May, three days before Sam was to leave for New York, they set out for his parents' home in Oak Park, a Detroit suburb with post-war houses made of brick and built shoulder-to-shoulder.

Bayla and Shlomo Waldman had lived in the same 900-square-foot home for fifty years. They'd moved in when Sam was a year old and Bayla was pregnant with Bracha. In typical Orthodox fashion, the couple had married young—Bayla was eighteen to Shlomo's twenty—and the house was a gift from Shlomo's parents, a formidable and respected Hassidic couple whose surviving relations had emigrated to America after the Holocaust. Shlomo's father, Rabbi Shmuel Gavriel Waldman, had led a German yeshiva before the war and was a rare rabbinic leader who saw the danger of the Nazis and vowed to resist. Most of his brethren ignored the signs, and his warnings, while Rav Shmuel gathered his family and fled before the war broke out in earnest, committing his energies to the resistance and hiding his wife and nine children in a forest until the war ended. They were not without scars, but they were alive, and the family gained access to America thanks to a cousin who had emigrated earlier and sponsored their arrival. That cousin had settled in Detroit, so the Waldman clan followed suit.

Rav Shmuel was a matchless leader ahead of his time, seeing the wisdom in not entirely isolating from the modern world. He was steadfast in his commitment to a Torah-observant life, but he didn't shun his more secular brethren who comprised the majority of American Jewry. He had an almost entrepreneurial consideration of the long-term. Many of his children went into professions of medicine, law and business, guided by their faithful father to choose a path that would shore them up in case a calamitous future repeated the dangers of the past. The youngest son, Shlomo, followed in his father's footsteps, devoted to yeshiva and attaining ordination to lead a community of Torah-dedicated Jews, believing immersion in religious study was the best and only way to ensure continuity of the Jewish people.

Named in memory of his paternal grandfather, Sam could not remember a time when his gray-faced father looked different. His scraggly beard and thinning hair matched the pallor of his skin, giving him the air of a wizened and feared scholar. His black suit, black hat and white button-down were the uniform of the Hassidim, the white fringes of his *tzitzit* swinging at his hips, his scuffed black shoes and rough-bitten nails the only evidence that anything weighed on the stalwart man with a gruff voice that had inspired fear in Sam's childhood friends and neighbors.

In contrast, his mother was quiet and smelled like sugar. A large, shapeless woman, Bayla Waldman wore waistless dresses in blue, black and gray and opaque stockings with sturdy shoes. Her hair was always covered in public by a stiff brown wig. Sam had never seen his mother bare-headed, not even as a boy. In the house, she traded the wig for a snood that covered her ears, lest wisps of hair escape. But while his mother's appearance was formidable, her personality was soft and loving. Sam could remember many a hug pressed into his mother's chest, her sturdy arms holding him in a tight and reassuring embrace.

He had loved his mother and feared his father, which was what Sam had been raised to believe was how a family operated. His father's stern reprimands, which sometimes became physical via a cracked leather belt kept in the front hall closet to keep the kids obedient, were a great contrast to his mother's even voice, which never rose in anger or frustration.

The Waldman clan consisted of Sam—the estranged eldest son—a diminutive faithful daughter and three rigid, religious sons—Moshe, Eliezer and Yoel. One of Sam's brothers lived in Lakewood, New Jersey, a bastion of American Orthodoxy, the other in Boro Park, Brooklyn, and the third in a religious suburb of Chicago. All of his siblings had big families; his sister lived on the same street as their parents, with her brood of twelve in a similarly small house. Sam was the only one who had left the fold, and he was sure he hadn't been missed. He wondered if his nieces and nephews even knew he existed, and he had no plans to contact his New York-based brother when he moved in with Simon.

Sam was explaining all the limbs of his family tree as he and Eve careened along M-14 to I-696 to the Greenfield Road exit that would take them to the world he had never looked back on.

The closer the car drew to the insular enclave, the slower Sam drove, until Eve said, "You have to go at least the speed limit, Daddy, or you'll get a ticket for disrupting traffic." She laughed lightly.

Sam's knuckles whitened as he gripped the steering wheel of the old Volvo.

Seeming to sense his distress, she stopped laughing and laid a hand on his shoulder.

"It'll be fine," she said. "They can't take me from you."

He huffed and nodded. "I don't know what I'm nervous about. Just sick at the thought of seeing my father. He was not a kind man."

Off the highway, Sam turned into the neighborhood and drove slowly, memories washing over him. Where once there had been boys wearing black yarmulkes and prayer fringes swinging as they ran and played in the yards and girls in long-sleeved flowery dresses puffing in the wind, now there was a mix of residents. Oak Park had become a hipster haven, with young, upwardly mobile couples paying top dollar for old abodes that needed a lot of love. He couldn't imagine why they'd want to live here. Some driveways were crammed with pickups and VW bugs rusting at the corners, while others featured extended vans to accommodate all the children of a religious family. He saw tattooed twentysomethings with long hair and baggy jeans playing with toddlers and teenage girls sunning themselves in bikinis.

"My father must hate this." He laughed.

"Hate what?" Eve didn't see anything unusual, which reassured him that he'd made the right decision to leave and raise her in an open-minded, accepting community.

He parked on the street in front of his childhood home. The black paint on the shutters had faded to gray. His father wasn't one for repairs. He'd hire some unsuspecting young man, likely African-American or Hispanic, pay less than minimum wage, and then harp on the guy to finish the job faster than humanly possible. Sam's father had never known how to live in a non-Jewish world.

"Here we go," he muttered as Eve slipped her hand into his.

The door opened before they stepped onto the small porch. Bayla pushed open the screen and smiled.

"My boy!" she said, engulfing Sam in a hug. She peered over his shoulder at Eve. "And you! You're so grown. What a beautiful girl." She cupped Eve's face with her soft, doughy hands. "*Shayna meydl*," she muttered in Yiddish—*pretty girl*, Sam knew—tears shining in her eyes.

"Come, come." She waved them inside.

Sam's chest vibrated and his hands shook, but Eve was all comfort and ease as she swept into the house. The door opened onto a small slate foyer that led to a carpeted living room with a varnished oak table covered in plastic and surrounded by upholstered chairs whose seats were faded and worn from use. A sagging gray couch backed to the window beside a small table with a single lamp. In the corner, a glass cabinet showcased a magnificent silver kiddush cup that poured like a fountain into a dozen thumb-sized cups. There were other ritual items, too: a gleaming silver menorah, a metal box to hold an etrog—or citron fruit—on Sukkot, his mother's silver candelabra. And on the very top shelf, framed photographs of the Waldman children at various stages of their lives—the five siblings young and smiling, them as poised, serious teenagers and then four tall frames bearing the wedding portraits of Bracha, Moshe, Eliezer and Yoel. *At least they kept some evidence that I exist,* Sam thought, gazing at the images from his childhood. His wedding portrait was not displayed with the others. After his teen years, he had simply been erased.

The gray-white walls were bare, except for one photograph of the family as it was today. Women in dark dresses and tights sat on one side, and men in black suits and black hats were on the other. The men didn't smile, but the women did, and they were arranged so no unrelated men or women came into physical contact. Sam could not imagine how long it had taken the photographer to get everyone together in a modest fashion and snap the picture before the children wilted into tears or ran off to play. Including the spouses of grandchildren already married, the family totaled sixty-two at the time the photograph was taken, according to the quick math in his head.

"From Estee's wedding," his mother said, coming up behind him. "Bracha's oldest."

She waved them over to the couch.

"Come, sit!"

Eve sank into it, hunched by the way the cushions sucked her down.

Bayla squeezed her leg. "I've missed so much! Are you married?"

Eve laughed. "I'm in no rush," she said.

"Rush? You're thirty-one. I was a mother of five by then," Bayla said.

Sam pulled a chair from the dining table and sat across from Eve.

"It's different in our world, Mama," he said.

Bayla shook her head. "Everyone wants to get married," she said, not meeting her son's eyes.

The door opened as Bracha stepped into the house. She smiled as she straightened her snood.

"Shmueli!" she exclaimed, shuffling toward Sam but not touching him. "It's good to see you."

Her smile was genuine. Sam felt a rush of warmth as he gazed upon his sister. She looked so much older than her forty-eight years. But then, she was a grandmother already, with little ones still at home, too. He smiled feebly, wanting to hug her but knowing she'd recoil at his touch, even though he was her brother. It just wasn't done.

Bracha was petite and bespectacled, and she wore a long-sleeved, striped cotton shirt and soft black skirt to her ankles, her feet in socks and Crocs. Her hands were small and bony, her left ring finger encircled by a simple gold band and her right ring finger encased by a dainty ring with a small stone. She had a kind face and a soft voice, and she hadn't stopped smiling since she arrived.

"This must be my niece," she said, reaching for Eve. Struggling to lift from the sagging couch, Eve wiggled forward until she could press into the floor and stand. Bracha laughed. "You need a new couch, Mama," she said.

Bayla *tch-tched* and swatted at her daughter.

"You're absolutely beautiful," Bracha said, pulling Eve into a firm hug. "It's so good to meet you. Finally!"

Sam watched the exchange, jaw set, eyes steady. He wanted to trust this outpouring of affection, but his stomach flipped every time he heard a sound, bracing for his father's entry. His heart pulsed in his temples, a *ratatat* like a woodpecker at a tree.

"Get a chair from the table, Bracha," Bayla ordered. The dutiful daughter obeyed and sat to her mother's left, in Sam's sight line but at a careful distance.

"Chava was just about to tell me about her life."

"Mama, she goes by Eve," Sam corrected.

Bayla ignored him and kept her gaze on Eve.

But before Eve could speak, Shlomo thundered into the room as if from out of nowhere. He pulled a chair from the dining table to join their circle. He didn't look at Sam; the old man just stared at Eve. His eyes softened at the sight of her.

"Chava, is it really you?"

His voice was quieter by several octaves as he gazed at his granddaughter. Eve's smile was hesitant, showing her nerves.

His father was still formidable, but now Sam could have empathy for the old man, with his rough-bitten fingernails, the skin around them angry-red and flaking. To hack so fiercely at your own skin must mean that the man was besieged by worries and perhaps fear. He'd never thought of his father as a man with insecurities, but this much time away had given him the gift of distance to see him as human.

Still ...

"She goes by Eve." Sam's voice was quieter this time but firm.

Shlomo turned a pointed gaze at him, his eyebrows angling together in a glare.

"Are you still *that way*?" The comment came out in daggered words, little drops of spittle flinging from the old man's pink lips and catching in his frizzy beard. He offered no *hello*, no words of welcome, and in that moment, the budding empathy vanished. Sam breathed steadily through his nose, steeling himself not to respond. But Eve's face reddened, and she stood.

"How dare you!"

Shlomo's gaze whipped back to his granddaughter, startled.

"Isn't it bad enough that this is how Jews have been treated throughout history? It's a *hillul Hashem* to see Jew turn against Jew, father against son," Eve said. "You should be ashamed. My father is kind, generous and loving. He's the best person I know."

She was trembling by the time she finished, and Sam reached out a hand. Bayla and Bracha were stunned into silence, and even the old rabbi was at a loss for words. Eve took a breath and looked at her father. Tears shone in his eyes, and he smiled, proud of her strength.

"How do you know that phrase?" Bracha asked, looking curious and kind.

Eve turned to her.

"Just because we aren't religious doesn't mean I don't know what it means to be Jewish," Eve said.

She turned to Shlomo.

"I'd hoped this would turn out differently," she said. "But I can't stay if you're going to be cruel to my father."

"Eve, wait." Bayla reached for her. "Give us a chance."

A wave of gratitude coursed through Sam's body as he heard his mother use Eve's name properly. *Thank you, Mama,* he thought.

His mother's soft face was ridged with lines along her forehead. There were dark circles under her eyes. Their life was so hard, but of their own making.

"I would really like to," Eve said. "But we are a package deal."

Sam stood by her side, and she took his hand in hers.

"It's both of us or neither of us," she said.

Bayla and Bracha turned to Shlomo for permission, but his jaw was set, his mouth a straight, stern line. There was no give in his expression, no surrender. Eve searched through her purse and pulled out a scrap of paper and a pen. She scribbled something and then handed it to Sam's mother—her grandmother.

"If you change your minds, here's how you can reach me. But I meant what I said. There is no me without my father."

And with that, she headed for the door. As she stepped onto the porch, Sam turned a final glance to his father, offered a soft nod toward his mother and sister and followed his daughter out.

They were on the highway, heading west, before Eve broke the pulsing silence.

"I'm sorry, Daddy."

"For what?"

"For making you go back there."

Sam shook his head. "No apology needed," he said, smiling as he stared at the ribboning road. Cars whizzed past on either side, and Sam's hands were light on the wheel, his body relaxing. He was silent as tears striped his cheeks.

Eve whispered for him to pull off the highway and stop the car.

He headed up an exit ramp, turned into a school lot and parked. He gave in to audible sobs, his head bowed to his chest. Eve threaded an arm over his shoulders.

"No one has ever loved me that much," he said.

"I don't think that's true," Eve said softly.

He smiled, thoughts of Simon filling his head. Soon, they'd be together, forever.

He bent his forehead to hers.

"Sometimes the people we love deserve second chances," he said.

She nodded, and he started to drive again, back onto the highway, heading for home.

Chapter Forty-Seven

Sam, June 2015

When Sam gave his notice at the *Ann Arbor News*, his boss looked sad.

"You're the best reporter I've ever known and a really nice guy," she said. The editor had replaced Mitch and come to rely on Sam as the longest-running reporter in the newsroom. She'd only been there a year and a half.

He smiled and nodded his thanks.

"You're an excellent employee! You could go anywhere with your careful talent and reliable writing," she said. "Are you applying to the *New York Times*?"

Sam blinked to hold back the emotion. Did he stand a chance against younger reporters coming from bigger media markets? Probably not, but he had nothing to lose, so he decided right then to apply for any open position.

***

He approached a variety of smaller outlets in Manhattan, Brooklyn and even Staten Island. He'd take whatever he could get, for the steady income and to help him get to know his new home.

He was more than surprised when the call came from a hiring manager at the *Times*, offering a phone interview for a beat reporter position covering local courts. When that went well, Sam was invited to interview in-person before a panel of three editors. He didn't want to spend the money on a flight at such short notice, so he drove the ten hours east to New York. Simon didn't want to ruin the surprise of their new home—he'd already moved out of his studio—so they sprang for a Midtown hotel. Sam aced the interview—the editors loved his Midwest humility and made an offer on the spot.

He couldn't quite believe this was his life.

***

Eve, June 2015

The galleys arrived on a Tuesday with a handwritten note from Delta asking to meet. Eve texted her a thumbs-up and a party hat emoji and the words *Meet Friday?* Delta's response came in less than a minute—laughing face emoji and the words *Take at least a week.*

Eve spent the bulk of the day marking the pages with pencil, adding notes in the margins where she spotted an error or reconsidered a sentence. She drank copious amounts of ginger-lemon tea out of a travel mug for fear of spilling on the manuscript. To hold her first book in her hands! It was a wonder and a delight, and her stomach tumbled with excitement.

She texted a photo of the galleys to her father in New York, who responded with a *Yay!* and a heart that made her smile but feel lonelier than ever. She was staying at Kate's house, which was empty most days while her friend traveled.

When she was in town, Kate dragged Eve out. *"You've been avoiding us for months,"* she insisted. *"This is the only way to be redeemed."*

"I know, I'm sorry," Eve said.

That night, as she dried her hair and debated between a silk top and fitted jeans or an emerald-green tank and tailored white pants, her phone pinged. She glanced at the screen, but when she saw who it was, she dropped the dryer on the counter, cracking the edge of the cone and sending it scudding across the floor, the whoosh of hot air like a jet stream.

"Shit," she muttered, picking it up and setting it on the counter.

It was a message from Mac. A long message. A surprising, unexpected, delightful message.

All I do is think of you, and I've been afraid to write, to call, to text, to do anything, for so long. All I want is you and me together. I've tried to move on. To get over you. But I can't. Can you?

A thrill coursed through her as she scrolled.

Things are different here now. Give me another chance! I miss you. I LOVE you. Please. Come back to me.

She stared at the screen, reading and rereading the words. All she'd wanted for months, and now, she didn't trust it. What had changed? Mac's mother had to resent her. She shook her head as the words swam into floating letters.

She'd had enough of family rejections. Her fury over the visit with her father's relatives had cooled but not entirely disappeared. She'd only discussed it once with her father.

"Honey, I made my peace long ago about who my family are," Sam had said. "We can't change who people are, and we shouldn't try. It's their problem. They've missed out on a life with me."

It had felt like a punch to the gut, she thought. She still couldn't get over how absolutely her grandfather could reject his son.

"How did you know how to be such a good father with no role model?" she'd asked her father. "You're so loving. So accepting."

He had shrugged. "I don't know," he'd said. "One step and then another, I guess. Maybe I poured into you all the love I never got, all the love I wanted. Or maybe I just did the opposite of what was done to me." He'd chuckled.

As crickets chirped in the summer night, his arms had come around her and pressed her close, the still, slow wind caressing their skin.

Then they'd gone into the house, and her father had ordered a pizza heaped with all kinds of meat just for the sake of eating the most non-kosher food he could think of. They'd eaten it on the couch while watching a movie, strings of melty cheese trailing from their mouths to their fingers. He'd left days later for New York.

Since then, she'd buried her disappointment over her grandparents' behavior but never resolved it. Now, reading Mac's text, it bubbled to the surface with great force.

He had his chance! she railed, returning to the hair dryer, seething with misplaced anger.

The voice in her head was suddenly two voices, arguing. The second one, laced with longing, pleaded with the first. *But you love him. You tried to move on with James. You tried to distract yourself with the book. You fled to another continent. He never says something he doesn't mean. Do you really want to miss this chance?*

The voices volleyed back and forth until her hair was done, her makeup perfect, her bare shoulders warm in the closeness of the bathroom. She tapped on the message, read it once more, and then shoved her phone into her pocket. *I'll respond later,* she vowed. *When I have the right words.*

She and Kate met up with Melissa and Molly at the Roadhouse, ordered heaps of cheesy, meaty, bready foods to share across the table plus tall cold glasses of dark beer. Later, they traipsed along Main Street, kicking back shots, laughing loud and long, and Eve forgot about Mac and his text and everything that had weighed on her for months.

It was in that fog of Friday night fun that she stumbled into James. He held a glass of pale beer and stood in a semicircle of men wearing polo shirts and jeans who were taking turns spearing a board with darts. He leaned against a stool but didn't sit. The noise of the bar hummed around them. She wanted to prove to herself that she could live without Mac.

"I'm going over," Eve announced, and her friends followed her gaze.

When they saw James, they shook their heads.

"No, you can't. It's not nice," said Melissa, gripping Eve's wrist to hold her back. "The poor guy was so into you, and you blew him off. Don't play with him."

Kate pursed her lips and watched the exchange. Eve turned to her, begging for an ally. "You agree with me, right?"

Kate shrugged and bit back a smile. "I don't know, babe. Melissa's got a point."

Eve glared at her, and Kate threw up her hands. "But, I mean, he's a grown man, right?" she said.

Melissa scowled at Kate, shooting daggers. Kate looked chagrined, and Melissa rolled her eyes.

"It's not that big a deal," Molly chirped. "Hook up or don't—it doesn't require conversation. And you don't need our permission." She patted Eve's arm.

"Alright, then," Eve said, setting her beer on the bar and wiping her hands on her pants. "Wish me luck."

The walk to James wasn't far, but it felt like ages to get to him, pushing through sweaty, warm bodies. The bar doors were propped open to let in some air, though it was so still with late-day heat that it didn't make a difference.

"Hey," she said when she reached him.

James nodded but didn't smile. He gulped his beer. "She emerges from the dark tunnel of no contact," he muttered.

"I deserve that," she said, hovering a hand over his arm then letting it land. "I'm sorry."

He nodded and took another swig. Glancing behind her, he spotted Eve's friends and lifted his chin in acknowledgement. They smiled a little too big and waved.

"Can I buy you a beer as an apology?"

He ran his tongue over his lips, drained the glass and plopped it on the high-top behind him. "Sure," he said.

She returned with two sweating bottles, an IPA for him and an amber for her. They sipped in silence, the heat and the din pulsing around them.

"Listen, I really am sorry," she said. How had she missed how hot he was? Sure she was a little drunk—maybe more than a little. Drunk enough to forget that James's attractiveness hadn't been the issue.

"I didn't realize how much I was still reeling from my breakup," she said. "I needed time to heal. I should've seen that."

James was nodding, drinking his beer, his eyes trailing around the bar.

"I understand," he said. He wasn't making it easy for her, which inspired her to want him more. She admired the soft skin of his face, the strong slope of his shoulders.

"The thing is, I don't want complicated, and I don't play games," he said. "A woman either wants me or she doesn't. I don't chase anyone."

He gulped the rest of the beer, placing the empty bottle on the high-top.

She moved closer. The noise of the bar blurred into a low hum. She could hear nothing except the flow of his breath.

Pressing onto her toes to reach his ear, she whispered, "Take me home."

He nodded and took her beer, placing it next to his empty glass, and aligned his fingers against her spine, directing her through the mass of pulsing bodies and the still dank heat of the overcrowded bar to the open doors and out into the night where the air was no cooler but freer. They walked without speaking down Main Street to the corner then south three blocks down and three blocks over until they reached his place.

They weren't even inside before he bent to kiss her bare shoulder. No one on the street, no sound from the sleeping houses on either side of the little house where he lived alone.

The house was quiet and still, and they moved through it, feeling their way in the dark, not flicking lights on, only feeling for the harsh corners of furniture, their bodies pressed together in urgent need. He was minty with a whiff of cologne and good soap. His hands were firm and pressing to awaken her, and it was working. Her nerves were on fire, electric currents blazing as her hands held on to him like a life preserver as he pulled her through the rooms to his bed, where they let go of the floor and closed their eyes and fell into the abyss that had been pulling them the whole way home.

Eve had always wondered how a one-night stand could be so fulfilling. You didn't know the person or their body, and they didn't know you, so how could the chemistry be so good? When she was younger, she'd hooked up with guys and enjoyed the spontaneous coupling so much that she returned for a repeat, and it was never as good the second time around. James was masterful, and she submitted to his direction, let him take charge, laid back and surrendered. It felt wondrous to not be in control, even for just a few hours.

By morning, she was numb and tired, every point on her body dulled in the aftermath of their intensity. She felt like she could sleep for days. But, waking in an unfamiliar bed, beside a tousled red-haired man with whom she had no intention of falling in love, Eve gathered her things and crept outside. It was only six, though the sun was bright. It was a long walk home, but Eve took her time, shaking off the fuzz of a hangover. The town and the campus were still asleep, the only movements the skittering of squirrels, the only sounds the tinny cheeps of birds.

She felt sad. And empty. The night had been fun and the sex good, but she didn't want him, and she felt the crush of leading on a good man in a most unkind way. Though he probably knew this would be just one night and nothing more. He'd known what he was walking into, as Kate had said.

The sky clouded over, and the light turned to gray. She thought of Mac's pleading text, and her heart leapt. Just thinking of him, even after all this time, sent tingles through her body. She'd respond eventually—when she figured out what to say. She knew beyond a doubt now that the only man for her was in a little Scottish town across the ocean.

***

The week passed slowly, as Eve scanned the galleys again and again, spotting new errors or typos or places to add a detail or a sentence. Finally, she took the marked-up pages to Delta's office and sat in a plush, hard-backed chair across from her editor.

"You've taken this very seriously," Delta laughed as she glanced at the marked-up pages. "Bravo on such thorough edits! I wish all my writers were like you." She sat back in her chair.

"Let's talk timeline. I want a February pub date to launch a tour of signings and talks."

Delta's eyes were serious. "The British press is going to love this! The Monteiths will not. But we'll weather it. Those stuffy aristocrats can put their objections where the sun don't shine."

Eve rubbed her hands together. She was suddenly and inexplicably cold.

"What's happening here?" Delta pointed to her hands.

Eve shook her head. "I'm nervous to go back."

"Because of him? The Monteith kid?"

She nodded.

"You're going back as a successful author with an explosive book. You're not going back to him. You might not even see him."

Eve shook her head. "Scotland is a small place. I'll see him. He wants me back—but what if now, with this book, he changes his mind?"

Delta shrugged. "Too late to worry," she said. "And I can't be concerned with your love life, no offense. This is what you wanted. And you're not going to fuck up your career or mine. This book does well, who knows what comes next for you."

Eve shrank into her chair. She was thirty-one-years-old, and it was time to grow up. She was embarrassed. Delta was right.

"So, the book tour ... " Delta coughed to bring them back to their earlier conversation. "You're going to be cool with all these UK gigs, and you're going to make me a boatload of money and raise the profile of the University of Michigan Press, and then we'll talk about your next book when you're back." She winked. "If you come back."

Eve smirked. "I'm coming back."

"We'll see," Delta said with a smile.

Chapter Forty-Eight

Eve, February 2016

When the book was ready for launch, Delta had booked Eve at the 92nd Street Y, along with a New York bookstore, two universities and three synagogues in the greater metropolitan area. The *New York Times* had requested an interview as *Family Secrets* shot up the bestseller list—a first for a University of Michigan Press title—and it was on the short list for a few awards.

Eve inhaled the scent of wet pavement, a surge of energy coursing through her. People walked briskly up and down the sidewalks. She loved the aliveness of the city, the purposeful gait of so many people standing tall, eyes forward. There was so much motion all the time—traffic in both directions, lights blinking green, yellow, red, streams of people walking in all weather. People waiting on subway platforms and for buses, eyes buried in books or glued to phone screens or lost in thought or the music pulsing through their headphones.

To be here on a book tour, with interviews at *Good Morning America* and the *New York Times*, well, Eve was riding high on the adrenaline of seeing her story resonate with so many people in unexpected ways. As uncomfortable as it was to see antisemitism on center stage in America during the presidential campaigns now gaining momentum, it proved to be perfect timing for Eve's book to be a counterpoint to the running big-oted commentary of the extremist far-right. That had been the angle the *GMA* anchors had taken when they invited her on. "Give us a context for historical antisemitism," their booker had urged the press's publicist.

She felt like a bit of a fraud, presenting herself as some sort of expert on historical antisemitism, but she'd spent the better part of a year researching the British history of it and was fairly well-versed in the Levenson, Monteith and Belzer clans. With more than two dozen talks under her belt and equally as many media interviews, the big-picture impacts now rolled off her tongue with ease. She even gave a historical perspective on how a rise in antisemitism usually forecast turmoil in society, the economy, even the world.

After a full day of interviews, Eve caught the subway for Brooklyn. The sounds of the city faded as the reverberating echoes of the subway tunnels took over, the slap of footsteps and turnstile clicks echoing against the cool walls. A train screamed through and stopped, its doors banging open and people streaming in and out. The tracks were damp and dark.

It was nearing five when she arrived at her father's brown-stone and let herself in with the key he'd given her. "I want you to feel like this is your home, too," he'd said. She'd nodded and smiled, but although she'd gone to college there, New York would never be her home. Eve wondered where home was at this point. She needed a place that felt like hers, a place where she belonged.

Inside, the house gleamed. Her father was fastidious, and Simon was so in love that he went along with her father's demands to keep the place spotless. Eve smiled, knowing that when the novelty of their renewed relationship dimmed, Simon would likely revert to his less-exacting ways, and her father might face his first real hurdle. Her father channeled the rigidity of his upbringing into a maniacal urge to clean, a rather acceptable outlet, she felt. But they'd overcome whatever challenges came their way. She just knew it. They'd waited a long time to come together, and neither of them would let anything threaten their long-term happiness.

They'd done a great job of renovating the brownstone. The entryway shone with a black-and-white large-square tile floor and snow-white walls with detailed crown moldings. An antique mahogany table with brass drawer handles stood beneath an oval mirror with a gilded brass frame, which magnified the space. Sam kept a potted orchid on the tabletop, with a slim, sensual neck and elegant magenta petals.

"I'm home!" she called.

"In here!"

The scent of meat, tomatoes, cinnamon and coriander drifted from the kitchen. Eve hung her coat in the closet and slipped off her shoes, leaving them on the mat by the door.

Her father stood over the stove, wooden spoon in hand, an apron tied around his torso with the words *Kiss the Cook* in block letters. She planted a kiss on his unshaven cheek, running her fingers over the stubble. "That's not like you."

He blushed and swatted her fingers away. "Simon likes it." His cheeks went from pink to beet to wine.

Eve peered into the pot. "Smells delicious." In the oven, fingerling potatoes were softening on a baking sheet, drizzled in olive oil and sprinkled with fresh rosemary. An uncorked bottle of Cabernet sat on the counter with a half-filled glass beside it that her father was sipping from. He rested the spoon on a folded towel and pulled another glass from a glass-fronted cupboard.

"Want some?"

Eve nodded and perched on a stool at the island. "What's the occasion?"

"You're here, and we're together." He stirred the contents of the pot—meat so tender it was breaking into shreds, carrots, onions and celery in soft chunks, bubbling in the fragrant sauce.

"Where's Simon?"

Her father covered the pot and wiped his hands on a towel. Violin strings sailed from a speaker on the counter. He took a swig of wine and licked his lips.

"He wanted little cakes for dessert, so he went to the bakery to pick some up as a treat for you," he said.

"Aw, that's sweet," she said.

The room was awash with the last fringes of daylight. Soft pendant lights hung delicately over the island, and the bulbs on the intricate glass fixture over the table were soft, too. Eve opened the sheer white drapes framing the window to let in the remaining natural light and went to a cupboard to pull out plates so she could set the table.

"Thanks," her father said, pulling utensils from a drawer. "The cloth napkins are over there."

He pointed to a drawer by the desk built into the far wall. Even that was neat—papers tucked into compartments of a wooden organizer or tacked to a linen pinboard. A mid-century modern dark wood chair with an oval leather seat was tucked into the desk. Everything in its place. Her father, included.

By the time Simon returned, the potatoes were soft and crispy, and her father had scraped them into a bowl. The stew steamed in a lidded tureen, and their wineglasses were topped off.

"You started without me?" Simon chuckled, opening a new bottle and pouring himself a glass. A white box tied with string sat on the counter. Eve tried to peek inside, but Simon swatted her away. "Let the anticipation build." His eyes sparkled as he smiled.

Eve liked him. His sandy hair was gray-streaked, his green eyes glimmered, and he was tall and lean, soft-spoken and friendly. He'd secured a position managing an off-Broadway theater and seemed to hover above the ground when Sam was near. She liked the man and loved what he brought out in her father.

The chemistry between the men pulsed like a live wire. They had an unspoken language of familiarity that she'd never seen her father exhibit with anyone.

Sam lifted the lid from the tureen and stuck a ladle into the stew. "Dig in!" he said, smiling.

Simon rubbed his hands, his eyebrows lifting with delight. He reached for Eve's plate and scooped some stew for her.

"Thanks," she chirped as he handed it back and then served Sam then himself.

They passed the bowl of potatoes around, and everyone took some. On her plate, the stew bled into the potatoes, the sauce flavoring the soft flesh.

The night before, Eve and Simon had settled into the soft, white living room couch with mugs of beer and fresh-baked shortbread cookies on the table, a fire licking at logs in the stone fireplace. Her father had gone to bed early, tired from a long day accompanying Eve to two media interviews and an evening talk that went late, but Eve had been wired. Simon had grilled her about the book, her tour and, of course, Mac.

"Tell me again why things ended," he prompted.

Eve shrugged. "Honestly, it seemed like there was no other choice at the time. You know how, in the moment, everything seems bigger than it is? I thought I was doing the right thing. Preventing future heartache."

"Yeah…"

She continued. "I believed that he'd resent me for distancing him from his family with this book, and I didn't want to abandon my book project. It felt so 1950s misogyny, a woman choosing a man over a career. And then his mother was threatening lawsuits, and I wanted to fight with everything I had. Can you imagine her as my mother-in-law?"

Simon chewed at his lip.

"What?"

"Nothing is ever as important as we think it is, honey," he said, crunching into a cookie.

She took a sip of beer, sweet and tangy, a pecan-infused brew from the South, then told him about Mac's text that she'd never answered.

"Well, you're a complete fool," Simon said. "It's like you're out to sabotage your own happiness."

He chuckled.

"What?"

"The apple doesn't fall far."

"You think I'm like my father?"

Simon nodded.

She froze, her heart stalling in her chest. And suddenly everything became clear. "I should call him," she said.

Simon was nodding. "You should've called him ages ago."

But she hadn't. Instead, she'd lain awake, staring at the ceiling and pondering how to reach out to Mac, how to repair all the damage she'd done. It had been months—months!—since he'd reached out and bared his heart to her in that text. And he'd been met with silence.

Eve snapped back to the moment, to the warm kitchen and the stained plates now empty of food. To the laughter and the grins and the beating hearts. She gulped back a lump in her throat.

"Daddy," she croaked. "I'm so sorry."

"For what?"

Her lip shook. "For keeping you from this love," she said, choking on the words. She swept her hand around the room. "You could've had a partner, not been alone all those years when I was little. Even after I was grown and gone to college and in my own career. I should've seen it, should've encouraged you to go after your heart. I'm so, so sorry."

Sam slid back his chair and, in three quick strides, loped to the other side of the table. He pulled her to him.

"It's not your fault, and it's not your responsibility," he said. "I made my choices when you were little, and I was happy enough then, I promise you. If anything, you gave me my freedom."

Simon watched them, his eyes soft.

"I have only myself to blame for not coming to Simon sooner," her father said.

She nodded. "I'm nervous to go to Scotland."

"Of course you are."

Simon sighed. "Oh, the drama in this family!" he exclaimed, laughing.

They looked at him and burst into laughter.

She told her father about Mac's text and her lack of response. Before he could respond, Simon jumped in.

"Girl, you still haven't responded, after we discussed it last night?"

His gaze pierced into Eve.

"I'm an idiot," she said. "It's probably too late."

It was quiet in the kitchen, their even breathing like a soft wind in a still space. The music on the speaker had moved to a lone wail of a trumpet and the plink of piano keys. Simon and Sam shared a knowing look.

"It's never too late," Simon said.

"Don't waste any more time," her father said.

She nodded as a memory jumped to mind, of Mac in her little cottage on a cold night, a fire crackling in the hearth, and her in thick socks and sweatpants, his beating heart a soothing rhythm in her ear. She could almost smell him. She thought of how hard it must've been for him to send that text and how brazenly she'd ignored it.

Chapter Forty-Nine

Mac, April 2016

The drive to Sukkat Shalom took an hour and a half in the half-light of early spring. Mac had given his Friday night shift to an eager manager, allowing him to sleep in that day and chill after a busy week, so by the time he set off for the city, he was full of pent-up energy. Nerves, too.

What would it be like? If only Eve were there to shepherd him through. He'd avoided church services like the plague whenever his mother urged him to attend with the family, and he'd never stepped foot in a synagogue. But he was curious. Especially after she'd revealed his family's Jewish ancestry and left him to tell that story. He'd tried to win her back from afar, but without a response, he felt adrift. What *was* he doing running a pub in the Highlands? Was there no greater purpose for his life? It was time to figure out who he was and who he wanted to be. And if Eve wasn't there to share his life, he'd figure out how to make it meaningful without her.

The falling night played tricks on the road, casting shadows and highlighting odd patches of asphalt. Mac drove carefully, if not slowly, until he hit the A905. He was used to the narrow, dark country roads that wound through the trees, but his somersaulting stomach made the drive seem longer. Why was he so nervous? He didn't have to go, and he didn't have to stay. No one knew he was checking it out. There was nothing riding on this, no one waiting at home for his eager response. Even if he liked it, he didn't have to do anything more. It could be a one-and-done experience in a lifetime of experiences. So why did it feel monumental?

He wedged the car into a streetside spot and parked, then killed the ignition. The night was cold, the streets lined in a fur of snow. Edinburgh was aglow in streetlights. Even the silence seemed alive. The city crawled with people scurrying by, huddled into their coats. The air felt heavy with foreshadowing. He thrust his hands into the pockets of his down coat and strode toward the door of the nondescript building with a small metal plaque nailed to the frame that read Sukkat Shalom. The congregation had graduated from a rented university space to its own home in the tight city.

Pushing the door open, Mac stepped into a warm, low-lit space. The service was set to begin at six, and he had arrived just minutes before.

He hadn't told anyone that he was doing this. His mother may have softened and started taking an interest in his life, but he still didn't know what to expect from her. As the favorite child, he could get away with a lot, but he didn't want to push his luck. Exploring the Judaism of his ancestors was a whole different thing.

In the year since he'd lost Eve, Mac had replayed their parting words again and again. He loved his family, for all their quirks and complaints, but he loved Eve more than anyone he'd ever known. Why had he let her go? Why had he waited so long to reach out to her? And why hadn't she responded? Had she moved on, found someone else?

The first months after their breakup had him feeling sorry for himself and pouring his energies into work. He'd hooked up with a few pub patrons—mostly Americans on vacation because they'd fallen in love with *Outlander* and booked silly tours through the Highlands to map out Jamie and Claire's journeys. It was easy to have a fling with a tourist—there was never a chance of it becoming anything more. But each time he hooked up, he felt lonelier after and cursed the notion of becoming intimate with anyone who wasn't Eve.

Except she was far away and had shut him out of her life. When she didn't respond to his text, he vowed to move on.

But he couldn't.

The rabbi called out the page number, and Mac fluttered until he found it. There was English on the left and what he assumed was Hebrew on the right with an italicized transliteration underneath it. He followed along while the congregation recited and sang. At times, the rabbi instructed them to stand and then he'd tell them to sit. Some sections were read aloud, and others were mumbled. A man stood at a podium with a white fringed shawl around his shoulders, leading the prayers.

Finally, they came to a section with a musical refrain. He read the English translation. Sabbath bride? My beloved? How romantic! Was this a religious service or a love poem?

At the end, the congregation rose and turned to face the door. Mac followed along. At the end of the lines, the people bowed left and right and then turned back around. It was … riveting. Poetic. Mysterious. And the voices—Mac's thoughts muted as the rise and fall of the congregational song entranced him, as if he were under a musical spell.

In his Highland church, there was singing, of course, from a majestic and formal choir. His family attended a Presbyterian stronghold full of pomp and propriety. Ladies wore elegant hats and fancy dresses, and the men were buttoned up in suits and ties. The looks on the faces of the congregation he grew up in were somber and serious, and while the choral refrains were enigmatic and shadowy, they were not soothing in the way the singing was here. It was as if he were being lulled into the oncoming Sabbath and also energized around it.

The service concluded. Mac closed his prayer book and slipped it into the wooden holder on the back of the seat in front of him. People shuffled out of the small sanctuary and slipped on coats. Excited chatter lifted the room. And then the rabbi was standing in front of him.

"Shabbat Shalom and welcome." He thrust out a hand, and Mac shook it. The rabbi wore charcoal gray dress pants, a blue-checked button-down and a light blue paisley tie under a navy blue cable-knit sweater. He was young, and his eyes sparkled when he smiled. His dark curls were flattened by a black yarmulke that was bobby-pinned in place. "I don't think we've met. I'm Stephen Raimi, the rabbi here."

Mac pumped his hand.

"Mac Monteith. First-timer."

The rabbi smiled. "And? Think you'll come back?"

Mac looked around. People were hunching into the cold as they pushed outside. A cool wind sifted through the room. A few lingerers talked in close corners. He nodded. "I'd like to."

"Do you have somewhere to go for Shabbat dinner? If not, please come home with me. My wife would be thrilled to have a guest."

The rabbi had kind eyes, gray as a stormy sky. Mac hadn't planned on staying for dinner. He hadn't planned ... anything. He had no idea why he had even come, other than he was curious about Eve's claim that he might be Jewish and he wondered what that might mean for his life today. Or if they ever found their way back to each other.

He hadn't had dinner with a family in ... how long? And he was hungry. Better than a burger and chips in a pub, alone with a pint of beer that would make the drive home even longer.

"I'd like that, thank you," he said.

"Great!" Rabbi Raimi clapped him on the shoulder and directed him toward the coat room. "Grab your coat, and let's walk home."

"I can drive," Mac offered, but the rabbi shook his head.

"I don't drive on Shabbat," he said. "My wife and I are *shomer Shabbat*. We don't do a bunch of other things from sundown Friday until Saturday night. I'll tell you all about it on the walk home."

Mac looked horrified, and the rabbi chuckled, clapping a hand on his shoulder. "Don't worry—you don't have to do any of that to belong here. You just have to want to come."

Chapter Fifty

*E**ve, April 2016*

She'd spent most of March in England, riding trains between various book talks, but Eve didn't get nervous until she arrived in Edinburgh on the first of April. She hoped to stay through Beltane, the spring fire festival symbolic for shedding what no longer serves and celebrating the growing light and warmth of the season. She stepped off the train and breathed in Edinburgh's damp scent.

She'd asked Delta to send a hardcover to David MacLaren before the launch. She'd devoted an entire paragraph in the acknowledgements to him and the archives. As the date of her arrival had loomed closer, she'd emailed him with all the information, including the dates she'd be in Scotland, and he was eager to meet her at the train and take her for a dram and a chat. She pulled her wheelie bag through the glass-domed waiting room of Waverley station, which was awash with the gray light of a mild afternoon. She scanned the room, looking for David's dark brown wispy hair and signature sweater vest and button-down. He sat on a bench with a folded newspaper in his left hand and his right waving furiously in her direction.

He tucked the paper beneath his arm and took long strides to close the gap between them.

"Ach, look at ye," he said, grinning. "Aren't you a sight?"

Eve beamed, let go of her suitcase and threw her arms around the man. She breathed in his papery scent.

"It's good to see you!"

"So we're hugging now, aye?" he laughed. "I suppose it's alright now that you're not my employee."

"Oh, I'm sorry. I didn't mean to make you uncomfortable." She stepped back. "See what happens when I'm back in America for too long?"

His smile returned. She gripped her suitcase.

"Let's get that dram," she said.

"Right," he said, pointing toward the exit. Her case clacked against the ground as they walked briskly into the bright day.

It was warm for April, a tease of spring on the air. Over heavy crystal tumblers with two-finger pours of vintage Macallan 12—"It's a celebration, you're back and I want to hear everything," David said—they talked about the book, the lawyer's letters, her publisher and her father's move to New York. Everything but Mac.

Each swallow burned her throat and warmed her belly as Eve settled into the hard leather bench. *This place.* People hunched into one another, eager conversations lighting their faces. The animation of Scots—bright faces, dancing eyes, she could almost hear the swirl and lilt of the words, though of course she couldn't hear a thing above the collective hum of a busy pub.

David signaled to the waiter for another round.

"So, are you going to see him?"

"I want to."

"Then you will."

He read the confusion on her face and changed the subject. "What's next? Another book? Or can we get you back at the archives? A real position."

Eve looked questioningly as she emptied her glass with a generous gulp. The waiter approached with two fresh tumblers and whisked away the empty ones.

"I figured I lost that chance with the way I left," she said.

David cocked his head and sighed.

"Well, I might not have shared the details of your departure with my superiors. They might believe the fellowship ended naturally." He looked skyward, then cracked a grin.

Relief flooded through her.

"Aren't you a sweet man," she said. "You didn't have to do that. It was unprofessional, leaving the way I did."

"Perhaps," he said. "But you were a great contributor to our work. You discovered some important materials that created a new collection and built a relationship for us with the Scottish Jewish Archives. And you turned your research into an internationally acclaimed book, bringing the archives to global attention. I'd say that promotes you above mere fellowship to budding archival professional—if that's what you want."

Scotland was her last stop on the tour, and she had no plans for after. She'd filled bookstores and libraries for talks in North America and England, and these next two weeks would be the pinnacle—planned strategically by Isla Macleod, her Scottish publicist. Delta had hired her to create an enviable itinerary of talks in the land where the story was based. Edinburgh was her main focus, though she'd ride the train to Glasgow for talks at Hyndland Bookshop, Young's Interesting Books, the radical and independent Calton Books and Thistle Books—which, while specializing in secondhand and rare Scottish tomes, wanted her to talk about her research.

She sipped the whiskey, following the burn from her lips to the back of her throat, down the center of her body until it fanned out across her limbs. The warmth that encompassed her from a good smoky vintage was like a promise whispered in the dark of night. Every whiskey she tasted reminded her of Mac, who had taught her to appreciate it in the first place.

"We need fortification," David said, waving at a waiter. A young man strode in their direction.

"Fish and chips." David held up two fingers, and the waiter nodded.

"Thanks," she said. "My publicist says a big story will make a splash in *The Scotsman* tomorrow. And *The Sun* on Sunday—I'll be in Glasgow by then."

"Impressive. Any pushback from the lofty ones?"

"They've been curiously quiet."

David drained his glass. "Maybe they'll stay that way. After all, there's nothing the aristocracy likes less than unwanted, negative attention. No one wants to be the focus of an accusation of antisemitism or homophobia in these enlightened times."

"Indeed," Eve said and emptied her glass.

She settled into a hotel not far from Sukkat Shalom. Since she'd left, she had kept in touch with Rabbi Raimi and emailed him before starting the book tour. He'd been overjoyed to hear from her and recommended a hotel within walking distance from the congregation's new location.

In Edinburgh, the first city named a UNESCO City of Literature in 2004, she was excited about events at Golden Hare Books, Blackwell's (the city's oldest bookshop), The Edinburgh Bookshop and Cornerstone—a Christian ecumenical store that wanted her to focus on the antisemitism of the church's earlier eras as a step toward making institutional amends. She'd have radio interviews and TV appearances and the two big newspaper splashes, and everyone would know who she was and what she wrote about. Her photo graced the windows of all the bookstores where she would speak, beside stacks of *Family Secrets*. She was growing into a sort of celebrity.

But at night, she tossed in the plush and spacious hotel bed, pumping her fists into the pillows as she tossed beneath the blanket. The first night went by with barely any sleep, and by the second night, Eve practically fell into bed from exhaustion. It was near two in the morning when she shook awake, her eyes wide, her skin cold and tingling. She looked around, forgetting where she was, and then, when she saw the angles of city lights shining through the window above her bed, she remembered. Edinburgh. Book tour. Back in Scotland, waiting to run into Mac and afraid of the possibility, too.

She scanned the room, the walls gray with night, the silence almost palpable. And then, beyond the bed, in the alcove between the door and the bathroom, she saw them. Two figures, surrounded by golden light.

Eve squinted to get a better picture of who they were. Shira and her mother again? But no, the second figure looked larger and darker, the face furred by a thick black beard, the oval head crowned by a mess of dark curls. She recognized Shira's sweet face and calm demeanor, but who was the man? Their hands were linked.

"Shira?"

"Hello, my dear."

The voice was like bells ringing.

"I thought I'd never see you again," Eve said. "I wrote the book. Completed what you wanted. Everyone knows."

Shira was nodding, her hand grasping the man's hand, their fingers almost forming the shape of a heart.

"I know," she said. "I've been with you this whole time."

Eve sighed. *Here we go,* she thought. *The melodrama.*

Shira smiled.

"I brought Benjamin," she said. "He wanted to know you."

"Hello, sweet girl," his voice rumbled, deep and sonorous. "Time is not linear. It's all connected. We're here even when we're not."

Eve wedged the nail of her right thumb between her teeth, thinking.

"Everyone is hiding something," she finally said. "So many secrets! It's like we live beneath a cloak, tucking the truth into the shadows. Why? It serves no one! I've lost so much to tell this story. I, too, come from a legacy of hiding. When will it end?"

She slumped against the pillows, tears staining her cheeks.

Suddenly, they were on either side of her. She wanted to shoo them away, to say this whole thing was ridiculous and contrived, but she felt a calming hum and she closed her eyes. It grew louder, like bees buzzing, and Eve felt the sound in her skin.

Then Shira's voice was close to her ear, and Eve felt it like warm air as she spoke.

"You will come home to love," she said.

Benjamin's large hand lay flat on Eve's forehead. Her tears flowed faster. *This must be what a grandfather would feel like,* she thought, sobbing for all the love she could have had, all the ways fear and hatred forced people to run, to hide, to live alone for far too long.

"You will come home to love, my dear," Shira whispered, her voice lulling Eve into an easy and restful sleep.

Chapter Fifty-One

E *ve, 2016*

"Miss!" the bellman called as Eve emerged from the revolving door.

His eyes were wide and serious, his face gray. She cocked her head in question as he beckoned for her to follow. A tall man in a dark suit stepped from behind the registration desk when they approached and ushered Eve into a back office, quickly closing the door. He pointed to the seat, and Eve sank into it, her mind a reel of worries. Had something happened to her father?

The hotel manager swallowed, then spoke.

"We've received a package addressed to you, and it's questionable."

"Questionable?"

"The authorities have been alerted."

Eve's heart thumped, its beat tapping at her temples.

"Can you tell me more, please?"

The man took a deep breath. "The box smelled of uh, excrement, and there was white powder dusting the outsides of it. We sent it off for scrutiny. We're concerned it might be anthrax."

"And this was sent to me? What was the return address?"

"There was no return address," he said. "We have it handled, miss. We just wanted you to know as your safety might be in question. There will be officers here to talk with you. I recommend not leaving the hotel alone until the matter is settled."

Eve pulled a hand through her hair. Her last talk, the one she'd been most excited about, at Cornerstone Bookshop, was scheduled for the following day. She could relax overnight in the hotel, have dinner sent up on a tray and binge old movies, but she would not miss that talk.

She shook her head. "I have a talk tomorrow night, and I'll be attending as planned. If the authorities want to accompany me, that's fine, but I'll be going."

"Miss, please, just wait to talk to them," the manager said. A flush of heat rode up his neck and face. He cast his eyes down to the desk. "We must think about the other hotel guests, too," he added.

"Thank you for your concern," she said, annoyed. "I'll be fine, and no harm will come to your hotel."

The man's lips were straight lines, the look on his face stern. He sucked his teeth. Then he forced a smile that looked more daggerly than sincere.

"Thank you, miss," he said as he stood. "I'll ring your room when the police arrive."

Eve understood that she was dismissed.

Although she had seemed the measure of calm in the presence of the hotel manager, her hands were shaking. As the elevator doors closed and she was finally alone, she tried to calm her racing heart.

Arguments swirled through her head as the elevator clicked through the floors. She'd seen skinheads outside several of her talks but thought nothing of it. Sometimes teenage boys cut their hair that way. She didn't automatically consider them dangerous. But maybe she should have.

She unlocked the door to her suite, flipped the light on and peered around the room. *I'm not nervous. Nothing to worry about,* she thought.

The room was clear, no shadowy murderer waiting to pounce. She dropped her purse on the desk and walked to the window to look out at the fading sun. She'd been enjoying the book tour—people lined up for her. Her message was landing with resonance; she was making a difference. Still, she hadn't seen Mac's face in any crowd, and she hadn't called him yet either.

Each night, after her talk was finished and she'd signed until her hand hurt, she returned to the hotel, buzzing with loneliness. She should be the one to reach out, as her father had said, but she had yet to do it. What was she waiting for? She'd been on some TV news shows and in the paper. He had to have seen her. She was being stubborn.

What she didn't admit to anyone was that she was afraid of him not coming if she asked him to. She'd understand if he'd moved on. She'd fucked up royally; she couldn't expect him to wait forever.

But Simon had waited for her father.

You're a fool, Waldman. Call him.

The bedside phone shuddered as it rang. Eve grabbed the receiver and gulped, "Hello?"

The hotel manager announced the arrival of the police and asked her to return to the lobby.

Downstairs, the reception staff ushered her quickly away from public sight and into the back hallway of private offices.

"Miss Waldman?" There were two officers, both young, one with a cap too large for him and puppy eyes, the other with freckles across the bridge of his nose. Both wore serious expressions and motioned for Eve to sit. They rested their hats on their knees.

"The hotel manager said you plan to attend your book event tomorrow?" the freckled one asked.

"It's the last talk on my tour, and I won't cancel it," she said. "It's been advertised, and people are eager to attend. I can't let them down. I'll be fine."

The man sucked his teeth. "I don't recommend it, miss, but we can accompany you, if you insist."

"Thank you," Eve replied.

The hotel manager crossed his arms in front of his body. She would not be swayed by domineering men. She planted her feet on the carpet beneath her chair and gripped the wood of its arms.

"Do you know who sent the package?" she asked.

"We believe it came from a skinhead group with roots in Sweden," the other officer chirped.

She suddenly felt cold.

"Do they pose a real threat?"

"It's an active cell we've had an eye on, but I don't believe so," said the puppy-eyed officer. "But it's a good thing the hotel intercepted the package."

"And that no one was hurt," chirped the manager.

She nodded but wasn't really listening.

"It's just a book," she whispered. "I haven't hurt anyone."

The puppy eyes seemed bigger. "We know, ma'am, but groups like these target gays, Jews, Asians, anyone not white and Christian."

"Attacks like these are not rational," echoed the other officer. "They're motivated by fear and anger. We'll keep you safe."

The officers stood.

"We'll scope the perimeter of tomorrow's event beforehand and position an officer outside the store to watch the crowd. If you decide not to go, please inform the hotel manager."

"I'll be going," Eve insisted.

"This doesn't happen here," the manager muttered.

"Actually, it does," said the puppy-eyed officer. "We have crime in Scotland just like anywhere else, sir."

A smile broke through Eve's stony exterior.

"Well, it does not happen in this hotel," he huffed.

"We can post an officer at the door if you'd like," the other officer said.

The manager's eyes narrowed, and he sighed, shaking his head.

CHAPTER FIFTY-TWO

*E**ve, 2016*

"And that's why we must stamp out antisemitism, homophobia, hatred of any kind, unfounded and inhuman, borne out of fear and a scarcity mentality, wherever and whenever we see it," Eve said.

People sat in rows of chairs wedged tightly together around book displays and stacks of shelves. Every seat was taken, and the Cornerstone overflowed with attentive, rapt readers hanging on her every word. In the last row sat an elegant woman who looked out of place in the crowd, with a strand of pearls around her neck and a soft pink cashmere sweater. Eve eyed her then lost herself to the lilt and rise of her story.

"Antisemitism is the oldest hatred," she asserted. "It makes no sense to be afraid of one of the smallest populations on the planet, and yet it not only persists, it's growing. Shira and Benjamin's story is one of secrecy and love lost, and it's a story we should never repeat. When I found those letters, my heart ached. Benjamin never knew his good fortune. And Shira's children died not knowing the beautiful legacy they were born into.

To be a Jew is to stand alone—and apart. We try, desperately, to fit in, to assimilate, to belong, and we endure. Beyond all odds."

Her heart thumped madly in her chest as she scanned the attentive crowd. She would call Mac after the event. It was time to face her fears.

"But there's another part to this story of hiding. Hugh lived his whole life in the public sphere, lying about his true nature. I was raised by a wonderful man who lived alone and afraid because his community would not accept him for being gay."

Her father's face flashed before her, and she smiled.

"I lost the love of my life because of secrets," she continued. "Hatred hardens us. And it prevents us from really living. It's time to let it go."

The bookstore thundered with applause. She smiled, closed the book that she'd read an excerpt from and watched the captivated crowd. The eyes of the woman in the pink sweater shimmered with unshed tears.

The store manager had allowed in enough people to fill the seats and amass two rows of standing, fidgeting folks at the back of the shop, and still people waited on the sidewalk for a chance to slip inside and pluck a signed book from the stack on the front table. Many wanted to meet Eve, after watching her on TV or reading about her in the news. The reviews in the local papers had been glowing. Rabbi Raimi sat in the front row beside his wife, who wore a simple denim skirt and soft sweater. David had brought his wife, and Isla the publicist stood to Eve's left, hovering and directing the crowd. She'd been a good shepherd, and Eve was grateful.

The event ended at nine o'clock, far past the store's closing time. It was another forty-five minutes before she finished signing books and chatting with guests. The manager generously allowed the last stragglers to hop in and make a purchase, which Eve was happy to sign. Her cheeks ached from smiling.

"You're returning to America soon?" Rabbi Raimi had hung back to let the crowd dissipate.

Eve paused. "I'm contemplating staying," she said.

"Really?" His eyes gleamed.

She nodded. "The archives has offered me a position, and I'm tempted to say yes."

"That's lovely! I hope we'll be part of your life here," he said.

She felt warm, content. She thanked the store manager, who gushed about sales.

"We've never had such a packed event or sold this many books in one go," she said.

Eve smiled. The book was a success. Her name was known in literary circles and among populations of people advocating for equality. Most of the audience had left, but the woman in the pink sweater lingered by the door. Eve cocked her head in the woman's direction and asked the manager for a few more minutes before closing up.

She strode over to the woman. "Can I help you with something?"

The woman stared at her as if they knew each other. Eve waited for her to speak.

"I can understand why Mac loves you," she said.

Eve froze. "I'm sorry?"

The woman was nodding. "I can see why. Your strength is admirable. I understand why you had to do it. Bang on you for seeing it through."

She waited for the woman to introduce herself, but she said nothing more. Only slipped out into the dark night.

The police officer who had shadowed Eve all night followed her out of the store. "Shall I call a taxi, miss?"

The city was quiet with night, the sky a sparkling purple canvas. The air held a soothing chill. She tilted her head to the heavens.

"I'd like to walk," she said.

The officer cleared his throat as a warning.

"I know, it's not what you'd advise," she said. "It's okay if you want to leave. I'll be fine."

"I'll just trail behind you," he said.

Her feet slick on the cobbled streets, Eve replayed the last month and all the people she'd met in bookstores and synagogues and the splendid black-tie fundraiser in London to gather donations for a Save the Night campaign to stamp out attacks against gay men in that city. So many good causes and good people. She'd made friends, started writing articles and essays, even jotted ideas for another book. There was a lot to say, and new people now hovered on the perimeter of her life. But at the end of it all, she was alone. She couldn't wait to get back to the hotel and call Mac. She'd say whatever it took to win a second chance. From here on out, she could focus all her energy on making things right, on filling her life with love.

She'd been walking for twenty minutes when she felt a presence behind her. But the dogged police officer didn't seem alarmed. His pace never quickened, and she heard him whistling in the night air.

The footsteps picked up speed. *Thump, thump, thump.* The pulse beat a tango in her wrists and temples. Eve's heartbeat accelerated.

"Wait!" a voice called.

She halted. She knew that voice. That sweet, husky, reassuring voice.

After so much time, after so long apart, after all the silence. After her self-righteous stupidity.

She stopped walking and turned on the ball of her foot.

Had he always looked this beautiful? Haloed in the light of a streetlamp, his blue eyes sparkling like the stars overhead, his dark curls consumed by the black night. He jogged up to her, his breath ragged, fogging in front of his face in the cool air.

She smiled. "What took you so long?"

His mouth made a perfect circle, and his eyes went wide.

"Me?" he gulped. "Are you crackin'? You've ignored all my efforts."

She pressed her lips together in a smile, nodding. "You're right," she said. "I'm sorry. I've missed you so much. I was a fool."

"That's more like it," he said, tracing her face with his fingers.

The officer coughed behind them.

"You can go," she called to him. "I know this man. He'll see me safely to my hotel."

"A guarded escort?" Mac said.

Eve sucked on her bottom lip as she remembered the package. "Um, well, yesterday a suspicious package came to the hotel addressed to me, and the police were called in. They believe it came from some skinhead group. Anti-gay, anti-Jewish."

"Seriously?"

She nodded.

He was shaking his head as he pulled her to him. "You don't do anything halfway, do you?" He stroked her hair.

She closed her eyes and felt the warmth of his fingers.

"Mum came around."

His words broke her reverie. She opened her eyes, stunned, and looked at him as he nodded.

"She was at the talk tonight," he said. "Pretty impressed with you."

The woman in the pink sweater with the pearls. Eve smiled. And felt such a surge of relief that she thought she might actually break open.

"She knows how much I love you and that I plan to spend my life with you," Mac said. "She's changed a lot in the past year. I told her to accept us, or she won't be seeing much of me. She gave her blessing. I have Emma and Shona to thank for paving the way."

Eve arched her eyes in question.

"There's plenty of time to tell you all about it," he said.

For a minute, they just stared at each other. She was lulled by the idea that they had all the time in the world to think of things to say. But then Mac spoke.

"Probably the threat of no access to future grandchildren got her to come around," he said.

She gulped.

Mac feigned seriousness. "I'm thinking three or four. And you're not getting any younger, so we'd better get started," he said with a smile.

"Um, uh ... " She stumbled for words, attempting to look angry, but she really didn't feel it and a smile grew across her face.

Mac pressed two fingers against her lips.

"Don't say anything. We can figure out the details together."

She leaned against him, listening for the heartbeat that tapped a symphony in her ear. The beat that helped her to sleep on cold nights near the mountains and the black lake. She loved the idea of no more sleepless nights, no more wondering and worrying and feeling so alone. She closed her eyes and whispered, "I'm sorry it took me so long. I hope it's not too late to have it all."

He stepped back and stared down at her with a look that she couldn't quite discern. Was he playing with her? Had this all been a dream? But then he broke into a big, goofy grin and pulled her to him once again in a warm and solid embrace.

"Nope," he said. "Not at all. I never make the same mistake twice. I'm not letting you go, lass. From now on, it's the two of us against the world."

ACKNOWLEDGEMENTS

Once, years ago, a guy I was dating insisted that he didn't want me to write about him. "If you don't want me to write about you, you shouldn't fall in love with a writer," I replied.

Life is full of stories. Everywhere you go, everyone you meet. Through writing, I figure out what I believe, how I feel, process what happens in life. Writing is how I make sense of the world. I've always written about my experiences. This collection of creative nonfiction essays represents decades of my life, my coming-into-myself, and I am grateful to all those who have supported and continue to support my writing, who encourage me to write and to publish, and who believe in the power of story to connect us.

Thanks to Dan, the love of my life, who has always seen me as a writer. I am my best self because I share life with you. All my love to my four wonderful children—Asher, Eliana, Grace and Shaya. Though you never read my writing, you support my right to do it.

Thanks to my mother, Sonny Cohn, for championing my writing. You are a wonderful mother, a fantastic grandmother, and a great friend. I was very, very lucky to be raised by you.

Thank you always to my sister Jody Charlip, my aunt Suzanne Zwiren and my cousin Amanda Zwiren, for being great cheerleaders and some of the most special people in my life.

Thank you to Jessica Fein, Elizabeth Gowing, Danny Hankner, Kim Kozlowski and M.L. Liebler for blurbing this book. Thank you to my Michigan writers workshop, women I love deeply who have become an important part of my life— Susan Chaplin, Karen Hildebrandt, Pam Houghton, Kim Kozlowski, Carrie Nantais, Anne Osmer, Lisa Peers. You've helped many of these essays grow stronger and become publishable! Thank you to my Tuesday co-writing group—Janet Bailey, Elizabeth Gowing and Rachel Weikel—the kindest, most supportive and encouraging global group of friends I could ask for.

Thank you to Jenny Rarden, my fearless editor, who is always available and great at what she does. Thank you to Susan Jones and Patrick McEntaggart for another fantastic cover design. It is great fun to work with you. I am grateful to the Women's Fiction Writers Association and all the friends I've made there who are the best support system an author could ask for.

About the Author

Lynne Golodner is the author of thirteen books and hundreds of essays and articles as well as a marketing entrepreneur, writing coach and retreat leader.

After working as a journalist in New York and Washington, DC, Lynne returned to her native Detroit to pursue a freelance writing career and teach writing. In 2007, she created Your People, a marketing and public relations company with a focus on storytelling that now guides authors in building their brands and marketing their work.

Lynne's writing has appeared in *45th Parallel, Moment Magazine, Great Lakes Review, Abandon Journal, Saveur,* the *Chicago Tribune, Better Homes and Gardens, Midwest Living,* the *Detroit Free Press, Porridge Magazine,* the *Jewish Literary Journal, The Good Life Review, Hadassah Magazine, Green Golem Magazine, The Forward, Valiant Scribe, Story Unlikely, The Dillydoun Review, QuibbleLit, bioStories* and *YourTango,* among many more publications. Plus, one of Lynne's essays was a finalist in the Annie Dillard Creative Nonfiction contest at

Bellingham Review and an essay won second place in the St. Petersburg Review/Masaai Land Retreat contest in 2026.

Lynne teaches writing around the world, leads writers retreats and facilitates The Writers Community. She fuses her marketing expertise with her writing background in webinars and masterminds focused on arming writers with the tools needed to market their work and build consistent and compelling author brands.

A former Fulbright Specialist, Lynne graduated from University of Michigan (BA, Communications/English) and Goddard College (MFA, Writing) and earned a Certificate in Entrepreneurship from the Goldman Sachs 10,000 Small Businesses program at Wayne State University. She is the mother of four young adults and lives in Huntington Woods, Michigan with her archivist-husband Dan.

Learn more at https://lynnegolodner.com and read Lynne's Substack at https://lynnegolodnerauthor.substack.com.

CAVE OF SECRETS DISCUSSION GUIDE

CAVE OF SECRETS by Lynne Golodner debuted on August 27, 2024 and soared to #1 in Jewish fiction, #1 in Gay Fiction and #1 in British and Irish fiction on Amazon on the first day! This book was named a 2024 FOREWORD INDIES Finalist IN LGBTQ+ fiction and Romance, a Reader's Choice Awards Finalist with a 5-star review, and a Finalist in the 2025 American Fiction Awards for Romance, General. CAVE OF SECRETS won the Bronze Medal in the 2025 IPPY Awards for Multicultural Fiction.

The author is always available to speak to your book club, virtually or in person! Please contact her directly at lynne@yourppl.com to schedule a talk with your book club.

"I have counted the days until you would return to my waiting arms, my insistent kisses.

But now I know you never will..."

On a rainy hike by Loch Lomond, Eve Waldman stumbles upon a perfectly preserved journal in a hidden cave. The time-worn lettering details the illicit affair of two Jewish lovers that sent a shiver of shame through a Scottish family — and echoes down the bloodlines.

Born of Highland aristocracy, Mac Monteith prefers to spend his days behind the bar of the family pub, rather than live the life his parents desired for him. Then Eve walks through the door, stirring more than Mac's long-dormant heart.

When Eve traces the cave documents to the Monteith line, scandals and secrets spill out from all sides. Eve remains committed to the truth, but when being truthful means hurting the man she loves, she is forced to make a bigger choice: righting the wrongs of the past, or building the future she's yearned for.

*A contemporary romance with hints of magical realism, **Cave of Secrets** is an award-winning, bestselling novel about family heritage, intergenerational trauma, and finding the courage to be honest with ourselves—and those who love us.*

"A layered story full of heart, wisdom and hard truths..."

~Annie Cathryn, multi-award winning author of *The Friendship Breakup*

"**Cave of Secrets** transports readers on a timeless journey to Scotland, sprinkled with secrets and a touch of magical realism. This novel is a must-read."

~ Merle R. Saferstein, author of *Living and Leaving My Legacy, Vols. l and ll*

"A masterful blend of suspense, romance, and self-discovery."

~ Lisa Williamson Rosenberg, author of *Embers on the Wind*

"**Cave of Secrets** not only addresses forbidden love of the past but also brings to light the struggles of love and relationships today."

~ Michelle Glogovac, award-winning author of *How To Get On Podcasts*

***

Discussion Guide

1. The family relationships that wind through *Cave of*

Secrets are powerful, but sometimes at odds with the individual identities of the characters. How have your family relationships filled you up, and how have they broken you down?

***

2. This book highlights the challenge of aligning with religious values or communal values versus individual values. Sam must suppress his attraction to men until he can leave his community and live free, but it scares him and for much of his adult life, he has never been comfortable being fully out. Is this because his family didn't accept him as he is?

What do you think of the idea of communal values that most people should adhere to?

Is it ever possible to accept a variety of perspectives and identities all within the same community?

***

3. Scottish identity, like Jewish identity, revolves around culture, music, work, and language. And, both identities are very communal. What's more, the Scottish Diaspora and the Jewish Diaspora have a lot in common.

What is the most prominent way that you find your identity expressed?

Is it through music? Does the music come from the work like with Scottish tunes?

Is your identity more aligned with language or storytelling?

Or ritual?

Or is it connection to a particular place?

***

4. Eve feels that she has to choose between her book project and her relationship. Do you think she indeed had to make that choice?

And in the end, do you think she made the right choice?

Have you ever had to choose between two things that were important to you? And if so, how did you make that decision?

***

5. Margaret wants so desperately to reinvent herself as an aristocratic wife that she suppresses her origins throughout much of her adult life. But it costs her her relationship with her husband and with her kids. In the end, she ends up realizing this, and Alex welcomes her back when she has a change of heart.

Do you think that her identity needed to change so much to be accepted into the aristocracy?

Or was that a myth that she created for herself?

And do you believe relationships like the one between Margaret and Alex can be as elastic as theirs was? Why or why not?

***

6. Eve begins her career as a journalist, and then transitions into being an archivist. Her life revolves around storytelling and is largely driven by the idea that she doesn't know her own story and her own history.

How much of your life's work has been motivated by what you've had or have lost?

***

7. When Sam and Eve return to Oak Park, Michigan to visit Sam's family, it seems like his mother and his sister are welcoming. Do you think that they built a relationship with Eve after that fateful meeting? Why or why not?

***

8. All of the characters in *Cave of Secrets* feel that they need to leave their place of origin to truly find themselves. Do you think that is helpful? Why or why not?

And has this been true for you?

***

9. Food and the creation of meals together is part of the dance that Eve and Mac do as they become closer. Later, Eve prepares a meal for Sam's friends, and that becomes a relationship-building, restorative endeavor as well. How else are relationships built, aside from making food and nourishing one another?

***

10. Were you surprised by the ending of *Cave of Secrets*? Why or why not?

IF YOU LIKED THIS BOOK...

You'll love other award-winning novels by Lynne Golodner!

Available wherever books are sold, in e-book, audiobook and paperback...

WOMAN OF VALOR

Sally Lieberman chose to become an Orthodox Jew in her twenties because it was comforting, calming and full of community and family. It didn't hurt that religious observance brought her to the man of her dreams—her patient, sexy husband, Barry.

Ten years in, Sally has everything she ever wanted, a passionate marriage with three children and a best friend she can count on. She loves everything about her chosen life.

Until her son is abused at school, and she's shocked by her husband's response. That's when Sally's first love finds her online and wants her back—something she dreamed about long before she became a religious wife.

It would be easy to abandon the community that is abandoning her—but she's not the same person she was when she first fell in love with John. Sally is caught between two worlds. Can she give up the life she's built with Barry?

Experience the sensory-rich, food-filled Orthodox community of Skokie, Illinois in WOMAN OF VALOR, and step inside Sally Lieberman's loving family along with her often-difficult, yet surprisingly-inspiring way of life—even when everything seems stacked against her. Ask yourself what you would do if you had a second-chance with your first love.

Winner of the 2025 American Fiction Awards for religious fiction and an honorable mention in the 2024 Eric Hoffer Awards for spiritual fiction!

I LOVE YOU, CHARLIE TANNER

When Charlie Tanner's soulmate dies suddenly in a remote commune, she loses her voice—and everything she thought she knew about love, loyalty, and truth.

Seeking refuge in a quiet Vermont cottage, Charlie begins to rebuild: tending a garden, reconnecting with estranged family, and falling for a widowed rabbi who sees beyond her silence. But the past isn't done with her.

As secrets unravel and danger draws near, Charlie must decide: will she reclaim her voice and the life she deserves—or stay trapped in someone else's vision of love?

For readers who love *Where the Crawdads Sing*, a book that evokes the unlikely romance of the Netflix series *Nobody Wants This* plus the intrigue and passion of Lucy Score's *Forever Never*, **I Love You, Charlie Tanner** is a steamy story of second chances, midlife love, and starting over, with a whiff of intrigue and surprising twists that'll keep you turning pages.

Winner of the 2025 Pencraft Fall Seasonal Book Award for Women's Fiction!

And...consider checking out Lynne Golodner's essay collection, **FOREST WALK ON A FRIDAY**!

www.ingramcontent.com/pod-product-compliance
Lightning Source LLC
Chambersburg PA
CBHW031844310726
48972CB00005B/1406